BEAUTIFUL SALVATION

EMMANUELLE

USA TODAY BESTSELLING AUTHOR

SNOW

Smart Lily
Publishing

Dahlia &
BRIDA
GREEN   UNTAIN, TN

Emmanuelle Snow
emmanuellesnow.com

CARTER HILLS BAND UNIVERSE
(SUGGESTED READING ORDER)

Carter Hills Band series
False Promises

HEART SONG DUET
Blindsided
Forevermore

Whiskey Melody series
Sweet Agony

SECOND TEAR DUET
Cruel Destiny
Beautiful Salvation

BREATHLESS DUET
Wild Encounter
Brittle Scars

Upon A Star series
Last Hope

Midnight Sparks

Love Song For Two series
LONESOME HEART DUET
Fallen Legend
Rising Star

TWO OF US DUET
Snowbound

Wicked Love

All titles available at
emmanuellesnow.com

For the best experience, read in the order as shown above

TRIGGER WARNINGS

Disclaimer

My books are realistic and emotional romance reads.

I'm an advocate for mental health, and some topics could be sensitive for certain readers since they are portrayed as close to real life as possible.

I've listed the potential trigger warnings for each title on my website.

Be advised that those trigger warnings could potentially be spoiler alerts for the storylines.

Those sensitive topics have been written with the utmost care and respect. Please reach out if you have questions or comments.

All books contain sexuality, mature content, and language
not intended for people under 18 years of age.
For other readers' sake, please avoid spoilers in your
reviews.

Thank you and have a wonderful day!

Emmanuelle

emmanuellesnow.com

BECOME A VIP

TO NEVER MISS A THING

Snow's VIP

Join **Emmanuelle Snow's VIP newsletter**

Be the first to know about new releases, giveaways, sales, and special events. And step into a space where big emotions are celebrated, love is messy and beautiful, and stories linger long after the last page.

emmanuellesnow.com

Snow's Soulmates

Join Emmanuelle Snow's Facebook VIP group, **Snow's Soulmates**, to chat with her and other readers, get updates, and more bonus content.

facebook.com/groups/snowvip

Chapter 1

Dahlia

The four of us sat at a round table in the middle of the pub. The booth's blood-red leather back curved up high enough to block us from the rest of the patrons, giving us a bit of privacy.

Stud had ordered a bottle of champagne and after the server poured each of us a glass, my ex-bandmate lifted his. "To Dahlia and her great new venture, and to Nick, who I'm happy to call a friend. Man, we have a lot more in common than just our shared love of woodworking. Cheers."

Nick bowed his head, and Stud exchanged a quick glance with his wife, sharing a smile.

"Thanks for being here," I said to my friends. "We don't see each other often enough. Next time, you gotta bring Tristan along." Belinda—or Belle as we all called her —and Stud had a boy a little younger than Jack, who'd stayed back in Oregon with his grandparents.

We all drank to that.

The whole time, my eyes stayed fixed on the man sitting next to me. The firm line of his jaw. His tousled blond hair. When he laughed, the amber of his eyes glinted. My heart skipped a beat each time his fingers skimmed mine over the table. He slipped his arm over the backrest behind me, and as if it were the most natural thing in the world, he pressed a gentle kiss to my lips. Not earth-shattering, but enough to make my breath catch and send jolts of desire and happiness coursing through me. I let myself sink into the familiarity of his touch—and the woodsy scent of him.

In that instant, I felt at home. Exactly where I should be. Exactly where I belonged.

Tonight, like so many times before, it felt as if Nick had always been there—woven into the fabric of my life without me ever realizing it—but waiting for the right moment to walk in and wake that part of me I believed had been quelled years ago. That spark in me I thought had vanished when my heart had gone missing. The one that now begged to express itself, to shine, and conquer the world. Nick's world.

"Okay, one of these days, you'll have to come visit us," Stud said.

Lost in the contemplation of my date, I had missed most of their conversation.

"Our property has a few acres, and we'd like to add a B&B. Right now, I'm building a new barn because my little woodworking business is really taking off, and soon I'll be running out of space."

"Man, we were destined to meet," Nick said, bumping his fist with his.

"If you ever go into business, you and I are gonna have

a talk. Right now, my brain is running at full speed," Stud continued. "I see a future here."

"The day I decide what I'm going to do, you'll be the first to get the memo," Nick added.

They clinked their glasses.

Belinda watched me, amusement dancing in her irises, and shrugged.

I knew the meaning of every twitch of her lips and every twinkle in her eyes. In the time we'd traveled the world together, she had become a sister to me, but also a confidante and a friend.

Don't let him go, she mouthed my way.

I knew it. Since the shop's pre-opening celebration, she had become a Nick fan too.

I'm serious, Dahlia. Hold on to him. He's good for you, she continued.

I sipped my drink, etching the moment into my memory, hiding my flaming cheeks behind the rim of my glass. *I will*, I mouthed back.

The blood rushing to my face burned even hotter now, as I made the commitment in front of my friend.

Five hours later, Nick drove me home. I didn't want the night to end. We sat for a few minutes in comfortable silence, engine idling, my head resting on his shoulder, his arm stretched across the center console to pull me close.

"Thanks for inviting me tonight. I had a blast. Stud and Belle are great. If Tucker were here, he and Stud would be a terrible match. It would be a very tiring night."

"Yeah, Stud is pretty intense. He has energy for days. He just never stops. No pause button. But he's a true artist. Everything he touches turns to gold. And on top of that, he's the sweetest guy. Now I can't wait to meet *your* friends and learn interesting things about you too. I'm sure they have great Nick Peterson life stories to share."

Whoever that Tucker guy was, I bet he'd have a lot to say about Nick's antics over the years. Was I moving too fast? I'd kind of blurted out a not-so-subtle request to meet his friends…without really meaning to say it out loud. The last thing I wanted was to freak him out or make him think I was rushing things instead of letting us take our time.

For a short moment, I looked away, breathless, my pulse beating at the realization. First Belinda. Now, this. I swallowed. Nick had made it clear we needed to take things slow and get to know each other first, and I had agreed. I just couldn't seem to remember that with him sitting beside me, so close it short-circuited my common sense.

"How's the house renovation project going?" I asked, steering the conversation toward safer ground. Less personal. Much better.

"Good. So far, I've focused most of my energy on the exterior. The haunted-house vibe is fading, one wall at a time. Soon it'll look sharp. The interior doesn't need nearly as much work."

"Sorry I haven't had much time to help you out…been pretty busy. Tonight was nice, though. A well-earned rest after the whirlwind of the past few days."

He let his fingers glide up my arm, stopping at my shoulder where a tight, stiff spot made me wince. "Tensed?"

I rotated my head and rolled my shoulders to loosen up. "Yeah, I guess I am."

"Turn around."

Nick shifted closer and placed his hands on my upper back. My body responded instinctively, relaxing under his touch. With skilled hands, he worked out the tension, using his thumbs to knead the knots from my back.

"Oh, Nick… Wow. It's even better than what that

woman at the spa did the other day. Yes, right there." I moaned, unable to hold the sound in. My whole body seemed to sing beneath his palms. "Keep going." I purred and dissolved under his soothing touch. Nick kneaded my flesh, moving his fingers down the length of my arms and along my back. "Where did you learn this?" I asked. "No way you're this good by accident."

He snickered from behind me, and I savored the intimate closeness between us in the truck's cab. "My mom is a massage therapist…or used to be. She trained my sister and me at a young age. It's been years since I offered someone a massage, though."

I turned my head and grinned at him. "I feel like a VIP. Thank you. Do you also offer foot massage? I'm a sucker for those."

Nick laughed with me, the baritone sound clear and contagious."Yeah, my magic touch also goes to feet." He paused. "And other places…"

My cells tingled at his words. I could've tilted my head and locked lips with him, but refrained, lost in the pleasure he brought me, and in our promise not to rush things. Because right now, if I gave in, nothing would hold me back—not until we reached the edge and free-fell, together, into whatever came next.

Nick's hands continued their wonder, grounding me to the present.

I gasped every time he loosened a knot.

He trailed his hands down my arms, stopping on my thighs. This could be it—the moment we'd combust together. I could throw caution to the wind and give in to whatever was brewing between us.

Air barely reached my brain as a flood of sensations surged through me. It had been years since a man had touched me this way.

My head spun in a rush of dizzy heat. The flutters his touch had sparked the other day now surged, pulsing in a steady rhythm low in my belly. A single spark could blow the entire truck to pieces.

Nick moved his palms to my hips, kneading the tender flesh there with his thumbs.

Could I climax just from a massage?

I heard his breath hitch behind me, sharp and shuddering.

We were playing a game neither of us seemed able to step away from.

"Dahlia."

Ohmygod. My name rolled off his tongue, slow and deliberate, sending shivers down my spine. His mouth traced the curve of my nape, and I saw stars.

I hadn't been touched, or loved, by a man in so long. It felt like I was seeing the sun after a few years of hibernation, and I savored the feeling. I wanted more. No, scratch that. I needed more.

I twisted in my seat, ready to set aside all our pseudo-friendship rules and give in to what my body, mind, and soul craved most when a ringtone broke the lust-filled silence.

Nick groaned, and the throaty sound only heightened the desire coursing through my bloodstream. I wished to hear it again, but with our bodies entangled, and blissfully satisfied. God, keeping those thoughts—the images I'd painted in my mind—at bay grew harder with every passing second. I felt bereft when his hands left my body to grab the phone and decline the call. Why were we always interrupted? Panting, I watched his face over my shoulder as he scowled at the device.

The phone rang again.

"Tuck," he muttered, his eyes shooting daggers at the flashing screen.

The interruption—unwelcome, but maybe necessary—diffused the storm raging inside me. Within minutes, the air in the cab felt normal again, and I sank back against the seat.

My voice dropped to a whisper. "I have to get inside. I told the babysitter I wouldn't come home too late."

The man who could so easily steal my heart nodded as I traced the shape of his mouth with the pad of my thumb. My breath sizzled as his tongue darted out to lick the tip. "Yes. We'll talk later, okay?"

We intertwined our fingers, and I had to summon superhuman effort to let go as longing rose inside me, swelling and refusing to be tamed. Now that Nick Peterson was a part of my life and held an important place in it, I found myself savoring the way we existed together. Every hour with him strengthened our bond, yet I had no way to explain the effortless chemistry between us.

I ran my fingers through my hair after I closed the front door behind me and pressed my back against the panel, begging my heart to quiet its violent thrum.

What had just happened?

Chapter 2

The next few days went by quickly. I was so busy with everything that I barely had any time to myself. I hadn't seen Nick since that night we went out with Stud and Belinda almost a week ago.

We texted a few times, exchanging *hellos* and *good nights*, but with both of us so busy, it lacked its usual warmth. Ever since that night at the barn and our double date, things between us had shifted from good to something truly amazing. Our bond felt stronger and deeper. Nick had become a huge part of my life in a short period of time, and if I was being honest with myself, after days without seeing him, I kind of missed him.

Each time we talked, a smile lingered on my lips for hours afterward. The man had a way of teasing me, challenging me, and caring for me all at the same time, and I relished the feeling.

"Dah, you've been talking about Nick for the last ten minutes. You should call him or pay him a visit. Are the sparks between you still there?" Addison asked as we video chatted once I'd put Jack to bed.

I grinned like an idiot. "Yes. And they've only intensified with each time we spend together."

"Then don't let him walk away."

"The other night when we had dinner with Stud and Belle, it was…huh…it was… I'm not sure I possess the right words to explain it."

"Try anyway."

"When we're together, it feels as if we've always been like this. Dahlia and Nick going out with friends. Easy. Simple. Matter-of-factly. During dinner, he kissed me like it was the normal thing to do… It's like we've known each other a long time."

Addison's voice turned high-pitched, and she clapped her hands in joyous enthusiasm—just like a kid. "Okay, I hear you. It's perfect. You didn't scare him away by bringing up his grief the other night or by suggesting he talk about it. And I'm pretty sure your near-orgasm during that massage only turned him on. Either he needs time to deal with everything going on in his life, or with whatever he left behind, or he's just busy with work. Don't wait. What you two could have is precious. Priceless. Fight for what you deserve, girlfriend. What are you waiting for? Call him already."

"I know we're both fairly occupied and stuff, but what if he's changed his mind?"

"What do you mean?" my friend asked. "You told me yourself that you almost came the last time you were together, when his hands traveled all over you."

"I did." Oh God, if I shut my eyes, I could relive that

instant with great details. "But he's the one who insisted we take our time. Maybe he could tell I was on the verge of giving in, and he's not ready for that yet."

"Don't be silly. If it's not his work, the only logical explanation is that he got spooked because you brought up his late friend the other night. Guys aren't exactly known for talking about their emotions. Not all of them are Carter Hills. He's one of a kind."

The words lingered between us. Addison once had a serious crush on Carter, but since he didn't reciprocate her feelings, it never went anywhere. Sometimes she still wondered what might have been. She admitted it one night after a bad breakup, when she came over to vent and talk shit about her ex.

"Back to Nick.Give him time. Maybe he needs to work through some emotional stuff…on his own. Anyway, grow some balls, girlfriend. If your words opened his wound, use them to help heal it. Be brave. Be fearless. Be the friend you promised to be—the one he can share his sorrow with, even without words. You're Dahlia Ellis. You've been through much more than this. Woman up. Take the lead. Take action."

"Ever thought about leading group therapy sessions?" We both chuckled until I spoke again. "Addi, I know you're right. I'm just not sure what I should do. Or rather, how to do this."

"Dah, I'm just thinking out loud here. Do you think the whole "star thing" could have scared him? Like, you used to be super famous, and maybe that intimidates him. You said he and Carter didn't click… Perhaps he finally decided it's a bigger deal than he realized."

I sighed. "Nah. If it were the case, it would have happened sooner, no? Why now?" I nibbled my thumbnail. "No, it can't be that. We were good, I swear. After the night I brought up his late friend, we went on that double date, and the sexual tension between us was undeniable. But now, he's sending short texts and is suddenly too busy to spend time with me…" I sighed again. "Nothing makes sense."

"Ask him. Plain and simple. Or take a page out of my Wilde's playbook and do something crazy. Go to his place, kiss him—you're both being too reasonable by sticking to that friendship rule, by the way—and show him what he's missing. Use that sexual energy you've both been basking in to rock his world. He'll thank you. I know I would."

I snickered. "Yeah. This is the perfect recipe for disaster. I'm not sure I remember how to flirt…or be upfront. The night at the shop pre-opening, I kissed him first, and…he…he recoiled."

"Forget it. He explained why. You two have spent a lot of time together since, and you kissed many times. Go to him. Set the record straight."

"Why are you always my voice of reason? You're right. I should. I will. Tomorrow."

"See? Easy peasy. Keep me updated. I'm rooting for you."

I giggled. "You better."

I moved to my bedroom and unclasped the chain around my neck. The one that held my wedding ring.

"What are you doing?" Addison asked as I stored the ring into a box after pressing it to my lips.

"Moving on. It's about time. Jeff lives in here," I said, pointing to my heart.

"You sure?"

I nodded. "Yes." I blew out a long breath. "It feels right. It's time…to let go. If I wanna move forward, I have to put the past to rest."

"Dah, I'm proud of you. You're amazing. Nick is a

lucky man. Don't worry, okay? Things will work out between you guys. I can feel it."

"I love you. Night, Addi."

"Love you too. Night, girlfriend."

In the upstairs bathroom, I undressed and slipped into a hot bath with a glass of red wine in hand. Country music played on a small speaker set on the countertop as I sealed my lids, my thoughts drifting to Nick—for the thousandth time today. He'd been center stage in most of my dreams since the day we met, taking up way too many of my brainwaves during the day.

Addison was right. Our friendship was too precious to let it go to waste and not explore it further.

As I sank into my thoughts, the sound of the doorbell startled me. In one swift movement, I dried off and wrapped a towel around myself. Who could it be at this late hour? The only person who ever stepped onto my front porch, day or night, was Carter, but he wasn't in town, so I really had no clue who it could be.

Hurrying down the stairs, I rushed to the front door. The man on the other side looked nothing like Carter Hills. Blond hair, broad shoulders, tanned skin.

Nick stood there, his head hanging low, kicking the deck with the sole of his shoe, still in his work clothes—a white T-shirt, a dark plaid vest, dirty jeans, and tan boots —looking hot and messy, his stubble longer than usual.

"Hey," I said, folding my arms over my chest, remembering I wore nothing but a towel. A smile tugged at my lips at the sight of him.

"Dahlia, I'm sorry for coming here so late." He paused. "I-I just wanted to apologize, and…huh…it couldn't wait."

"You are? Why?"

He shook his head. "I ghosted you, but I didn't mean to. It has nothing to do with you, and everything to do with me. The last week has been crazy, but now I was afraid you'd think you did something wrong, which is far from the truth. I shouldn't have come here at this late hour, but I wanted to explain."

"Did you just leave work?" Or had direct access to my naughty thoughts? Because seeing Nicholas Peterson dressed in construction attire was something my eyes would never get enough of. He looked effortlessly masculine, hot, and focused, like he'd just stepped straight out of a fantasy.

A black smudge grazed his upper brow, and several more marked the front of his white T-shirt, which clung to his toned abdomen.

His tousled hair gave him that boyish-manly look I loved so much.

I ogled him with no shame as his irises, two golden gems, scanned the length of me.

I blinked, breaking our silent flirtation.

Nick gave a single nod. "I pulled a lot of overtime this week. An unplanned project landed in my hands, and I wanted to get ahead. I was used to working much longer shifts in Chicago, so adjusting to the shorter schedule here has been tough. Anyway, someone asked for my help—"

"Wanna come in? I can warm something up for you… or huh…make you a sandwich. If you haven't eaten yet. In a past life, I was crowned the Sandwich Queen. That's how good they are, I'm telling you. You won't want to miss one."

His lips curled at the corners, and the sight sent bursts of longing through me. "It's tempting, but I'm not staying. It's late, and you must be tired. I just wanted to clear the air. Friendship is sacred to me, and I'm never letting my friends down. Oh, and I brought you something."

He handed me a small, square cardboard pastry box.

"What is it?" I asked. "I love surprises."

"Every night this past week, I've been working at that cookie shop that's opening next weekend. The owner gave me this as a thank you. I thought you and Jack would like it. There are frog and rabbit-shaped cookies in there. Oh, and they're organizing a kid's cookie decorating workshop in a couple of weeks. Maybe Jack would like to go. Just in case, I booked him a spot—"

My eyes rounded. "You did?"

"Yeah. It lasts about twenty minutes, and he'll get to decorate a bunch of cookies with frosting and eat them afterward. I thought it could be fun. The lady told me even a toddler would love it."

I blinked. "You brought us cookies and booked my son a workshop?"

"Oh shit. Is he allowed to eat sugary treats? I didn't think about asking first."

I grabbed his hand between mine. "Yes, he is. Just not every day. Anyway, that's very sweet of you. Now come in, you must be starving. I'll feed you." I winked, and he snickered with a shake of his head. "For the record, I'm not taking no for an answer. Also, I could use the company because I've missed my friend this week."

After I changed into a pair of lounge pants and a seafoam-green cotton long-sleeved T-shirt, Nick and I sat on the opposite sides of the table, and I watched him engulfing his sandwich. No. Attacking his food would be a better word.

"This is amazing," he said with a mouthful.

"For how long have you been underfed?" I teased.

"Nah. I'm not. Just haven't eaten all day. Too busy."

A smear of mustard clung to the corner of his lips, catching my attention.

"You have—" I pointed to his face.

A soft blush colored his cheeks. "I what?"

On my feet, I neared him, and using the pad of my finger, I wiped away the yellow blot, then brought the coated finger to my lips.

Time stood still.

The air froze between us, around us, enveloping us.

A warm tide rose from somewhere deep inside me.

I swayed, leaning on the table to stay upright.

I couldn't find the right words to explain the swarm of butterflies in my stomach, each bigger and more beautiful than the other. They multiplied at a vertiginous speed, and I had to blink to break the trance I'd fallen into.

Nick swallowed, and it soon cast another spell on me. One I wished to never escape.

The heat radiating from his muscular frame stirred something deep within me. With a deep inhale, my eyes fluttered closed as one of his hands molded around my nape while the other rested on my hipbone. My body drank in his masculine scent, and my soul basked in his glow.

Every touch of him branded my skin through our clothes.

My thundering heart pounded in my skull, its rhythm dizzying.

I closed my hand around his elbows, my anchors to stay grounded in this world.

Nick skimmed my forehead with his warm lips, and a new tide, now flooded with raw lust, surged within me.

A small gasp left my mouth when his lips trailed to the side of my cheek and lingered there for a long moment.

My head spun as Nick's grip on me tightened, and I reminded myself to breathe.

Caressing the shell of my ear, his rough voice sent shivers through my heart. "Thanks for dinner. Again, I'm sorry I've been distant. Never again. I've missed you too much."

If only I could hold on to him like this forever. Through the storms and the fun times. Through darkness and complete illumination.

A long exhale escaped his mouth, and his shoulders slouched slightly as he stepped back, breaking the moment. He gathered the empty glass and plate and loaded the dishwasher while I stood there, still entranced by everything he was.

After a while, he came back and pressed his forehead to mine. "Are you gonna be okay?" he asked, the whiskey-deep tone of his voice, diffusing shivers through me.

I nodded.

"Good." Why did the word sound so painful coming from his mouth? As if he hoped I'd plead for his help, his presence, his care, so he wouldn't have to leave.

He lowered his head and pressed a kiss to my cheek— so soft, that tremors shook me. And so intoxicating, I believed for a moment I was drunk.

Nick stepped back, my hand nestled in his. "Night, Dahlia."

He flashed me a hint of a smile, and my heart kindled.

I blinked again, and he was gone. The door clicked behind him, taking a piece of my heart in its wake.

Air returned to my lungs, oxygen made its way to my brain, and I regained control of my body. I blew out a long breath, wondering if I'd dreamed the entire scene. My hand flew to my cheek. The whisper of his kiss was all he left behind, the sole reminder of him.

———

The next day, I surveyed the business I'd created from scratch. Gowns made by local and foreign designers, prom dresses, bridal attires, accessories like shoes, purses, tiaras. Dahlia's Bridal Shop had something for everyone. Including a kid's section with smaller versions of high-fashion labels. It even carried an exclusive line of bridal wear by a coveted designer from Milan, along with a more affordable collection bearing my name that I co-designed.

As the owner, I spent a lot of time dealing with orders and numbers. Even though I enjoyed the business side of things, I also loved meeting with women and helping them choose the most beautiful gown for their perfect day—making their princess dreams feel within reach.

The shop was busier than I'd ever expected, which forced me to hire another employee. I couldn't keep working ten-hour shifts seven days a week. Jack spent most weekdays with Paula, but his nights and most weekends were mine. No matter what, that wouldn't change.

Truthfully, I could have chosen never to work another day in my life. My future was already secure. But I still had dreams—I still wanted to reach for them—and this bridal shop sat at the very top of the list.

Right after finding love again.

And maybe having another child.

Someday…one day.

Anyway, being a retiree in my early twenties didn't suit me. Not at all.

Today, I came home early, wanting to spend some quality time with my baby.

"Jack's still asleep, Ms. Ellis," Paula said as I dropped my purse on the kitchen island.

"Thank you, Paula, and please call me Dahlia." She nodded, but I knew she wouldn't—just like the fifty times before I'd asked her. "You can go home. I'll take it from here."

She left, and after I changed into a pair of cotton shorts and a hoodie, I climbed into Jack's bed, molded my body to his, closed my eyes, and let exhaustion lull me to sleep by his side.

We woke up from our nap two hours later, rested.

"Nick came over last night and brought you something. Hungry for a cookie?" I asked my baby boy as we sat on the back deck, watching squirrels jumping from trees, basking in the final hour of daylight.

"Yay," he screamed, hopping all around me. "Cookies. Cookies. Love cookies. Mama, gimme."

After fishing the pastry box out of the kitchen, I joined him back outside and lifted the lid.

"Oh," Jack said. "Frogs. *Boing. Boing.*" He paused to imitate the animal. "*Boing. Boing.*"

I watched my son, his adorable grin in full bloom, clapping his hands as he reached for a green-frosted sugar treat.

He licked his lips, and I couldn't hide my smile.

"Good?" I asked.

He nodded, gulping down the last bite, his fingertips green with frosting.

Unable to resist, I tasted one too. "Ohmygod, you're right. Wow, these are delicious."

"*Deciliticious,*" he repeated, scooting over to settle on my lap.

With my palm, I ruffled his thick hair and kissed the top of his head.

Soon he squirmed out of my embrace and dashed toward the slide, sending the squirrels scattering as he ran after them.

Left alone, my thoughts drifted back to Nick and how

much I missed him. Last night had been nothing but a tease, making me yearn for him even more.

Jack called my name, and I joined him, scooping him up in my arms and tickling him while he laughed his heart out.

On the swing, with my arms wrapped around him, I rocked my son back and forth as an idea popped into my head.

Chapter 3
Nicholas

I got home early, ready to paint another wall of the house. The sun sparkled in the azure sky, not a cloud in sight. I stood atop a ladder with a paintbrush in hand, letting the warm mountain breeze brush my face. Country music—something I'd come to really like, thanks to a certain redhead I couldn't get out of my head—played from a portable speaker I'd set on the banister below. I hummed softly, lost in my task when Chaz joined me, Buddy trailing behind him.

"Hey, guys," I greeted. "Bud, I thought you weren't coming today," I added with a smile.

The bloodhound made a noise that sounded like a sigh and huddled in a quiet corner beneath his favorite tree.

Both Chaz and I exchanged a laugh and a shrug.

I leaned back to admire my work. The top of the wall looked fierce with a fresh coat of white paint.

"From down here, it looks pretty great. Need a hand?"

the teen asked, approaching the base of the ladder where I was still perched.

"Are you skilled with a paintbrush?"

"Huh…not sure, but I'm afraid of heights. Please don't ask me to come up there with you."

I let out a warm chuckle. "Not a chance. You can paint the windowsills if you wanna give it a try. It's pretty straightforward. I already sanded them the other day. Grab a can of paint and a brush from the back of my truck, and you'll be all set."

In no time, Chaz got to work. After an hour of painting in silence, he asked, "Do you miss Chicago?"

"Everybody in this town has been asking me that question." I smiled with a shake of my head. "The truth is, I don't. Which, to be honest, surprised me at first. I love how simple life is around here. The absence of traffic is a huge plus. People here are happy, and friendly. I'm still not used to the rumor mills, but other than that, I get why people would want to move to Green Mountain and raise a family." I climbed down the ladder, shifted it to the right, and climbed back up. "Have you been to Columbus yet?"

"No," the teen said. "My parents and I are going soon, so I can get to know the city and everything before the big day. We'll go to—"

My phone rang.

I reached for my back pocket, only to realize I'd left it on the banister."Chaz, can you get that?"

"Sure." A pause. "Hi, this is Nick's phone." Pause. "No, I'm his neighbor." Pause. "Yes." A longer pause. "No."

I snickered. By the sound of the interrogation going on, I'd bet Tucker was on the other end of the line.

"Nick," Chaz said, "this guy named Tucker says it's an emergency." He held my phone above his head.

With a huff, I climbed down and snatched it from his grasp. "Hey, Tuck, what's up?"

"Man," he said, "where have you been? I've been texting and calling you nonstop like a clingy girlfriend, and you never reply or call back."

"Sorry," I said, wiping my stained hands on my jeans. "Been busy. Working overtime and all that stuff."

"Yeah, yeah. We almost never talk anymore since you moved. I'm beginning to think you prefer the company of a dog to mine." He sighed, and I was pretty sure he rolled his eyes too. Tucker was always aiming for the drama.

"Seriously, you should leave the finance world and go straight to Hollywood. You'd be a much better actor. And knowing you're the best at your job, it's saying something. What's the emergency?"

"None. Just a marketing strategy to make sure you wouldn't avoid my call this time."

"Huh…okay, but I'm in the middle of something, and you're being paranoid."

"No, there is actually something. How is it going with that girl you told me about? Still in the friend-zone or did you score a goal like pussy-whipped Jace would say?"

Why did I open my mouth about Dahlia to him of all people? "Yep, we're friends. For now."

From the cooler on the ground, I fetched a bottle of water, uncapped it, and took a long swig.

"What does that even mean? You get sucked on the side, or you tap that pussy only on the weekends? Unless you jerk yourself off to oblivion every night. Do you fix roof leaks in Green Mountain too? I bet your services are in high demand. Uncle Mike could start a new department."

Water spilled from my mouth as I burst out laughing. "Fuck, Tuck. No roof leaks. And don't drag Mike into your kink. No need to brand these images into my head. C'mon, man." I shook my head and wiped my dripping chin with the back of my hand. "For what it's worth, and I can't believe I'm actually laying out the facts for you, our relationship is not like that. Why am I even trying to explain myself?"

Beside me, Chaz faked to be fascinated by his phone screen, but he was clearly listening to our conversation, judging by the grin on his face.

Tucker continued as if I hadn't said a word. "Nick, you're confusing me. Why no sex? This is fucked-up. Are you sure you're okay?"

"Tuck, I'm great. Never been better."

Chaz mouthed, *I gotta get going*, when my eyes landed on him.

I moved the phone away from my face. "Thanks for your help. See you around."

The teen waved and disappeared behind the line of trees.

Buddy raised his head to watch him leave, but didn't make the slightest move to follow him home.

I exhaled a chuckle. This dog.

"Neighbor?" my friend asked once I brought my attention back to him.

"Yep. Was helping me paint the house." I sat on one of the front porch steps, elbows resting on my bent knees. "To answer your question, that woman and I are friends, but I'd like us to be more. Eventually. When we're both ready to give it a real shot. I don't want us to be a fling. She's long-term commitment material, man, not a woman you fuck and forget all about. She's special."

"Shit. So, she's out of my league then."

I spit a laugh. "Forget it. She's too good for you. They all are. I have to go, not done with the wall yet."

"Call me later."

"Sure thing. Please stay out of trouble."

Tucker's deep laughter filled the line before we hung up.

Soon my thoughts drifted to Dahlia. As if she'd read my mind, she sent me a text message followed by a picture of her and Jack eating cookies.

DAHLIA

> You should have at least kept one. These are amazing. Can I join the kid's workshop? I'd do anything for cookies.

My stare locked on their happy grins as my thumbs typed.

ME

> You like cookies? My bad, I pictured you more as a joystick kinda woman.

DAHLIA

> Dear God. You're the worst.

ME

> You make it too easy for me. Anyway, you've got green frosting at the corner of your mouth. If you were here, I'd take care of it.

I pressed *send*, savoring the flirting we always indulged in. Since the night at the barn and the double date happened, I wasn't convinced we could stay just friends for much longer.

DAHLIA

> Wish you were here with us.

> Can we talk tonight?

ME

Wine and midnight talk? Sounds good.

I pictured her laughing with her head tilted back.

DAHLIA

Let's say nine o'clock chat and wine. Deal?

ME

I'll be there.

DAHLIA

It's a date then.

———

At eight fifty-seven, my phone went off. Not that I had been checking the time. Okay, fine, I had. My pulse raced when Dahlia's name flashed on the screen. A warm flush hit me. Great, now I felt like a teenager on a first date.

I scratched the column of my throat before answering and smoothed my T-shirt as if Dahlia could see me. "Hey you," I said the moment I accepted the call.

"Hey, Nick. Free for our chat and wine?" she asked, her voice low, with a hint of a smile.

"I wouldn't miss it for the world. Since I don't have the honor of picking you up for our date, I have a few questions for you first."

"Go ahead. Hit me."

My lips curled. "It's just one, in fact. What are you wearing?" I asked, slouching on the couch with my feet resting on the square ottoman.

Dahlia's sharp intake of breath resonated through the phone, followed by a low chuckle. "It's not really sexy, but it's comfy. Cartoon PJ pants and a T-shirt Jack painted for Mother's Day. It's a modern-style piece of art with blue as the dominant color. Very fancy and unique. Every designer's dream."

"You should frame it. Could be worth a fortune someday." My phone pinged, and a photo of Dahlia, gorgeous with her hair loose and rosy cheeks, her wineglass in hand, and wearing that piece of clothing, filled the screen. "Yeah, I agree, definitely museum material. Jack is awesome."

"He is. Being pregnant at twenty was a surprise, but in the end, it was for the best. He's the greatest thing that has ever happened to me. As if life knew I'd need him to keep living. Now your turn to send me a picture. You've seen my outfit. Let me see yours."

I pointed the camera of my phone at me and smiled. Okay, I looked stupid. I ran a hand over my face and tried again. It took me about five poses to get a good enough result.

"You know, I've never done this before," I said.

"What? Being charming over the phone?"

I sipped my wine, shaking my head. "No. Sending a selfie to someone… Well, not exactly… I mean sending a selfie to a woman."

"So, I'm your first?"

"You are."

"Oh, I like the sound of that," Dahlia teased.

And, for some stupid reason, it made me proud. At that moment, I missed being able to touch her. To kiss her. To hold her.

"Please don't judge me if I didn't nail it. I might need a couple more tries." I lowered my voice. "Or a private lesson."

"Nick, stop. You're perfect." Her gravelly voice turned my insides to mush. "Nice shirt, by the way. You're a solid nine out of ten. Don't let it go to your head."

"God, you're a tough one to please. Dully noted. You subtracted a point. Why?"

"The lighting. There's a shadow on your left side. Other than that, it would have been a perfect shot. I'll still keep it, though."

Dahlia's laughter lit up a thousand fires inside me.

"I had no idea you were also a photography critic. Is there something you can't do?" I asked, taking another sip.

"A million things. But you'll have to stick around to find out."

My playfulness faded, my tone turning serious, every cell in my body vibrating. "I can't wait to learn about them. I'm sure you're being too hard on yourself."

"We'll see. And just to be clear, you'll be allowed to grade me too." Silence stretched between us. "Nick, I just wanted say…thank you."

"For what?"

"For being you."

My heart swelled and pushed against my ribs as her words streamed through me.

"Thank you for being you too. Walking into your shop by mistake that day is the best thing that's happened to me since I got here." I breathed in some air and a hefty dose of courage. "Can I tell you something?"

Her voice became a throaty whisper. "Yes."

"I wish I could see you right now."

Was she panting? "Open your video chat. I wanna see you too."

"Hey," I said when her face filled my screen.

Dahlia was sitting on her bed, holding her phone in one hand and her wine glass in the other. How much would I give right now to be able to kiss her? Just another kiss to relive the ones we'd shared and feel her warmth against my chest. And get lost in her green irises. Trace the curls of her hair between my fingers. Touch her. Hold her. Fuck her.

Uncomfortable on the couch, I moved to my bed, my phone resting against my folded legs, my glass in one hand and the other cupping my junk, the tightness in my crotch becoming unbearable.

"Do you believe in soul mates?" Dahlia asked, breaking the painful threads of my thoughts.

"Sure. I believe we're all destined to be with someone for a reason nobody can explain. A force greater than us placing people on our road for a purpose. Why?"

"Because I've been asking myself this question a lot lately. Can someone have more than one soul mate in life? Don't answer…it's silly."

I searched her gaze through the small rectangular screen. "Dahlia, it's not silly. If I were in your shoes, I'm sure I'd be asking myself the same question. I love when you're offering me a window to your thoughts…and to your soul."

I'd trade everything just to hug her right now and chase away the doubts shining in her eyes.

Silence fell between us, both of us lost in our own minds for a moment.

"What's your favorite travel destination?" I asked, trying to get rid of the heaviness enveloping us.

"Why?" Dahlia furrowed her brows, and I traced them on the screen with a fingertip, as if I could smooth them out from here.

"Because. I think people's tiniest preferences tell a lot about them."

"New Zealand. Favorite food?"

"Chicken wings."

"Sweet or spicy?"

"Spiciest, the best," I said. "Favorite season?"

"Spring. I love how everything wakes up. Favorite sport?"

"If I'm playing, baseball. If I'm watching, hockey. Your middle name?"

"Elisabeth. I love this game. Yours?"

"Jake."

Dahlia's eyes flared. "Nah, you don't look like a Jake. I much prefer Nicholas."

The sound of my name—my full name—leaving her lips sent shivers up my spine to the very tip. Nobody except my mother—and strangers—called me this, and it had never sounded as sexy as coming from Dahlia's mouth.

"Nick, thanks for doing this with me. Talking, sharing, laughing. Being a mother, sometimes it…it scares people away."

I set my empty glass on the nightstand and turned to my side, my phone propped up against a pillow and one arm folded under my head. "It would take a lot more than that to chase me away, Dahlia. I think it's amazing that you're a mom. I'd never see this as something negative. It's part of who you are. Part of what makes you, *you*. What makes you amazing."

A faint blush colored her cheeks. "I have no idea where you come from, Nick Peterson—"

"Chicago," I whispered while she grinned.

"Now that I know you, if you didn't exist, I would have to invent you. I'm kind of a fan."

The way the last word left her mouth with that southern drawl broke me in the most delicious way. All I craved now was to drive up to her place and kiss her senseless until neither of us could breathe on our own anymore. And to do nasty things to her. I remembered the taste of her lips, and every night, I prayed to taste them again and devour all of her right after.

"So, you're telling me I have my own fan club now?"

"And I'm the president. I'm not crazy, I swear," she said, using the words we exchanged the day we met.

"First, don't get ahead of yourself. I'm sure there are things about me that would drive you nuts."

Dahlia chuckled. "I doubt it. I've learned a long time ago that people are complex individuals with many layers, but the truth lies within their hearts. That's where you gotta aim. In your case, your heart is pure gold. I'm a good judge of character. Don't try to sell yourself short." She stared at me, her tongue tracing her lower lip. "Tell me something annoying about you. I'll tell you if it's *that* bad." She arched a brow, challenging me with her eyes.

Damn, I loved how her power over me made me confess all my sins to her.

"I hate lies. My temper usually flares up when people tell me half-truths or lie right to my face. I also hate when things get chaotic. It drives me insane, and I withdraw into myself until I straighten them up."

"If those are your flaws, then we're good." Dahlia yawned, and I followed suit.

"You tired?" I looked at the time. "Whoa, it's already past midnight. Where did the time go?"

"A little, but I don't wanna hang up. I like our late-night talk. It feels like I know you better…or in a more intimate kind of way." With my finger, I traced her lips on the screen. "I enjoy being your friend tonight."

"Anytime."

Dahlia's voice grew warm and steady. "After Jeff passed away, I've made it my mission to end each day by telling the people I care about how important they are to me." Her eyes turned glossy in the dim light. "It's something I have to do… I-I never got a chance to tell him those words or to hear them from him one last time…"

My throat worked. A truckload of emotions knotted around my stomach and rattled my heart. "I know what you mean. Been there too." I pinched my lips together, holding back my emotional overload before it could spill over. The last time I went to see Derek, he slept the entire few hours I was there, and I never got a chance to tell him one last time how important he had been to me. "I'm glad we found each other." Through the screen, we gazed at each other for a long moment before I spoke the words lingering on the tip of my tongue. "Dahlia Ellis, you're passionate and strong. And fearless in your convictions. Your energy is soothing. I'm sure everyone around you feels loved."

She locked her eyes on mine. "Nick, there's something about you... A vulnerability. I'm not sure what it is, but it's there. I sense it." She paused. "Not a lot of people reflect the wisdom you possess. It's a great quality. You left everything you'd ever known behind to start afresh. That's very brave of you. You should be proud of yourself for being strong when you could have been weak."

"Guess we both ran away when things got too tough."

She shrugged. "You and I, we both had two choices. Stay and be miserable and haunted by our past, or leave, rise from the ashes, and wish for something new. Something better. We're very much alike."

"I wouldn't say my level of courage equals yours, though."

"Having a broken heart isn't a competition. When facing it, we each handled the pain as best we could. For what it's worth, I'm glad you left Chicago."

Something twisted in my stomach.

I didn't want to let her go. I wanted to hold on to her for a little longer. "Me too."

We contemplated each other. Something passed

between us. Fascination. Understanding. Interest. And flakes of lust too.

I was right when I said that from the moment we met, it felt like I'd known her forever.

Right here, right now, our souls were living a journey of their own as if they had to connect because they could understand each other, learn from each other, and heal together.

I cleared my throat. "Now, go to sleep. I'm here, and I'll watch over you."

"Why?"

"Because. You're important to me."

"Good night, Nick," Dahlia said between yawns.

"Night." Our gaze bored into each other for a few more seconds until she looked away, moving to turn off her bedside lamp.

Watching her drift into sleep, the steady rhythm of her breaths stirred feelings in my heart I'd never experienced before.

This was the most surprising date I'd ever had. Dahlia was her own person, and I loved how careful, yet willing to open up to me, she had been tonight.

I hadn't dated lots of women in my life—my dating records didn't compare to Tucker's—but Dahlia had an almost virgin record. She'd told me once Jeff had been her one and only. Deep down, I loved how sweet and innocent she was about everything, a contrast to the self-assured woman she usually projected. This new side of her grew on me. From an outsider's point of view, she appeared to have everything figured out, but this version of her tonight showed me just how fragile she could also be.

And damn, everything about her enticed me.

With my thumb, once I made sure she was deep asleep,

I ended the video call. A pinch squeezed my heart when her face faded on the screen. "Good night, Dahlia."

For the first time in a long time, my last thoughts before dozing off didn't travel to my memories of Derek and the day I pressed that awful button.

Sleep claimed me, and my dreams swarmed with the woman I was beginning to crave more and more every single day.

Derek's Bucket List – ~~*20. Nick. Go on a different kind of date*~~

Chapter 4

Dahlia

"How are you doing?" Carter asked from across the ocean a few days later. I squeezed the phone between my cheek and shoulder as I hung up the new bridal lingerie I'd just received. A teal lace babydoll set with matching panties caught my eye, and I held it up in front of the wall-length mirror, imagining myself wearing it.

I had no idea when was the last time I'd dreamed of wearing something sexy and beautiful underneath my clothes. The realization filled me with a heady rush of secret thrill.

"Dah, you there?"

Carter's voice brought me back to the present.

"Huh, yep. Sorry. Distracted. I'm great." I put the lingerie aside, ready to take it home. "How was the concert last night?" I asked, giving him my complete attention. Carter's new tour had kicked off in Europe yesterday.

"Uneventful. Is Jack through the night these days? He was having more nightmares than usual the last time he stayed over."

"He hasn't had any in a few days. He woke up once last night, and that's been the only time so far."

"And the fever?"

Yesterday, my little boy had woken up with a fever, but it had subsided during the day. "Gone. He was still asleep when I left him with Paula this morning, but he was in top shape before bed last night."

"Call me if it returns. I hate knowing I won't be there to help you out if he's sick or something. If you need me, I can hop on the jet and be there within a few hours, though."

"Stop worrying. Nightmares aren't life-threatening. And the fever only lasted a couple of hours. Nothing serious. We'll be fine. Do your thing. Anyway, Nick is around if I need a hand."

"Dah—"

"Stop it, Cart. Nick and I are friends. Like you and I."

"Fuck. It's not the same, and you know it. All that guy wants is to get into your pants."

"And that's not what you want?" Carter remained silent as I apologized. "Sorry. That was a low blow. You care about me and want what's best for me. Listen, I'm just enjoying the idea of having someone around to spend time with. Nick is good for me. We get along great, and he makes me smile. Our relationship is new…and exciting. No matter what, the best friend title will always be yours, Cart."

"Dah, just say the word, and I'll drop everything and stay with you forever—" His voice cracked a little on the last word.

My heart too.

"I know, and I love you even more for saying this, but it wouldn't be fair. You shouldn't have to choose one or the other. Anyway, we'll never be together *that* way. For what it's worth, you're incredible onstage, and I'd never ask you to throw your gift away. Even if you begged me to. The stardom has always been yours, and I can't wait to see you the next time you play around here."

"In the fall, I'm playing in Nashville. You guys are staying with me at the penthouse for an entire week. We'll find someone to manage the shop, but I need both of you with me. I fucking miss you when you're that far away, and I'm stuck in some impersonal hotel room, on the other side of the world."

"Gosh, we always miss you too. How's Spain?"

"Just landed my ass in the suite. You are my one-call." I chuckled at the pun. "Can you believe I haven't done a show here since the Band days? It will be weird to be up there on my own tomorrow night."

"Carter, I'm always onstage with you…even if I'm not physically present."

"I know… Do you remember that guy we met who showed us around town the last time we came here? He's still working at the hotel. I saw him minutes ago, and he remembered us. Called you the fiery angel."

"Ohmygod. He did?"

"Yep."

We talked some more, then hung up.

At fifteen past four, I left the shop and hurried home to relieve Paula of her duty.

"Baby, wanna go see Buddy?" I squatted to hug Jack as he squealed in delight.

My son pulled away from me, and a heartwarming smile tugged at his lips. "Buddy," he singsonged. "Buddy. Buddy my *bestest* friend."

His contagious optimism warmed my heart.

Something clicked inside me as I watched my baby, sending tingles of excitement through me. Not because of the dog, but because of the man the dog had befriended. I couldn't help it—my heart ran wild for him.

"Let's go then," I said, gathering what we might need after I changed into denim cut-offs and a loose shirt, ready to leave. "We're having dinner there. My friend Nick invited us over. We wouldn't want to keep him and Buddy waiting for too long, right?"

A permanent grin was now etched on my face. No matter how ridiculous I looked with a smile too big to hide, nothing could wipe it away. Honestly, the idea of seeing Nick again sent sparks shooting through me.

With Jack's tiny fingers wrapped around mine, I knocked on the door. My pulse had started its berserk dance the moment I parked the car, and with every passing second, the rhythm grew even more berserk.

"Here you are," a masculine voice greeted me from behind. I nearly dropped the bag slung over my shoulder at the sound.

Nick.

He looked scrumptious.

My insides clenched.

There was no denying it. Nick Peterson possessed a hold on me and my hormones—and every inch of my womanly parts.

Jack's here. Act cool, I repeated in my mind because there was nothing calm about me or my demeanor right now. I was an explosive device on the edge of detonation. My insides twisted with need. My body amplified every signal Nick sent, tugging at every string of my composure.

Somehow, that phone date the other night had proven to me that we were meant to be. That what Nick and I shared was bigger than we could comprehend, that our connection was beyond words.

Jack let go of my finger and rushed toward the man who was looking at me with a barely concealed desire—something unfamiliar I hadn't noticed until today.

Nick picked him up and ruffled his hair. "Hey, little guy. I thought I heard you arrive. I was in the garage. Wanna gimme a hand? I made a bird feeder and was waiting for you to choose the perfect place to hang it."

"Yes," Jack said, squirming to be set down.

"Buddy's waiting for you under his favorite tree. Let's go see him first."

Jack ran toward the backyard as I climbed down the stairs to meet with Nick.

His arms pulled me closer the second I neared him, my heart now a throbbing mess inside my chest.

"You know you're wonderful with Jack, right?" I asked, breathless.

"Just with Jack?" he asked with an arched eyebrow, his smile hitting me straight in the heart.

I rose onto my tiptoes. "Not just Jack," I murmured against his lips before kissing him. Because that was all I'd been thinking about since that phone date.

"I've missed you too," he said, voicing the very thought in my head. He intertwined his fingers with mine, and hand in hand—as if we'd done this a hundred times—we walked toward my little boy.

Our smiles grew as we watched Jack tell Buddy all about his day. The dog twitched his ears in response, as if the stories were the highlights of his canine day.

"Little guy, ready to feed those birds?" Nick asked after their conversation was over.

My son moved to his feet and nodded.

"Great." Nick swiveled to face me. He traced his lips

down my cheek, leaving a trail of goose bumps in his wake. "There's a glass of wine waiting for you on the back deck. Make yourself at home. We'll be right back." I closed my eyes, my heart hiccupping in my chest, as Nick kissed the side of my face. "I won't be long, and I'll make it up to you later."

Air sizzled, and I almost lost my footing, drunk on his promises.

He turned to grab Jack's hand, and my lungs deflated with a woosh. How long had I been holding my breath?

After dinner, we went for a walk with Jack and Buddy, then my son fell asleep on the living room floor again, next to his best friend. Nick and I spent countless minutes watching them, enjoying the picture-perfect moment: Jack lying on his side, his arms wrapped protectively around the dog's neck.

"I feel bad about moving him," I whispered.

"They look so peaceful," Nick said. "We could try slipping a blanket underneath him, then cover them both without disturbing either one."

"That could work. Let's try."

We repositioned Jack alongside Buddy and spread a quilt over them.

In the kitchen, we refilled our wine glasses as I settled on the cool surface of the island, and Nick sat on the countertop next to the sink, three feet away from me.

"Thinking about moving here full time?"

His lips stretched. "I am."

"Told you. The mountain air."

He raked a hand through his hair. "Not sure it's the air, Dahlia."

Why was he looking at me like that? As if he were starving.

In a swift move, he jumped to his feet and stalked toward me.

"Gotta tell you something."

I gasped, choking on my own breath.

The room temperature soared to searing levels.

His lips parted, and my grip around the wine glass tightened, my heart bracing for whatever Nick was about to say.

I inhaled through my mouth to put to rest the jitters awakening inside me.

Nick stopped a foot from me, and I was pretty sure I melted as his eyes rested on mine.

My throat was parched from the heat radiating off him. My lips parted, my tongue tracing their length, but no sound followed. I swallowed hard, the silence thick between us.

Tremors shook me.

Nick stepped forward, and my gaze drifted to his mouth, waiting for him to say something—anything—to soothe the tension rising at my core.

Chapter 5
Nicholas

"Fuck, Dahlia. I'm not sure I want to be your friend anymore."

Hurt flashed in her eyes. Replacing the intensity that had been burning there all night. "W-why not?"

"Because I wanna kiss you so bad."

Her voice became a throaty whisper, and it tormented my agonized cells. "We already kissed. Many times."

"Dahlia, friends aren't supposed to kiss each other. Not the way I'm itching to. Not how I intend to. It's not in the rulebook… I checked. Believe me, I'm sure. And your being here right now, all beautiful and sexy, is driving me crazy." I paused to breathe properly. "Big fucking time."

Her breathless murmur quivered in the air. "You do? You…you did? The thing is"—she inhaled—"maybe it's time to change the rules. Nick, we've played long enough. I'm a mess because I think about you kissing me *this way* all the time. I do."

Pure unleashed electricity traveled through my veins. A fire sparked through my body as I discovered the depth of her desire, every nerve ending alive and hungry for more.

My lower body twitched just at the thought of her lips on mine…and mine, well, all over her soft flesh.

The woman was like a drug. She got me addicted to her essence with just a glance my way, and now I was a junkie craving her.

Dahlia's sharp intake of breath commanded my undivided attention. "Kiss me, Nick. Like you mean it. Like you want to. Like I belong to you."

She nibbled her bottom lip and molded her upper body to mine. Each thump of her heart reverberated through my chest. She captured my eyes, and I lost the battle within me.

With deliberate slowness, I took the wine glass from her hand and set it on the counter behind me, desire making my fingers tremble. A rising tempest within me made it hard to be gentle. I wanted to take her hard, the way I pictured myself doing so every night—every day. And every aching minute in between.

I slammed my lips on hers, tilting her head back, claiming her as mine, wanting to inhale her completely.

My heart probably skipped a few beats.

Dahlia gasped, and I thought I'd lose it.

Nothing was delicate or slow in the way I captured her lips. All the restraints I'd held onto for the past few weeks flew away. The roughness of my jaw brushed against the softness of hers. Desperate whimpers whirled around us. My torso pressed against hers, caging her and keeping me upright as my body convulsed, her lips savage against mine, accepting everything I demanded.

This wasn't a kiss. It was a seismic wave of desire washing over both of us. A tsunami of burning want.

I closed my eyes as I imprinted this moment on my heart.

Dahlia anchored herself to me. She fisted my T-shirt, urging me closer. Her other hand curled around my neck, a vice grip forbidding me to step back.

I stopped breathing. Only Dahlia existed for me in that instant.

She sucked on my tongue, and I swore I could have come right there.

Blood boiled in my veins as a sudden surge of need electrified me. I tangled my fingers in her hair, clutching her to me. My lips crushed hers. I bit them before soothing them with my tongue.

Her whimpers were my undoing.

I tugged her bottom lip between my teeth, barely able to contain myself. My eyes fluttered open, just enough to notice how beautiful she looked, lost in the moment between us.

Shivers of pleasure shot down my spine as she half-moaned and half-growled and pulled my lips back to hers. My tongue darted into her mouth, hungry and intense, eager to play with hers. I clamped my fingers around her hips while sensations spiraled with a searing need inside me. She shuddered in my arms, and my heart swelled as if it would burst out of my chest. My dick was about to drill a hole through my pants. Heat flared between us as we lost control, Dahlia's sounds awakening something wild within me.

Feral.

Animalistic.

Wild gasps and yelps.

Her body undulated against mine, hot and untamed. Mine dissolved under her touch as she caressed my chest and pinched my nipples between her fingers. I felt more alive than I ever had before. Thrilling. Only desire existed between us. We were lost in each other, in this connection, breathless and dazed.

This time, I looked at her. A thunderbolt called Dahlia had cleaved my body, igniting my core, scorching my spine.

She owned me. Every single bit.

We were about to crash and burn, and it scared me as much as it excited me.

Soon, we would explode together, consuming each other. I tried—I really tried—to talk myself out of it so our friendship could blossom for a little longer, but my body had a mind of its own. My soul too. And I gave in to both.

I curled a hand around her nape, my fingers digging into her skin, hating even the slightest space between us. Our mouths collided again. She tasted like a forbidden fruit, sweet and addictive. The taste of her wasn't enough —it would never be. If we crossed that line, there'd be no going back. Dahlia Ellis had become my *raison d'être*. My sin. My obsession.

Our lips moved in perfect sync, like a rehearsed choreography. No teasing. No hesitation. Just raw need and the urgency of wanting each other. Dahlia was offering herself to me, and like a greedy man, I intended to take all of her and give back ten times stronger. I wanted to blow her mind until she couldn't think, her body completely satiated.

Fire traveled through my bloodstream. My lower body pulsed, desperate for an immediate release.

Dahlia quivered in my arms, wild moans echoing from the back of her throat.

My brain went blank.

My senses sharpened.

My heart pounded in my chest.

One look into her eyes, and every nerve in me ignited.

Without another word, I cupped her cheeks as her gaze, demanding and scorching, found mine. So heavy, I almost forgot my own name.

I angled my mouth and sucked at the seam of her lips, dueling with her tongue in a delicious tango. Dahlia pulled me closer, her hands charting the searing ridges of my abdomen, goose bumps rising in their wake. I slid her forward until her hips reached the edge of the counter. She pressed herself into me, her body chasing the ache of something deeper. Tension wrapped around us until we were coiled tight with an urgency we could no longer ignore.

Every breath she took sent aftershocks through me, turning my flesh into a blazing inferno.

My hands roamed all over her still-clothed body. Too many layers of fabric separated us, preventing me from touching her, like really touching her in the way I'd been dreaming of since the day we met.

"Where have you been all my life?" I whispered against her mouth, ravenous for the woman rocking my world.

She moaned, her need for me woven through her words, the sound waking the beast inside me. "Here. Waiting for you to show up."

My hand ventured between her thighs, and she shivered when I traced the seam of her cut-offs, sensing her heat through the denim.

I drew circles over her clit through the fabric with my thumb, and she gasped. Taking advantage, I pushed my tongue deeper into her mouth, meeting hers in long, enticing strokes.

"Nick." Dahlia cried as she pushed her breasts forward while I traced her jawline, the column of her throat, and the contours of her collarbones with my mouth. "More," she demanded. "So much more."

With one arm, I lifted her into my arms and locked her ankles behind my back. I slid my hands beneath her shirt, my fingertips enjoying the feel of the warm skin of her back, before moving to her front. Squeezing her plump breast, I rolled a nipple between my fingers, the lace of her bra adding to the fiction. A low growl rumbled from her throat as she fisted my hair and consumed my lips.

I ground against her center, my dick seeking her warmth. Dahlia rolled her hips in an age-old dance, a symphony of purrs escaping her luscious lips.

"Shirt off," I ordered as I unclasped her bra, my hands greedy, not wanting to let go of her breasts, even for a second.

She lifted my shirt over my head, her eyes singeing my torso.

My body pulsed, and my heart rattled inside my chest.

This woman was killing me.

Taking her sweet time, she removed her top, her unclasped white bra revealing the most perfect mounds I'd ever seen. Creamy, round, big enough to fill my hands. My dick, now rock-hard, twitched in my pants.

I grazed the skin of her arms with my fingertips, from her shoulders down, freeing her from the dangling piece of lace. We both watched it fall as it landed on the planked floor. Our palms came together, and our fingers wove around each other.

"You're beautiful," I breathed out, still wrestling with myself not to give in and take her right here on the kitchen island.

Tilting her head back, Dahlia bit her lower lip, eyes alight with sparks.

My mouth grazed her earlobe, slowly tracing its way downward, licking and tasting. I nipped the flesh of her neck with my teeth, trailing over to the fullness of her chest, famished for the stiff buds pressing against my torso, pleading for attention.

"More," Dahlia begged, her voice husky, the sound orgasmic.

My dick pushed against the zipper of my pants, wanting to be let loose in this game.

I close my lips around one stiff nipple, and I sucked on the tip, flicking it with my tongue.

Dahlia moaned, a dark flush rising from her neck up.

"You taste like summer."

A low gasp escaped her lips.

"What does summer taste like, Nick?" Her voice shuddered, pleasure building inside her as I attacked her other nipple with my tongue, so hungry for her I could never stop.

Fuck, Dahlia's sex voice was like pure ecstasy shooting through my veins. And the way she said my name, with her southern inflection, destroyed me in the most delicious way.

"Sweet. Smart. Sexy. Sassy. Irresistible. Delicious. You. I have to taste all of you now."

She cupped my face in her hands and drew me up, her mouth claiming mine, plundering it with her ravenous tongue. "I can't wait…to know…what you taste like too," she said in between kisses, panting.

Those words. They shattered me. My brain, my resolve, my willpower, they all left me. Only my mouth, my dick, and my hands existed.

Dahlia unbuttoned my pants, her fingers set on their own mission. Her tongue darted out, tracing the curve of her lips.

I groaned, and another chain of my restraint clattered to the floor.

Before I could feel her touch on the burning piece of me aching for her, I stopped her with a hand.

She raised her gaze, question marks floating in her moss-green eyes.

"You first. Let me make you come. If you touch me, I won't last, and it will be over before we even get started. I'm about to explode just from the way your lips taste."

"But I—"

I silenced her with a bruising kiss, the kind that would sear itself into my lips forever. "You'll have plenty of time."

With steady fingers, I unbuttoned her cut-offs and pushed a finger inside her panties, relishing the wet warmth of her coating my digit. Dahlia screamed in delight, and I swallowed it as our lips sought more, never satisfied, never still.

"Fuck. Even your pussy is addictive."

I slid a second finger in, and Dahlia gripped my biceps, digging her fingernails into my skin, and arched her back, mewing like a kitten.

"Oh, God, Nick… Yes. It-it's been so long since someone touched me like this. Please, don't ever stop."

I cupped my junk, making sure my dick hadn't drilled a hole through my pants. Everything was fine. Except that I was so hard, I wondered if all the blood in my body had pooled to the tip.

"Oh, yes. There… More—"

Giggles reached us from the living room.

My brain didn't really register them.

More giggles.

This time, there was no mistaking the sound for anything else.

Dahlia and I froze, my digits concealed deep inside her, her wetness and heat wrapped around them.

Bubbly laughter spilled from the other room this time.

I fished my phone out of my back pocket.

Ten thirty-seven.

Dahlia and I exchanged a quizzical stare.

I extracted my hand just in time as Dahlia jumped to her feet and buttoned her shorts. She offered me an apologetic smile and a shrug.

I grabbed both our shirts from the floor and handed Dahlia hers.

Dressed and decent, we made it to the other room.

The scene playing in front of us made me smile, but it also put to rest my horny self.

On the floor, Buddy was licking a sleepy Jack's face, the boy laughing his heart out.

Dahlia and I shared another look. She winced, and our eyes traveled back to Jack and Buddy cuddling on the floor, and we both burst out laughing.

Dahlia angled herself to face me, her arms circling my waist. "Nick, I'm so sorry."

My lips found hers. "Don't be. Look at them." We turned our faces in their direction. "This is priceless."

Half an hour later, I walked the woman of my dreams and her son, now fully awake, to their car, Buddy in tow, listening to Jack singing to him, energized from his power nap.

Once she buckled Jack in his car seat, Dahlia joined me. "Again, sorry," she said as my lips found her in the darkness of the night. "I'm already counting the days when we can continue where we left off."

I lowered my palm to her ass and gave it a squeeze as she kissed me one last time.

"Night, Nick. Sweet dreams," she said with a wink.

My body overheated. "After what we did, I'll never be able to sleep. I'll have a hard-on for days to come."

She ran her hand along my erection. "How rude of me

to leave you like this." She offered me a lopsided smile, palming my hard flesh.

My knees buckled. "Geez, this is as much incredible as it is torture."

Humor left her features. "I don't know when we'll be able to resume this." A long huff broke the silence. "I'll miss you."

With one finger, I lifted her chin up, staring into her eyes. "As I already said, I'll wait for you. We'll be fine. Each time we get interrupted, I'm just burning hotter for you afterward." As if to corroborate my words, a rush of heat spread through me. "I'll see you soon. Go now, or I'll kidnap your pretty ass and lock it in my cave and never let you go."

A smile returned to Dahlia's face, and I silently congratulated myself for putting it there."Thank you, Nick. One day, I'll let you capture me and do nasty things to me."

If only she knew. *You've already captured my heart, Dahlia Ellis.*

"I can't wait. Go. Now," I ordered, teasing, as I kissed her forehead and opened her car door. "I'll miss you too."

She waved at me, and as soon as she rounded the corner, I escorted Buddy home in a rush to return, the tension still clawing at me, knowing it wouldn't relent until I took care of it—myself.

Chapter 6
Nicholas

The next morning, I woke up at dawn, too restless to stay in bed. I had tossed and turned for hours, my mind drifting to the woman who had taken a chunk of my heart hostage last night.

The taste of her lingered on my lips for a long time after she left, and I hoped it could stay there forever.

My thoughts churned in my head. I dragged a hand over my face, trying to ease the new wave of desire pulsing through me.

"Fuck," I screamed to relieve my frustration, as my fist connected with the kitchen counter. This thing between us had me all bothered, and now I was in my kitchen, wishing she'd appear at my front door and we'd pick up where we left off last night. With my tongue in her mouth and my fingers playing her body.

With a mug of coffee in my hand, I watched the

sunrise from the back deck. The sight helped me pull myself together. For a moment, I simply appreciated the view, pushing away the images in my head. This brief moment of peace and quiet—taking in the beauty nature had to offer—had become my ritual on most mornings.

My mind stopped spinning, and my racing thoughts slowly fell into order.

I breathed easier.

Maybe it was the lack of sleep that had sent me into a state of mental agitation this morning, but now that the trepidation and angst had eased, I could see more clearly.

"Hey, bro," I said, slouching in my chair, glancing at the sky.

Derek and I were due for a meaningful talk.

"How are you doing? Touching base with you. Things move fast around here. Just so you know, you were right. I can see it now. I have no clue how you could, but hey, I'm not questioning the process. Back home, I was missing out on so many things. Home… Why does my chest tighten whenever I think about Chicago as my home? Is it weird? Now I can only picture myself living here, in Green Mountain."

I paused to regroup my thoughts.

"Anyway, I'm glad you sent me on this journey. And guess what? I checked another item off your list. I made three best friends so far. Our lives entangled in a way I can't explain, but there is something there. It's real. And powerful."

I let the silence hang in the air after I spoke.

"By the way, I never thought I'd befriend a dog, but here he is, proving me wrong. It's like Dahlia, Jack, and Buddy were destined to enter my life. Some way… Some day… When I was truly ready to welcome them. It feels so damn right to share pieces of my life with them. If you're the mastermind behind all this—and I truly hope you are—thank you. I can't wait to see how far our relationships will go, but I know in my heart I'll forever be grateful they've become part of my journey."

I closed my eyes to chase the emotional turmoil shaking me.

"I miss you, Derek. Every day. I wish you were here. I wish you could meet them. I wish you could have come on this adventure with me. Go, have fun, okay? Love you, bro." With my fingers, I saluted the sky.

A scratching noise echoed through the ajar patio door. Buddy yapped from the front porch, and I hurried inside and crossed the kitchen to let him in. He sniffed around, and after pacing the main floor of the house twice, he curled into a ball on the floor with a loud sigh.

"You miss them too?" I asked, wishing he could talk back for once. "Yeah." I sighed. "I know the feeling."

I refilled my mug and was about to start my day when Chaz, my young neighbor, came knocking. "Hey, Nick. Can I talk to you?" he asked through the screen door.

"Yeah. Sure. Come on in. What's up?"

He sat on a stool and buried his head in the bent of his elbow.

"Coffee?"

"Sure," he muttered.

"Everything all right? Huh, you looked…confused?" I asked, lacking a better word.

Chaz nodded, not meeting my eyes. "You know the girl—"

"The one who dated your best friend?"

"Yeah. Jolie. She asked me to this dance in town next month."

"That's great, man."

The teen groaned, his face still hidden in the crook of his arm. "No, it's not. She was *his* girl first. He'll kill me if I go with her. He told me many times she was off-limits. I'm screwed. I really like her. And I…I think she likes me too."

"Your coffee, black?"

"One milk and too much sugar," he muttered.

"Tell me the truth, Chaz. What do *you* want?" I asked, making my way to the refrigerator to get the milk.

He lifted his head, his face flustered. "Her. I've been in love with Jolie since third grade. And she'll be in Columbus too next fall."

"Did—what's his name?—your friend know about your crush when he asked her out?" I placed the cup of coffee before him and leaned back against the counter next to the sink, sipping mine.

Chaz was about six or seven years younger than me, but right now, I felt like decades separated us. He looked so clueless and inexperienced that it made me smile and I felt for him.

"Yeah."

I shrugged. "So. He broke the bro code first."

"You think?"

"I'm sure. Come on, man. He made a move on the girl you loved. That's really shitty of him. Best friends don't do that."

Chaz's face lit up as if I'd shot him with pure caffeine through an IV line.

He cast a glance down, and a single deep wrinkle carved a line across his forehead.

I followed his gaze and cursed all the saints in my head. Nested underneath the kitchen cupboards, a foot away from me, was a piece of fabric.

White lace.

I blinked, urging my brain to think—fast.

With my index finger, I directed Chaz's attention to my right. "Look who came to visit me this morning?"

The teen turned his head, and I kicked my leg out to hook Dahlia's bra lying abandoned on the floor. In a ninja-style movement, I picked it up and shoved it into a drawer.

Chaz huffed a loud breath. "He's getting weaker by the day. At this pace, I'm not sure he'll be here by the end of summer. I got him when he was a puppy, you know. He's been my best friend forever. I'm glad he has you now that I'll be going away to college."

Tears glistened in Chaz's eyes.

I stepped around the kitchen island and clapped his back. "I'm sorry. I know it's hard, but I'm sure he's had a great life."

He shrugged. "I guess."

"I lost a best friend too. A couple of months ago. I know the pain, believe me." I forced a tight-lipped smile, though it felt anything but natural, hoping Chaz wouldn't ask questions I wasn't ready to answer.

"I'm sorry. That sucks."

He turned his attention back to the kitchen floor, scanning for the white piece of lingerie. He arched a brow, stared at me, then shook his head. "What should I do about Jolie?"

"Life is short, man. Seize the chance or you'll always wonder what could have been. Face your friend. Tell him the truth. If he's upset and throws a fit, then he's not worth your time and friendship, and you don't need him around."

Chaz listened to me, nodding, as if all of this occurred to him for the first time.

"What do you have to lose? You'll be gone in a few months, anyway. Will—"

"Hank."

"Will Hank be in Ohio too?"

"No. He's staying here."

"Go for it then. Don't let him ruin what you and Jolie could have."

Images of Jace and Pam flashed through my mind. Since I moved here, I'd barely had a chance to talk to him. Now my friend had no reason to drop by unannounced, and we had no more excuses—like poker nights—to see each other. Even Tucker mentioned the other day that he'd only seen him a handful of times since I left the city. But hey, if it meant Jace was happy in his marriage, what could I say? It wasn't my decision, but I missed him.

Chaz firmed his back, resolve now flashing in his eyes. "You're right. Hank has no right to pull the bro code card on me. Thanks, Nick."

Without another word, the kid left, his cup half-drunk, confidence radiating from him.

I took the bra out of the cutlery drawer and twisted it between my fingers.

Last night's memories swirled back in my mind, suffocating me as they replayed in my head.

My lower body hardened, and my mouth watered.

Was last night just a one-time thing? A flood of lust we had to tame? Or was Dahlia truly serious about moving forward in our relationship—just as much as I was? *Wait and see, man. You promised her friendship. Stick to it. Unless she makes a move,* the naughty voice in my head added. I breathed out. Could I do that? Wait and see? I had to. For both our sakes. Dahlia already had a complicated past, and she didn't deserve a fling. She deserved the real thing. Flowers. Date nights. Love. Commitment. And forever.

I was busying myself in one of the bedrooms upstairs, taking measurements to replace the broken window, when an idea hit me.

It planted a little seed of hope in me that shot jitters to my stomach.

After I changed, I hurried downstairs, ready to run some errands.

With my phone, I snapped a picture of Buddy, sleeping in the same exact spot he'd shared with Jack just the night before, and sent it to Dahlia.

ME

Look who's missing his new best friend?

She replied minutes later. For my plan to unfold, I had to know if she was at the store right now.

DAHLIA

I'm telling you. This dog is a keeper.

ME

I'll put a lock on his leash to make sure a redhead who's been seen lurking around him won't be able to steal him away from me.

DAHLIA

I wouldn't.

ME

Oh yes, you would. I heard you all right last night. And the other times before.

I can tell you have a plan.

Picturing you wearing a ski mask, dropping cookie crumbs to create an evasion path, waiting in a white van while your toddler sidekick eats those chunks, messing with your mission.

What would your thief name be? Firecracker? Red Devil?

DAHLIA

Firefly.

ME

Firefly? It doesn't sound badass enough. You sure?

DAHLIA

Why not? I like those bugs.

ME

Girl, you'll never cease to amaze me. Let's call you Fireworks.

DAHLIA

Why?

ME

Because. It fits you. You're no insect, Dahlia. You're a spectacular, colorful display, setting me on fire each time you rest your eyes on me.

Imagine the headline: "Fireworks Thief and her Spark sidekick have stolen a dog. Wanna catch them? Offer them cookies."

DAHLIA

Stop. I'm laughing so hard right now, my ribs hurt.

Be honest, though. Jack would look cute in a ski mask, eating pieces of cookies.

ME

Absolutely. But not sure he's the man for the job. If it were for any other mission, I'd drive the getaway car.

DAHLIA

You would?

ME

Without hesitation.

Big day at work?

DAHLIA

It was earlier. Prom dress fittings. I'm all
alone now.

I jumped into my truck, and minutes later, I parked in
front of Dahlia's Bridal Shop. In Green Mountain, I could
be about anywhere in only a couple of minutes, while in
Chicago it took usually over half an hour to get from one
place to another. I loved it. The small-town charm and
simplicity.

ME

Got something else you might miss.

DAHLIA

?

ME

*sending her the picture of her bra I took
before leaving my place*

DAHLIA

OMG I'm so relieved you can't see my face
right now. It must be neon pink. I'm sure it's
bright enough that it can be seen from
space.

ME

Don't be ashamed, it's a pretty piece of
lingerie. I'm just not sure it's my size. I may
have to return it to its rightful owner.

By the way, pink is a good look on you.

Through the store's big, square window, I watched
Dahlia as she perused around, searching for me. I waved at
her when our gazes met. She shook her head and ran a
hand over her reddened face.

I shrugged as I opened the door.

"You're the worst, Nick," she said, backhanding my chest. "I almost died of embarrassment."

"You're lucky I didn't bring it here." Her eyes widened. "Anyway, if you wanna get it back, you'll have to come over and have dinner with me," I said, raising my hands between us.

Dahlia looked thoughtful as she said, "I supposed it wouldn't be fair to Jack to deprive him of spending time with his best buddy."

And my body from the withdrawal last night caused me.

"It would be like another double date with friends."

A chuckle left her mouth. "Okay, fine. You won. You got me at double date."

I grinned like a fool because that was how spending time with this woman made me feel.

Long gone were those spells when I went through life mechanically, back in Chicago, where every day was almost a duplicate of the previous one. I used to love my job, but looking back at my life before I moved here, it missed the excitement. I wasn't unhappy. No, I didn't think it was that. But it was predictable—an awful lot. If I had agreed to the contract Cody urged me to sign, the next five years would have looked exactly the same. Thanks to Derek, I'd escaped the routine I thought I'd miss, but didn't. All the plans. The expectations. It would have soon become too much, weighing me down. I hadn't thrived like this in a long time, and I could easily become addicted to this slower, more content lifestyle.

"See you at five." I whirled around to leave when I remembered the paper bag in my hand. "Here." I handed it to her.

Dahlia gave me one of her quizzical stares. "What is it? I hope it's not a new bra." A pink blush returned to her cheeks. Her lips curled when she eyed what was inside, discovering the treat I got her.

"Saw it next door. It reminded me of you."

She halted, her hand midway between the bag and her mouth. "You saw a glazed donut in the bakery window, and it reminded you of me. How?"

I shrugged. "It's sweet and sparkly. Like you, Fireworks."

She tilted her head back, laughing. "Okay, it's actually nice of you." She bit into the pastry as if she hadn't eaten in days. "Want some?" she asked with a mouthful.

"Nah. You look like you can use it. When was the last time you ate?"

She flicked her wrist as if it was no big deal. "I had tea at six this morning."

"Glad to learn I'm not the only one starving himself. Still, you shouldn't run on an empty stomach."

"Sometimes I'm so focused that I forget."

"Gimme a sec," I said, hurrying outside, not giving her time to argue.

I crossed the street, reached Ivy's Café in a dozen strides, and ordered Dahlia a sandwich. After I came to an agreement with Ivy, I returned to the bridal shop and handed Dahlia the takeout container.

"Eat. I'll watch the store while you do. Take your time."

"You sure?"

I nodded.

"Thanks," she said, her hand finding mine and giving it a quick squeeze before moving to the back of the store.

Fifteen minutes later, I left, ready for the next step in my plan.

Back home, I carried the packages I'd bought to the bedroom upstairs, and after I fixed the broken window, changing the glass and sealing the edges, I sat on the floor and unwrapped everything, ready for phase three of my plan.

Derek's Bucket List – ~~24. Nick. Make someone smile~~ ~~my newfound mission~~

Chapter 7

Dahlia

Jack ran toward Buddy, a plastic firefighter truck in his hand, the moment his feet landed on Nick's doorstep.

"Thank you," I said after Nick lifted the bag from my arms.

He rubbed his jaw and turned to face me. "I've been thinking about remodeling the upstairs bathroom because there's a leak in the shower, and getting rid of the wallpaper in the master bedroom. I was wondering if your offer to gimme a hand still stands. I might need your help picking out tiles, faucets, and paint…those sorts of things."

"Yes. Absolutely. I'd like that. Already told you I used to be a master fixer-upper… Back in the day." My throat closed as images of Jeff and me fixing the old house he bought for us when I was seventeen resurfaced.

"You okay?" Nick asked.

I blinked and nodded. "Yeah. Got lost in old memories

for a second." I forced a smile and chased those flashbacks away. "Can I get a tour? To see what we're dealing with?"

He leaned in, and his lips grazed mine. "Sure, follow me. I can't believe I never took the time to give you a proper tour. Guess we've been busy."

I grinned at the teasing while Nick lifted my son in his arms, and climbed the stairs after them.

The farmhouse was old, but it had a lot of charm. Since the first day I came over, I could picture all its potential in my mind. The tour cemented my vision. One wall down here, an opening there, new windows, an updated banister, some black wrought-iron light fixtures, and a terrace off the master bedroom.

"Looks like your brain is in high gear," Nick remarked after we exited the bathroom, and he explained his vision for the room.

"I can see it clearly in my head. It's a shame we can't do it all. I love the bones of this house, though with the right budget, the right plans, and enough time, it could be so much more."

"My mission here is only to fix it up for future buyers, but I agree. With a bigger budget and a few additions, we could easily turn it into an incredible home."

"What's this room for?" I asked as we passed a closed door.

Nick breathed out and straightened his back. He looked around for a few seconds as if debating with himself whether to tell me or not. "If I show you, promise me you'll listen to what I have to say before freaking out, okay?"

I knitted my brows together. "Tell me you're not a serial killer and this isn't your trophy room."

He relaxed at my words before offering me a devilish smirk. "Only the heads."

"Then it's fine. I would've run away if you'd said only the feet. Not a fan of toes. Heads are safe."

He wiped imaginary sweat from his forehead with the back of his hand, pretending to be relieved. "Since I was hoping you'd embark on this remodeling journey with me, I did something. It's no big deal. You hate it, and we don't talk about it anymore. You love it, then great. Don't feel obligated to anything… I feel stupid right now. I should've asked you first. I'm sure you'll think I'm a weirdo—"

Before he could finish his sentence, I turned the knob, opening the door slowly as if it could detonate somehow.

My hand flew to my mouth, and my heart did a three-sixty-degree rotation in my chest.

Jack squealed and wriggled in Nick's arms, silently begging to be lowered to his feet. My child entered the room, a huge smile brightening his face.

"Is it what I think it is?" I asked, standing motionless, as though gravity had doubled beneath my feet.

Nick cleared his throat, keeping his eyes from mine, his head bowed as he rubbed the nape of his neck with one hand. "Yeah. Well… It's a…it's a playroom. It's not much, but I thought Jack could use a safe place when we're tearing apart the old bathroom. Assuming we do it together… Somewhere he could play or"—he pointed to a tiny plush sofa-bed in the corner—"nap if we work late. It's silly. Huh, I get it. In my head, it sounded smart, but now I feel ridiculous for not asking your permission first."

A street-patterned rug, a few plastic vehicles, and other toys were lined up against the wall. A shelf with half a dozen picture books was set up next to the royal-blue sofa-bed, decorated with two stuffed animals.

"You made this?" I asked in a voice so thick with emotion, it barely sounded like mine. "For my son?"

Nick nodded, his fleeting gaze meeting mine.

Without thinking further, I jumped into his arms, brushing my lips against his. "It's beautiful. And thoughtful. You didn't have to, but I like it. A lot. You're amazing."

"Look, Mama. *Vroommm. Vroommm*," Jack said, opening his fist to reveal an orange toy car.

"You like that, baby?"

He bobbed his head and grinned.

"Say thank you to Nick."

"*Thankliounick.*"

We both laughed as my son wrapped his arms around this incredible man's leg.

Nick kneeled before him. "You're welcome, little guy. I'm happy you like it. How about you and I go get Buddy? I'm sure he misses you very much. He was looking for you earlier today."

Jack bobbed his head and stepped back, holding out his hand to grab Nick's finger. "Cookie, *pleaseiounick.*"

Nick rolled his jaw back and forth, as if he were thinking it over. "Are you sure your Mama is okay with that?"

Jack bobbed his head once more as I watched their exchange.

"Then let's ask her." Nick, still on his knees, raised his eyes toward me. "Dahlia, can Jack and I get cookies? *Pleeeease.*" He glanced at Jack next and whispered, "You think she'll let me have one too?"

Jack nodded, giggling.

I rested one fist on my hip and tapped the side of my chin with a finger. "Will you two eat your dinner later?"

They both said "Yes" at the same time.

"Will you brush your teeth before going to bed?"

They said "Yes" again.

"Cookies it is then." I scrunched up my face. "Can I get one too?"

Nick jumped to his feet and winked. "Oh yes, I forgot how your Mama loves cookies."

My face heated up, no doubt, as I remembered our innuendos from the other day.

Jack lifted a finger. "Wait, Mama. *Nickandme* get cookies, okay? Wait."

Five minutes later, the three of us sat on the playroom floor eating our snack. Once we finished, the boys left to get Buddy, Jack tugging at Nick's hand, while I attacked dinner.

We sat around the table as if we'd been doing it for years, and Jack perched himself on Nick's lap. They laughed together at something Nick said, and in that instant, I wished I could stop time and savor this moment of bliss a little longer.

I had no idea how we had slipped into this comfortable routine, but I was thankful for every second of it. Most nights, when I closed my eyes, I still believed it was all a dream.

———

After dinner, Nick and I were seated on the kitchen island, wine glasses in hand, going over the pictures on his laptop, finding inspiration for the upstairs bathroom. At some point, Nick sauntered off—only to return seconds later with my bra folded neatly in his hand.

"I have this piece of equipment I gotta return to its rightful owner. I must ask, and I have a right to know. Did you leave it here on purpose? Was it to tempt me, or were you trying to find a not-so-subtle way to snatch an invite again?" He wiggled his eyebrows, and I buried my face in my hands, feeling warmth pooling in my cheeks.

"I figured it might add some personality to your trophy

room… Or give it a little edge, you know?" I pinched my lips together, not quite sure how I felt brave enough to speak these words out loud.

"Considering it's now your kid's playroom, I'll have to hang it on my bedroom wall instead."

My body tingled. I clenched my thighs as heat billowed between them. "Maybe it was the plan all along," I said, the blush on my face now hot enough to melt my skin.

"I'm sure we could find a way to make it part of the new decor."

The heated exchange between us was turning me on, my body melting into a molten pool of sizzling need.

We stared at each other, the chemistry between us so palpable, I could almost taste it.

"I have to get going," I muttered.

Nick framed my face with his hands. "I know. Our time together always flies by too fast."

In the living room, I scooped up a sleeping Jack from the little sofa-bed we'd brought down there two hours ago and made my way to the car.

"Thanks for the room," I said when what I really wished to say was: *you're awesome. All I hunger for is for us to pick up right where we left off last night. I'm a mess since you've entered my life. I think about you all the time. Every night I touch myself, imagining these are your hands on me, your heartbeat that's vibrating through my chest, your lips that are between my thighs.*

"You're welcome. Thanks for your help. Now I owe you twice."

I know exactly how you could pay off your debts.

I mirrored Nick's smile. "No, we're square. You fed me today, remember?"

I'm desperate for you to feed me every day, but I want more than sandwiches and dinners. I want the entire buffet. Every last bite.

What were all these thoughts popping into my head?

Nick leaned forward, and my heart skipped a beat. If he got any closer, we'd get burned. There was no way I could resist him. To try would only fan the blaze. We'd start a wildfire, and everything in our path would combust.

"Night, Dahlia," he said, his lips tasting the corner of mine.

His scent rushed through me, heightening all my senses. Man, soap, and wood. It imprinted itself on my nose.

"Goodnight." I climbed into my car, not looking back, desperate to be as far as possible from this man who could shatter my existence with a single flick of his tongue and a brush of his fingers.

———

The next five days flew by in a haze. I stayed busy at the store, training my newest employee. I'd talked to Nick a few times on the phone since Jack and I went over there the other night, but we hadn't seen each other—not even once.

Every day, around noon, I received a special delivery from Ivy's Café—wraps, sandwiches, soups, salads—with a note.

Friends take care of each other.
Don't go a day without eating.
Take a few minutes for yourself, you deserve it.
Life is brighter when you're around.

After three days, I begged Ivy to tell me the truth. Nick had asked her to bring me lunch every day since he told her I had a tendency to forget to eat. Ivy loved the idea, and together, they had planned the entire thing. I'd asked Nick about it on day four, but he told me he had no idea what I was referring to. This was one of the sweetest things someone had ever done for me, and now I couldn't wait to thank him the proper way.

In person.

My phone rang, and I answered it without checking the screen. "Hey, Nick. Still on for tonight?" We were supposed to go shopping for the new bathroom an hour's drive from here.

"Dah, it's me." The sound of Carter's voice startled me, but it also grounded me. My best friend had a way to calm my nerves just by talking to me.

"Hey, Cart. Still in Germany?"

"Yeah, leaving in the morning. Heading to Scotland next." His words were clipped. Carter was upset. I could read his moods even from thousands of miles away.

"Cart, it doesn't have to be like this," I said, trying to soothe him.

"Do you like him?" he asked.

I said nothing.

"Dah, be honest. Do you like Nick?"

I sighed. "We're friends. We get along and have fun together. He's nice."

"He's not right for you."

"Stop already. You don't even know him," I argued, strangling the phone in my hand.

"My gut tells me he'll break your heart."

"Well, your gut is wrong. He won't."

"Fuck, you like him. A lot. I can tell. Why am I always the one you push away?"

I closed my eyes, knots tightening my insides.

I inhaled—and exhaled—trying to calm my jumbling

thoughts. "Because. You and I, we're best friends, Cart. We're not lovers. We got too close once, and it complicated everything… We're still surfing the aftershocks."

"Dah, you never gave me a real chance. You gave one to Jeff. No, you granted him many. Even when he was acting like a shitty piece of shit. I loved my brother, but he was wrong. Still, you stayed with him through it all. And… and you forgave him. Now Nick. Why not me? You never even gave us the chance to prove how perfect we could be together. How incredible our relationship would be. That night we shared…it…it meant something. I know you. Better than you know yourself. It was out of this world. Don't try to deny it. Fuck, Dah…I'm the one who's been by your side all these years…through everything. No matter what… Never asking anything in return, but a chance at love. This is freaking hard. To see you fall for other guys while you refuse to just acknowledge what we are or what we could be. I'm so sick of being parked in the friend zone. No man relishes that spot. It's like being benched during the last game of the championship. It sucks. Bad. Life is much better when we're together, Dah. I only feel alive when I'm by your side. Gimme a shot too… to prove to you we belong together."

"Cart, I love you. With all my heart. You're one of the two most important people in my life, but I'm not in love with you the way you want me to be. I'm sorry… We've been over this a million times already. You have to move on and chase your own happiness… To find *your* person. Maybe Nick is mine or maybe he's not, but I won't know unless I try. It's not about giving you a chance or not. It's about what my heart desires. Believe me, I have no control over this. Things would be so much simpler if you and I were together, I agree. It would be so much easier with Jack too. I'm aware. But for a reason I can't explain, I can't go down that road with you. We'll always be more than friends, but we'll never be lovers. Friendship is all I can offer you… My heart breaks every time I think about how I'm hurting you."

I paused.

Carter said nothing, so I continued. "Every time I push you away, I fear you'll have one of your episodes. That you'll withdraw into yourself and lose touch with everything and everyone around you. I hate knowing I won't be there to care of you…to calm you down. To bring you peace. When you find the one—"

"I already have," he rushed out.

"No, Cart. You haven't. I swear on Jeff's grave. Your soul mate, your other half, she's out there, searching for you too. She wishes for you as much as you wish for her."

Carter remained silent on the other end of the line.

"Be open to give her a piece of your heart. Be open to love. Elsewhere."

I imagined him scratching his forehead. Or clenching his fists.

"Dah, I'm in love. With. You. Always have been. For over twenty years. It's a fucking long time, so I can tell you it's not just something that will go away. I want everything with you. Love. Family. It's us, Dah. Carter and Dahlia against the world. And Jack. We're a family, the three of us. My feelings won't go away just because you don't reciprocate them. In my heart, I'll keep hoping you realize I'm the one for you too. Be assured I heard everything you said, but it doesn't mean I have to believe it…or agree." His voice cracked on the last word.

Tears pooled in my eyes.

My best friend continued, "You are my destiny. The day you stop fighting it, you'll realize the truth. In the meantime, I'll put on a happy smile the next time I meet

Nick. If he hurts you, though, I'm killing him with my own hands, Dah."

I chuckled through my tears. Carter was the least violent person I knew.

"I'm not kidding."

"Cart, I wish things were different. I do. No matter how it turns out, I'll always be there for you. In every way I can. What would I do without you in my life?" I breathed out, drying my tears with my fingertips. "For what it's worth, you don't even kill spiders, but whatever. If you wanna act all rough and tough around Nick, suit yourself." I sucked in a jagged breath.

Carter sniffled.

My heart vibrated. "I miss you. All the time."

"Me too. I love you," he said after a moment.

I kept my eyes shut, fighting back my emotions. "I-I know. I love you too. Be safe out there."

"Talk to you tomorrow, okay? I'll video chat with Jack."

"We'll be here. Whenever you're ready. Bye."

We hung up, and tears streamed down my cheeks as I locked the store.

For a couple of minutes, I sat in my car, my heart breaking into many pieces as I thought about how much I kept hurting my best friend. Why did it have to be this complicated? Why couldn't Carter love someone else? I heard everything he said and it all made sense, but right now, I craved Nick's touch. My heart longed for him too.

"I'm sorry, Cart," I said out loud before starting the engine once I dried all my tears.

Nick was already parked in the driveway when I made it home.

The sight of him chased my emotional breakdown away. It brought a smile to my face, hope to my heart, and heat to my core. Yeah, Nick happened to be the one my entire body burned for.

"Finished early today. Thought you might like a hand with Jack while you get ready. If we feed him before we get going, we could grab takeout somewhere, both of us later," he offered, opening my car door.

That fuzzy feeling returned to my chest—and my lower belly.

I climbed out and moved closer to him. "Ohmygod, you're a savior. I thought I wouldn't have time to shower."

I hugged him, my pulse spiking when his arms curled around me in return. The way our bodies connected quieted every doubt swirling inside me. I tightened my grip on him, needing him more than ever.

We breathed each other in before finally breaking apart.

I smoothed the fabric of my powder-blue maxi dress with my fingers, trying to busy my hands.

Paula left, and after I snuggled with my son for a little beat, I put Nick in charge of feeding him some leftover macaroni while I got ready.

Dressed in a denim skirt, a teal tank top, and cowboy boots, I braided my hair and added a little makeup to my eyes and lips.

Satisfied, I went downstairs, only to find both guys sprawled on their stomachs on the floor, building a tower with wooden blocks.

Jack pushed it until it toppled over, his laughter warming up my heart.

Nick faked being sad, and together, they built it up again.

I could've stood there in the doorway, watching them for hours.

"Mama," Jack said, jumping to his feet when he noticed me and running into my arms as I crouched down.

"Hey, baby. Ready to leave?"

He bobbed his head. "See Buddy?"

I said no with my head. "Not today, baby. Some other time, okay?"

"Okay. Buddy my friend. My best *bestest* friend."

"Yes, he is."

Five hours later, Nick pulled into the driveway, the bed of his truck loaded with boxes of bathroom tiles and other supplies needed to start the farmhouse's interior renovation.

Jack snored in his car seat behind us, deep asleep.

"I had fun tonight," I said, not ready for the night to end.

"I did too." Nick leaned closer, tracing the rim of my lips with his thumb. "Listen, I can't stay away from you, Dahlia. There's something powerful that exists between us, and no matter how much I tell myself I should back off and be content being your friend, I can't. The line we crossed the other night can't be uncrossed. I don't wanna go back to being just friends."

I remained silent, searching for the right words.

Shivers tickled my spine.

My heart danced behind my ribs.

I blew out a long breath, doing my best to keep my fears at bay.

"I have no idea what I'm doing. I might be a mother, but my love life has been dead for years. It's scary to trust someone else with my heart."

"I—"

I spoke before he could finish his thought. "But I'm willing to try with you. My heart tells me you're worth the risk. That you'll be gentle and careful with it. It hasn't healed completely. It might still break again from time to time, but I'm okay. I just need the reassurance you'll be patient with me."

"Dahlia, I'll never hurt you. I'll be gentle, and we'll figure it out. Together."

"I'd like that."

"Can I kiss you?"

I nodded. "It seems like forever since you did the last time."

Shifting in my seat, I leaned over the central console, meeting Nick halfway.

Our mouths explored each other, careful at first, as if it were the first time, but soon we kissed with unchained zeal. And passion. And something else I couldn't name. Our tongues entangled together.

Nick feasted on my neck as much as he could with the console between us. "God, you taste even better than I remember."

My skin ignited. All rational thoughts left me. This. This feeling. The desire. I'd missed it more than I thought. A pool of scorching heat filled my lower belly.

"You wanna come inside?" I asked, breathless, barely holding it together.

"You sure?" he asked, his eyes full of sparks, his pupils dilated, sending my heart in high gear just by the way he stared at me.

"Yes. Don't leave already."

He cradled my cheek with his warm palm, and he said "Yes" against my lips as I melted into his embrace.

We broke apart, and eager to return to kissing the man who had turned my world upside down since he'd first wandered into my store by mistake, I released my baby from his car seat and lifted him into my arms.

Nick moved closer and extended his hands. "Let me. Show me the way to his room."

I placed my son in his arms, seized with emotion at the sight of them, when Nick's lips connected with the top of his head.

Once in Jack's bedroom, I tucked him in his bed as Nick stood beside me, watching my baby for a long time with cloudy eyes, his head dipped forward, and his shoulders low.

"Wanna go downstairs?" I asked, caressing his biceps with my fingertips.

He nodded and swallowed. "Sorry," he said, dragging a hand over his face. "I killed the mood."

"It's okay," I said. "Remember, I'm here if you ever wanna talk about it."

He averted his eyes for a few seconds before bringing them back to me. Caring. And hurting. All at the same time. "Not now. One day I will."

I fetched two beers from the fridge and offered him one as we made it to the living room.

"Whenever you're ready."

A sigh left my lips. I knew Nick had lost someone he loved. I didn't know what he'd been through, but I knew despair and heartbreak when I saw them—because I felt them too. I recognized the signs.

I scooted closer, and Nick draped an arm over my shoulders. With my head pressed against his ribcage, I drew figures over the plane of his abs with my finger, drunk on his heartbeat, strong and steady.

"It's nice," I said.

Nick cocked his head, waiting for me to continue.

"This. It feels right. And good."

With a twist of his upper body, he moved to face me. "I

was serious earlier. I want this. With you. Whatever *this* is."
I closed my eyes as he smoothed my lips with the pad of his
thumb, sending shivers to my core. "Can I kiss you again?"

"Do you really have to ask?"

When his lips, sure and warm, locked on mine, I
dissolved in his arms.

He groaned. I whimpered. He swallowed every sound
coming out of my mouth. My back arched as Nick trailed
kisses down my throat.

How did I survive all these years without this man's
touch?

"You wanna keep going or stop?" he asked, his voice
rough and rippling with lust.

"Stop."

He jerked away from me fast, and I felt the cool air
rush between us.

With my bottom lip between my teeth, I moved to my
knees, and without a word, I straddled him.

"Dah… What..? I-I thought—"

I placed a finger over his lips. "I don't wanna stop. I
just want to do it this way," I said, barely recognizing my
own voice, strained and husky.

Nick hooked his hands around my hips, and I shifted
over him, feeling the hard part of him taking residence
between my legs. He stared at me, waiting for me to make
the first move.

With a tilt of my head, I grazed his lips, savoring the
way they felt against mine. How they reacted to my
teasing.

"Now kiss me and don't stop," I said, almost pleading,
my entire body combusting with restrained need and
aching desire. And a whole lot of different sensations I
couldn't define.

His muscular hands ventured under my top, pushing the cups of my bra down, his palms hot on my bare flesh.

I threaded my fingers through his blond locks, tugging his head back to lock eyes with him. My heart raced in my chest. His tongue dived into my mouth, and the fire burning inside me turned into an inferno, fed by his oxygen as it mixed with mine.

With my hands splayed across his chest, we devoured each other with our eyes, his whiskey irises bright and dark at once.

I rolled my hips over his, relishing the sensations of his thickness as it rubbed against my most sensitive spot, sending bolts of electricity to the deepest part of me and igniting all my cells.

Nick clutched my hips and increased the friction between our bodies. I moaned so loud I feared I'd wake Jack upstairs, but I was unable to keep it bottled up inside.

"Come for me, Dahlia. Let go. Now." As if he possessed a special key to controlling my orgasms, his words acted like a magic formula. I hadn't reached a climax with a man in years. We were still dressed, and I became a pile of sizzling flesh in his arms as I dropped forward, pressing my forehead to his chest.

"Are you okay?" he asked, brushing the tendrils of my hair away from my face.

I grinned as euphoria flooded my veins. "Better than fine. I'm fabulous. I'm flying. You've unlocked something deep inside me…and now, I'll be craving more. So much more."

Nick mirrored my smile. "I'll give it all to you. This satisfied smile is a good look on you. I can't wait to see your *I just got fucked* expression. If it's half good as this one, I'll be addicted to it. I can already tell."

His hands found my breasts, and he kneaded them, making me hot for him all over again.

I sat on my ankles, and moving back, I unbuckled his belt and freed his erection. It pulsed in my fist, hard and warm, and ready for me. With my hand around the base, I worked him slowly, getting used to the feel of him.

I ran my tongue over my lips as wild and dirty fantasies whirled inside my head.

I pushed his shirt up, revealing his tantalizing abs, the ones I'd dreamed about since the day I saw him shirtless, water rolling down his chest. The vision had kept me warm most nights—and every time my vibrator showed up for a little private party of our own.

"I wanna taste you," I said, my voice sounding more like a sex kitten's than my own.

Nick nodded. Then shook his head. He nodded again, his head thrown back and eyes closed, as if torn between liking the idea or not. "I'm clean. Got tested a few months back. I haven't slept with anyone since," he said, panting. "Oh God, Dahlia, just your touch is enough to shatter me."

I smirked, relishing the power I had over him in that instant.

With my eyes trained on his face, I moved down and swept my tongue around the tip, enjoying the taste of him for the first time.

His hips buckled off the sofa as an animalistic growl escaped him.

I lapped at it again, eating him up as if he were made of ice cream. His pre-cum coated my tongue as I engulfed him deeper into my mouth.

"Fuck, you're good. Oh yes…God."

I sucked him harder. Pumped him faster. Pushed him deeper inside my mouth.

Every roar leaving his lips made me hornier for him.

Every pulse of his cock got me hungrier for him.

Nick grabbed a handful of my hair and set the pace. I had no time to catch a breath as he fucked my mouth. Our eyes found each other. His had never looked so dark before, the pupils dilated to the brim. Glints danced in his irises. The look on his face was a combination of pleasure, pain, and control. I had every intention of robbing him of the latter. I stroked him faster, drunk at the way he stared at me as if he was receiving head for the very first time and had no idea how to abandon himself to the pleasure, half-conscious and half-lost in it. A train of growls left his mouth, and he let go of me. A few bobs of my head later, his body stiffened.

"Dahlia, I'll—" He pushed my head back, fisting himself until his cum covered his stomach in jolts.

With a swipe of my tongue, I licked the swollen tip of his erection. Nick blinked, staring at me as if I'd blown his mind.

I shrugged. "Told you I wanted a taste of you. You stole that moment from me. I had to sample the product."

"Fuck, you're hot."

Pulling me to him, he crashed his mouth on mine, devouring my lips, our tongues dancing a tango. He wove his fingers through my hair and deepened the kiss, sucking my tongue in his mouth and sending a flood to my panties. His thick semen transferred to my tank top, hot against my skin.

"You are amazing, Dahlia Ellis. Now I wanna eat your pussy until you beg me to stop, until I drain every orgasm out of you. Fuck, you're gorgeous."

"I can't wait," I replied, leaning back to catch some air. "Not tonight, though. We both have to get up early tomorrow."

His gaze lowered after we broke our embrace. "Damn, I ruined your top."

"No, you just branded it. It might actually become my favorite one." I winked, and he groaned against my mouth.

Nick cleaned his abdomen using the warm washcloth I brought him as I removed my sticky top. We kissed goodnight in the doorway, our mouths still hungry for each other. After a long shower, I slid under the covers, sleep claiming me as I dreamed of all the things I couldn't wait for Nick to do to me, my lips stretching into a ridiculous grin, and my heart playing a cheerful melody in my chest.

Only then I realized something. Music had finally made its way back into my heart.

Into my life.

Chapter 8

Nicholas

"Can we talk?" I asked Dahlia a few days later while Jack was keeping himself busy with Buddy, rolling on the lawn after dinner as we sat on the deck. The sound of the boy's laughter healed parts of my heart, a little more each time, and I had to force my eyes off him.

Dahlia leaned over the table and grabbed my hand in hers and quirked an eyebrow.

My pulse quickened at her sight. We hadn't had a chance to be alone since the night we made out on her couch like horny teenagers. I couldn't wait for round two, but her responsibilities as a mother and business owner were her priorities—and only added to her charm—so I had to be patient.

I mirrored her stance and kissed her lips.

Something inside me grew quiet, a voice…a calm settling deep within.

For a long minute, we stared at each other until I could finally name the new sensation unfolding inside me. My pulse didn't even hasten at the thought of it. No, because it felt right. About damn time.

I exhaled. "There's a reason I left Chicago. You already know about my friend who passed away."

She nodded, a tiny wrinkle marring her forehead.

"His death hit me hard...huh...for many reasons. Anyway, one night, I received a delivery. Something Derek had put together for me. A letter... Stuff he loved... And somehow, as I was searching for the meaning of life, surfing through my grief, his words spoke to me. In a strange way, it was as if he wanted me to go on a self-discovery journey or something. As if he had planned the entire thing and knew I belonged elsewhere..."

I swallowed and tightened my grip on Dahlia's hand.

"I went to see the ocean first. There, I met a nice woman and her little girl. Their hospitality touched me. I patched their roof while they helped me patch my broken heart...or some parts of it, at least. A week later, I left and ended up meeting an old couple by the side of the road, arguing about a flat tire. After I helped them out, I spent three weeks working alongside them at their ranch. None of it was planned. It just happened... As if Derek was pushing me toward an ultimate goal...an endgame I couldn't really see at the time."

I shook my head, smiling at the memory of it all.

"Mike told my friend Tucker about the job here, and the next thing I knew, I was agreeing to move to Green Mountain. For a longer period of time than I imagined I would at first...but something in me whispered it was the right decision. That I had to do this. And now that I'm here with you, it feels like my instincts were right..."

Dahlia brushed my hair back with her fingers, letting her soft touch linger on my temple as she watched me.

"There's this list… Huh…how can I explain it?"

A curve graced her lips, and the tension in me eased.

"Well, Derek made it before he died. Some sort of bucket list. Or more like a 'Things he wished he had experienced in his life' list, as he called it. Somehow, it became our common bucket list. It was…it was in the package I received." I closed my lids for a split second and cleared my throat. "Derek was twelve when he died… Cancer."

Dahlia's sharp intake of breath vibrated through me. She squeezed my hand, offering me support. And a listening ear. "Nick, I'm sorry. It's devastating." Her gaze shifted to her son, and she watched him for a minute, her eyes soft and loving, brimming with unshed tears. "I can't imagine…"

I started speaking to avoid falling into the chasm of my grief and memories. "Anyway, when I set out on my big journey, I challenged myself to tick off everything on the list—and add a few personal goals along the way. That's why I drove to the coast. Since I left my hometown, many things I can't explain have happened—often matching the list, for some reason. Go figure. Anyway, there's one thing I haven't done yet, and I think we could do it together. The three of us… If you're up to it…"

Dahlia's eyes lit up. "What is it?"

"Okay. I don't know if you like the outdoors, but I've been thinking about it. A lot. And I'm sure Greta wouldn't object to Buddy having a sleepover."

"Nick, tell me what it is."

"Derek wanted to go camping…to sleep under the stars. Jack is little, and I'd never ask you to bring him into the woods with bears and all sorts of wild animals. And honestly, there's no way the dog would make it through the trek." My gaze shifted to the old bloodhound, panting next to Jack, as the boy hugged him and whispered into his ear. "What if I build us a platform? Nothing fancy, but some sort of stage, and we could add inflatable mattresses and sleeping bags, and camp here. Under the stars," I said, surveying the backyard. "We could light a campfire and roast marshmallows or have s'mores and even cook dinner or whatever. What do you think?"

Dahlia's irises glinted with thousands of stars. "Ohmygod, this would be so much fun. I haven't gone camping in forever. I'm not even sure I remember when the last time was." Her gaze darkened, and something passed in it. She closed her eyes and swallowed. When she glanced back at me, whatever memory had resurfaced had already faded.

I flipped my hand under hers, and she interlaced her fingers with mine. Leaning forward, I lifted her chin with a finger until our eyes met. "Whatever it is, you can talk to me. I know you had it all before me, and I'm okay with it. It's part of who you are. I'm just happy that we've found each other now."

A lone tear rolled down her cheek, and I caught it with my thumb. We got lost in each other's gaze for a moment before I stood and rounded the table.

"Come here," I said, sitting on a vacant chair and pulling her onto my lap. With Dahlia nestled in my arms, we watched Jack running around, Buddy puffing, too tired to follow him.

I really could get used to this life—more than I ever thought possible.

A simple life with the people dear to my heart. Love. And family.

I fastened my arms around Dahlia's waist, and she rested her head on my shoulder, soft and warm against me.

"Thank you for being you," she said, cocking her head until our mouths fused. "And I'd like to go camping with you. It sounds fun. As a teenager, I used to love stargazing and making out. Would it be allowed?"

"Absolutely. It's mandatory," I said, kissing the tip of her nose. "Next weekend. It's a date. Do you have sleeping bags and stuff like that?"

"Nah. But I'm on it. Build that stage and I'll take care of the gear."

"You sure?"

She nodded. "Yeah. Jack and I will go shopping sometime next week." She brought her attention to her son, now running in our direction, his friend snoozing in the shadow of a tree. "Baby, we gotta go soon. I have a long day tomorrow at the store."

"Not going. Stay with *NickandBuddy*," the boy said, folding his arms over his chest.

I let go of her, and Dahlia squatted before him. "I know, baby. You still have a little time before saying goodbye. Next week, we'll go camping together. The four of us."

"Buddy no camping. Silly."

"He will come. Nick will make sure he can sleep with you. But you must be a good boy. Do you think Buddy prefers marshmallows or hotdogs?" she asked, tickling her son's tummy.

"Buddy doggy, Mama. No people food. Doggy food, *Nicksaid*. You funny." He grimaced. "Buddy don't like *hontdogs*."

Dahlia nuzzled his neck and kissed him on the crown of his head. "You're right. What was I thinking? We'll find doggy treats for him then. Does it sound better?"

Jack bobbed his head with so much energy I feared it would fall off, and hurried toward the now snoring dog.

Dahlia and I busied ourselves cleaning up the table and filling the dishwasher inside.

"Before I go, kiss me," she ordered, her voice raw and overflowing with lust. She looped her arms around my neck, her soft breast pressing against my chest and sending so many signals to my lower body as our tongues danced together. "I've missed you."

With both hands, I pushed her hair away from her face, wanting to look at every inch of her.

"I'm sorry I've been so busy lately," she said.

"It's okay. Don't worry about it."

"It's not, but I'll make it up to you." She winked, and my entire body ignited at her promise. "Will you show me that list, or is it too personal? I don't want to intrude. I'm just curious. If I'm overstepping, please tell me. Your friend must have been wise to send you here…to me."

My stomach knotted.

I breathed in to calm my rumbling uneasiness away.

After all, Derek's list wasn't some secret. Tucker had seen it. Yeah, he'd even snapped a picture for good measure.

I tugged at Dahlia's hand. "Let's settle Jack, and I'll show you."

"It doesn't have to be today." She shrugged. "Next week is fine. Or some other time. You don't even have to if you're not ready."

At that moment, something unfurled inside me. I had no idea what it was, except for the certitude that this woman belonged in my life for as long as she would have me. Everything about her made me want to do better. Be better. Aim higher.

"Let's do it now. I hate secrets. Not that this is some world-shattering one, but I'm ready to share it with you.

Because it's important to me. And you're important to me too."

Jack lay in his small sofa bed, dressed in the monster pajama set Dahlia brought over, with a blanket in one fist and a sippy cup in the other, Buddy curled up next to him. As they watched bear cartoons with an annoying theme song, I led Dahlia upstairs.

Jitters surged inside me, my heart threatening to leap from my chest at any moment.

Now I would be sharing a past that only a few people knew about. It was scary opening up and showing my vulnerability. It felt like a big step in our relationship, but one that needed to be dealt with. Dahlia's sensitivity would heal the final rift in me. I had no more doubts.

We sat side by side on my bed after I fished the list out of a drawer.

Dahlia unfolded it with care, and I observed her expressions as I shared an important part of my life with her for the very first time.

She cleared her throat and read what Derek had written out loud. "Derek's *I wish I had experienced in my life* List + Nick's *Bucket* List. Ohmygod, this is so sweet." She sucked in a breath. "Okay, let's see. One. Go to a hockey game with Nick and the guys." Then she read the comment I added below. "*It was a great night, bro. Hope you saw the ribbon with your name on it after each goal. I'll forever remember that day.*" She turned to face me. "Wow." After blinking, she continued. "Two. Make one new…no, three new best friends. *I thought I already had all the friends I needed in Tuck and Jace, but I was wrong. Three new best friends came into my life unexpectedly, and they stole my heart the moment we met.*"

Her lips bent as she read my words.

"*Jack is a little boy. I'm sure you two would have hit it off in no time. He's sweet and adorable. And smart. Like his mother. He's always happy. Every time he's around, I can't help but smile. And it's amazing to be able to smile again. His innocence reminds me of yours. He has a way to appeal to my heart. Buddy is my neighbor's dog. You never specified if the friends had to be humans, so I take it upon myself to say it can apply to any living species. He came to me the moment I parked my truck in the driveway and has been by my side since. There's something between us. It's strong, and I can't really explain it, but I consider him my friend too. And there's Dahlia—"*

I recited the words out loud, knowing every line by heart. "I don't know where to start, bro. I feel like I've known her all my life, which is silly since I only met her not too long ago. There's a connection between us. Something powerful. She fits right into my life, her heart next to mine. Her smile makes my knees weak. You know like that song you enjoyed so much. I wish you could have met her because I'm sure you too would have fallen under her charm right away."

My gaze met Dahlia's, the blush covering her cheeks unmistakable. My heart rate kicked up at the way she stared at me.

"Nick," was all she said, her hand cupping her heart. She straightened her spine, and her lips found my cheek, filling me with new sensations, before continuing. "Three. Kiss a girl until my heart beats fast."

Once again, I interrupted her with words etched in my memory. "It happened. Go to point two. *She kissed me back. And I thought my heart would explode. It had never felt this way before. Never. She's special. I'm telling you. And she wanted to kiss me again, but like a fool, I stopped her. What's wrong with me? I yearn for more, bro. It's too soon to know, right?"*

Her voice was a breathless murmur, aimed for my heart, when she said, "You're not a fool. You're one of the best people I've ever met. You're smart, funny, caring, handsome… Definitely not a fool." She rested her head on my shoulder and kept reading. "Four. Go camping and sleep under the stars. Five. Watch the sunrise every morning. *I do that most mornings, talking to you as if you're listening to me. I hope you are, or if someone hears me, they'll think I'm going nuts. It's our moment, you and I. Buddy always comes to me right after. As if he senses I might need him in these moments. Yeah, Buddy is definitely one of my best friends now.*"

Dahlia smiled, her eyes glossy.

"Nick, this is beautiful. Six. Dip my toes in the ocean, even if jellyfish are gross." A snicker left her mouth. And one left mine too. "Seven. Go to a Carter Hills concert because duh, he's the best. Ohmygod, Cart would be so proud. Derek was a true fan?"

I nodded. "Yep. He could listen to his music every day, all the time, on repeat."

"I love it." She frowned, her brow knitting as she read my next confession. "*Okay, this one is tricky. See, for a reason I still can't wrap my head around, I've met Carter Hills. No kidding. I have no idea how this journey brought me to the rock star, but it did. Even though our first encounter was a bit tense, he seems like a nice guy. And he is Dahlia and Jack's family. He cares about them so much. Their love knows no boundaries…no beginning and no end. It's beautiful. I'm the guy getting in the middle of it. I understand his reservation. I really do, but I hope one day we'll be okay—for Dahlia and Jack's sake—because they mean a lot to me too. Oh, and by the way, Tucker gifted me two tickets for his show in Nashville in the fall. You'll get to see him in concert, after all.*"

Dahlia turned to face me. "Nick, about Carter—"

"It's okay. We only met twice, and I love that he cares enough about you that he's willing to scare anyone who's not good enough for you away. The thing is, I'm not scared easily, so he'll have to try harder if he wants me out of your life."

She moved onto my lap, straddling me, and grabbed my hands in hers. "Carter barks but doesn't bite. Believe me. And I'm big enough to choose who I bring into my life…and my heart. He doesn't have a say in it." Her lips widened into a smile, one that tipped my heart over. "But I'm really happy you're ready to fight for me. It's important to me. For what it's worth, I'd fight for you too. Any time of the day. Or night."

She kissed me, her lips light over mine, then continued reading the list.

"Eight. Do something deemed impossible. Oh, I like that. Nine. Build something with my own hands that I'll keep forever or gift someone. Ten. Nick, go on an adventure (now you must pick one). Wow, this kid was smart. I already love him." She read the words I added next. "*I did it. I packed my stuff and followed your advice. I don't know where this trip will take me, but it feels right. I'll keep you updated.*"

She paused, contentment painting her face.

"*Update. I'm in Green Mountain, bro. It was Tuck's idea. You know how he is. He even got me a job. And I'm fixing an old house. It's beautiful here. People are nice. They smile all the time. You would fit right in. I met someone this afternoon. Got lost and entered her shop by mistake. She stole my breath away the moment we locked eyes. We spent the entire afternoon together, chatting and laughing. She agreed to be my friend. We're having a date next week. Wish me luck.*"

Dahlia fastened her arms around my neck. "Nick, you didn't need luck. For the record, I was starstruck too."

I leaned in until our mouths were a hair's breadth apart. "You, Dahlia Ellis, the country music star, was starstruck by a guy like me?"

She nodded. "Nick Peterson, you're not just a guy. You're the guy I wanna spend all my time with. The one I never seem to get enough of. It means something."

Bringing her attention back to the list, she read the

other points. "Make someone smile my newfound mission."

I jumped in, gazing into the eyes of the woman still sitting on my lap, as I read aloud the words that spilled from my heart. "*Dahlia smiles all the time. Big gestures, little ones, she finds beauty in everything. Today I gifted her a donut, and she bit into it as if I had given her the world. I'm telling you, this girl is different. She's the best thing that has happened to me since I left the city. As if all my life, I was destined to meet her. To fall for her. I wish for her smile all the time and want to be responsible for every curve of her lips. Because her smiles make me smile too.*"

My voice faded out as silence enveloped us, my heart beating fast inside my ribcage.

"What's the last point on Derek's list? You left it blank," Dahlia whispered, her hands trembling, and a river flowing down her face.

I shrugged, battling the emotions stirring inside me. "I have no idea. He didn't finish it. I added a few and still do as I go. The last one has to be something meaningful. I haven't found what it is just yet."

Dahlia folded the sheet and handed it back to me.

"This is beautiful…and sad, Nick." She sucked in a shaky breath. "I'm amazed by you. You have such a huge heart. Derek sounds like someone great."

"He was."

Her moss-green eyes bore into my soul. They soothed me and shot me with doses of something close to love. Something that made me long to never leave her sight— and her side.

Our mouths collided, speaking everything we didn't say out loud.

"Point twenty. You're the reason I smile so much. And about points two and three," she said, whispering against my lips, "I agree too. Now kiss me again because I love it when my heart beats fast."

And just like that, Dahlia added another point to the list. One that mattered. A lot.

Derek's Bucket List – ~~22. Nick. Share parts of my life with the person who means the most~~

Chapter 9
Dahlia

"Nick, it's charming. I can't believe you made this for one night. Did you even sleep at all last week?" I asked, covering my mouth in awe as I took in the raised platform he'd built and stained in the same walnut color as the porch. Located behind the old garage in the backyard, it resembled a giant bunk bed on stilts. Fairy lights hung from the tree branches—as if he knew I loved them—casting a glow that made the whole scene feel magical. It would be even more enchanting once the sun set.

On one side, there were wooden stairs to climb up along with a ramp for Buddy's old bones. Okay, this was the cutest thing I'd seen in a long time. Nick's thoughtfulness and caring ways made my heart tremble with eagerness and need, lust or something I couldn't exactly define. All I knew was that spinning in his orbit made me happy—and content.

Before he could say anything, I turned and slammed my lips against his, craving the taste of him. He jerked and stiffened in shock, then leaned into the kiss as heat flared between us. I bit his lower lip, then soothed it with gentle, brushing strokes of my tongue before inviting his tongue into my mouth, sucking it hard. His lower body stiffened in greeting, a fitting reply to my bold move. Maybe I wasn't so rusty after all. The idea alone sent a thrill through me, filling me with jitters and excitement.

Breaking off the kiss, I panted heavily against his mouth. A new sensation washed over me. One I could easily get addicted to. Never before had I been so rough, taking what I wanted without restraint. But right now, all I craved was to play dirty. Silence hung around us, broken only by the harsh cadence of our breaths.

"Let's check out the view from the top. You'll see, it's fantastic," he suggested, putting my horny hormones to rest—for now.

I nodded and gestured for him to climb up first. He gave me a weird look, and a silent giggle escaped me.

Nick started up the wooden stairs, and I followed, pressing close, deliberately brushing my body against his. I gave his butt a hard squeeze, and he stumbled on the steps.

"Hey. You're not playing fair."

My eyes widened with fake innocence as a lascivious grin spread across my face. "What? Just admiring the view. As you said. With my hands. I agree it is fantastic and mouth-watering."

He waggled his finger at me over his shoulder as a wry smile overtook his lips. His gaze flashed with mischief. Clearly, he hadn't met my brand of naughtiness yet. "Woman, behave."

He wrapped his muscular arms around me when we

reached the top, and I sank into his embrace. The view was quite impressive from up here.

"I had no idea the property was sitting on such a big piece of land."

The trees lining the boundaries created a much-appreciated intimacy, offering us no view of the neighbors. I bet the owners had some great parties in this yard. If it had been me, I would've pitched a big white tent and hosted all my get-togethers here. Birthdays, anniversaries, weddings. A place to bring families and friends together. To create memories.

The pillows and sleeping bags we brought over were laid on the mattresses, and my eyes lingered on the cozy display.

"Perhaps this could be our thing. Sleeping under the stars once a week," Nick put forth with a shrug.

I agreed with a nod. "It's magical. Coming here once will never be enough." His hardness pushed against my back, and I whirled around in his arms. His grip on me slackened, and I watched him, amusement returning to my face, my cheeks heating up. "Oh, I'm not the only one feeling naughty."

His lips tilted in an innocent smile, the opposite of the heat flashing in his gaze. "W-what?"

I gave him a pointed stare, then deliberately dropped my eyes to his erection. The bulge in his jeans slowly swelled beneath the denim. "Dahlia, don't play with fire. You will get burned."

"Yeah, but what a way to go. I tried safe, now I want the inferno. The hotter the better."

My breath hitched as he combed my hair away from my face gently, then curled it around his fist and pulled until my lips opened. The flutters in my belly turned to raging fireworks. Hot air whirled between us. Mine or his, I couldn't tell. Nick's lips rubbed against mine as he cupped his junk with his other hand before pushing his hard-on against my softness. My insides melted as his length hit my sensitive nub. More. I wanted more. I needed more. Hungry for release as steam vaporized my sanity, I thrust against him. Demanding. Unapologetic. Anyone could walk on us, but I couldn't care less. I was finally taking everything I had been craving for weeks now. I bit his lips after he sucked on mine until they felt sore. I wanted to be marked by him and brand myself on him. Nick Peterson was mine. No one else's. It was about time we made it official, and I staked my claim.

We kissed for a few intense minutes, rough and hard. Playful and steamy. Bit by bit, sanity returned, and we separated, gasping for air. The desire that arose within seconds of our bodies touching each other couldn't be contained. I didn't want our first time to happen out here on the platform. I wanted it to be intimate, comfortable, and secluded. I wouldn't be opposed to it next time—but not today. Today, I had plans. For him.

Nick framed my face with his large palms, holding me in place. I grabbed his shirt to stop myself from tumbling onto the mattresses and dragging him down with me.

"Dahlia—" He was flustered, his gaze smoldering.

I tried to speak but couldn't find the words. The only thing that I could think about was our imminent release. Mine. His. Entangled together in bed sheets. And breathless. The only words echoing in my mind were "Fuck me." The tidal wave of pure need rising inside my core was demanding to be satiated.

Nick cleared his throat and broke the tension—the one wrapped tight around us. "Tonight, I prepped some food for grilling over the campfire and treats for dessert. Hope you're hungry."

Yes. *Hungry.* Not for food, though. For him. I salivated at the mere thought.

My body refused to temper down. To settle.

His hands all over me, his hard body pressed against mine—inside mine—his mouth mapping every inch of my bare flesh were what I craved. They were all I'd dreamed about since the day I saw him in my shop for the very first time.

With my arms wrapped around his midsection, I stared into his eyes. "Starving." Huskier than normal, rougher than before, the single word rose from the well of my desire.

Nick's eyes burned with a fiery heat. Tracing my cheekbone, down to my neck, right down to my cleavage, his finger hovered over the valley between my breasts.

Against his lips, I whispered, "Jack is still napping in the playroom. How about you and I have a little playtime of our own?"

Coils of heat snapped into my body as his pupils dilated.

"You serious?"

I gave a sharp nod.

"You sure?"

"Never been more sure."

"Gosh Dahlia, I want you so bad."

"I want you too. I don't wanna wait anymore."

Without another word, he jumped from the platform and raised his arms to give me a hand, allowing my body to rub against his slowly as he helped me down. A blaze snaked around us, between us. He swept me off my feet, scooping me over his shoulder and carrying me straight to his room. With my hands caressing every part of him I could graze, I stoked the fire, letting it burn hotter and brighter.

This moment would be mine—ours—and I would savor every second. Over the past few years, I had always put myself last. Not this time. This was my time.

Nick kicked the bedroom door shut and lowered me to my feet, my toes barely brushing the floor as I melted into a body of lust, conscious only of the thrumming pulse deep between my thighs, desperate for a release.

All the naughty dreams I'd had about our first time, about us, could now turn to reality, and none of them involved clothes or being rational.

The mere thought of us tangled together, enveloped by the scent and taste of him, sent a zing through me. The image in my head of his weight pinning me down, the feel of his rough stubble rubbing against my cheek, and the desire pouring out of him made me weak in the knees. Bits of me I'd long thought dead were slowly coming back to life, and now I wanted to take charge, to rock his world, to show him just how far gone I was for him.

His greedy palms molded to my ass, taking a handful. His mouth, as if under some magnetism, lowered over mine.

"Wait," I said, leaning back.

A frown creased his forehead as he looked confused.

I moved a step away from him, never breaking eye contact. With a twist, I unbuttoned my shirt, letting it fall open. The shadow between my breasts teased him with tantalizing glimpses.

His eyes widened as realization hit him. "No bra? Did you ditch it to mess with me on purpose? Had I known this, I would have lost my mind long before."

"None whatsoever. Lost it the other day, remember? Didn't wanna risk losing it again. So sad, I have nothing to hang on your bedroom wall this time. Maybe this shirt. Do you want it?" Nick's gaze could set the world on fire. With a seductively slow movement, I slid my hand lower, just under the waistband of my shorts. I tugged the dark pink lace up and winked. "Or maybe these."

"Yeah." Nick cleared his throat, his voice rough. "Yes. Gimme."

A victory smirk spread across my lips.

Sucking on my finger for a second, I glided it to the dip of my collarbone and down to my navel, swaying my hips, taking a few sideswipes over my half-hidden breasts, squeezing them, pinching my nipples until they poked out from under the fabric of the shirt.

Nick's eyes were at risk of bulging out, following every movement.

Feeling brave and beautiful under his ardent stare, I wetted my finger and dipped it into the waistband of my shorts, a low grunt escaping. I could see his restraint wearing thin, and I relished the power I held over him in that instant.

Keeping my shirt on, my way to titillate him, I used my other hand and unbuttoned my cutoffs, pulling the zipper down.

Nick's sharp intake of breath rippled through me.

Like a predator hunting his prey, he prowled toward me in one stride.

I shook my head. Slowly, I shimmied out of my denim shorts. I pushed the lace to the side, slipped a finger inside me, allowing the wetness to coat my finger. I added another digit and dived them in and out of me, chasing a release that would tip me over the edge. Removing my fingers from inside me, I showed him the evidence of my desire. "Look what you do to me. Want me to share?"

His tongue darted out to wet his dry lips, ravenous hunger etched across his face as he bobbed his head like a little kid.

Good. I loved that he was as hungry for me as I was for him.

I winked. "What about a striptease?"

"What?"

"Strip for me. Then you can fuck me as many times as you want, however you want."

Heat flared as determination rose in response to my challenge. He pulled out his phone, his thumb swiping across the screen for a few seconds. A low, soulful song—hot and heavy with beats—filled the room. His body began moving to the rhythm. I backed up until my calves brushed the bedframe, then slowly crawled backward across the mattress, all the while keeping my eyes locked on him as his body swayed to the rhythm.

In the most jaw-dropping move, he lifted his shirt, one inch at a time, enticing me with glimpses of his chiseled body—his sculpted abs, strong pectorals, and broad shoulders. As if he'd rehearsed it multiple times, he took a handful of the fabric behind his neck and peeled it off, the piece of clothing falling from his fingertips. His entire bare chest was now exposed to my gaze. So hot. He turned around, his back presenting me with another delectable treat. I would love to sink my teeth into those muscles and lick the golden skin that was tempting me.

Nick's firm butt twerked as he jerked to the music, then swayed, my mouth salivating at the sight. The sound of the zipper coming down became the biggest aphrodisiac. I wanted him. Every hard inch of him. He spun around and, in one sweeping motion, removed his jeans, his hardness pulsed, pointing straight at me.

"No boxer briefs?" I asked with an arched brow. "Did you ditch them to mess with me on purpose?"

"Didn't wanna hide the effect you had on me all night." He fixed his gaze on me.

I swallowed, my voice trembling, laced with unchained lust. "Nick. I want you. Right now. On me, against me, inside me." I slid out of my shirt, letting it drop to the floor, ready to lose every piece of clothing standing between me and him.

He inched closer. "I believe those are mine." He pinched the thin fabric of my panties between his fingers. "I earned them, no?"

The way he watched me, eyebrows dancing, had my throat dry and pulse racing.

"Yeah." My voice sounded as if it was coming from far away.

He crawled over me, his lips a hair's breadth away from my aching flesh, his harsh breaths caressing my bare skin. He curled his fingers into the waistband of my panties, and a shiver traveled the length of my spine. Tremors rattled me.

Nick's palms brushed against my ass cheeks as he pulled the flimsy fabric down.

I arched my back, aching, my head spinning, about to combust right here on his bed. "No more playing." My voice was shaking, barely sounding like my own.

"You started this," Nick argued, my underwear locked in his fist like a prize he refused to surrender.

With my legs spread wide, I beckoned him to taste me with a flick of my finger. My insides melted as his gaze became an erupting volcano.

With measured movements, Nick slithered in between my thighs, and his lips grazed my sensitive bundle of nerves as he inhaled the scent of me. His skillful tongue took a sweep of my lower lips, rubbing my clit, nibbling it gently. A rhythm overtook me as his finger joined in and entered me, hitting the spot that could send me over the edge in no time. He played me like an instrument. His hands, strong and calloused, took what they wanted. I twined my legs around his shoulders, opening my thighs wider to take more of his tongue.

How did I survive so long without this man devouring me in the most intimate way? My hips bucked to match his every move. I closed my eyes while he squeezed my breasts and pinched my nipples, then cupped my thighs almost painfully. Deliciously.

He firmed his tongue and dipped it deeper into me, reaching a spot that triggered spasms from my core. With the pad of his finger, he rubbed my clit to the same rhythm. I moaned as heat spiraled inside me. His hand moved away from my sensitive flesh to lift my hips further, leaving me bereft. I slid my fingers downward between my thighs and rubbed my bundle of nerves until I was filled with raw, explosive need.

Nick, his lower face shiny with my imminent release, watched me.

I arched my back further to meet with his expert tongue as he went back to his mission, hoping to take more of him, not ready to let go just yet. Desire lashed shivers through me. I gulped in air, savoring the sensation as it washed over me. Heat coiled within me, spiraling toward a point of no return—toward madness. My body shook, unable to postpone the climax any longer.

"Nick, oh God… More. Now."

He curved his fingers as they replaced his tongue, rubbing that aching spot inside me. His tongue joined my digits in massaging my clit, faster and faster as my head thrashed on the pillow, my breaths escaping in shallow pants. I reached a pinnacle where time stopped, and I convulsed against his mouth, gripping and releasing him, as waves of unleashed pleasure rippled through me in surges of exultation.

The pounding of my heart deafened me.

I surfed the climax, touched the high, breathing hard, dots dancing before my eyes as all my muscles tensed, then relaxed. I rode the surge of my release with soothing strokes of Nick's tongue as he licked every drop of wetness and stayed still until I returned to Earth, bliss flooding every inch of me.

On his knees, my lover watched me with a satisfied—part amused—glance.

A mischievous grin took over his face as he leaned forward. His greedy, and oh-so fantastic, tongue returned to my pulsing flesh.

I writhed my hips, trying to escape the hotness of his mouth. "Stop. Too sensitive," I pleaded. "I-I can't."

He snickered and pushed one, two, three—I had no idea—fingers back inside and I gasped, knowing the stars were still reachable if he moved them just the right way. Oh yes, this felt so good. So perfect. So intense. "Better?" he asked, positioning himself over me.

Could he feel how fast my heart was racing? How completely I had fallen under his spell? And how much more of him I still craved?

Gliding his fingers lazily in and out, his mouth found mine, hungry.

I tasted myself on his lips, the mix of us, sweet and musky, lingering on his tongue. My appetite for him had multiplied, feeding the yearning that had taken permanent root inside me, settling deep in every cell. Propping myself on my elbows to deepen the kiss, I wrapped one hand around his throbbing erection, unable to go slow anymore.

It vibrated in my fist, all thick and ready for me.

A hissing sound exited his lips as I worked him, loving how even his hard-on fit in my fist like it'd been carved just for me.

Nick pushed his head back, breathing heavy. "Dahlia, if you keep going at it like this, I will humiliate myself… Oh, fucking fuck."

Unable to hide my smile, I moved my hand up and down his steeled shaft, relishing the effect I had on his body and the control he could barely keep as I toyed with the hard part of him.

I bit my lower lips when our gazes collided, and I beckoned him closer with a finger.

Nick crawled over my body, and my hand curled around his nape, pulling him in.

One of his palms grazed my cheek, his eyes boring into mine, aiming straight for my soul.

"I'm ready," I said.

His finger tipped my chin up. "You sure?"

I nodded.

"I'll be gentle."

I shook my head.

"What?" A frown creased his forehead.

"Don't be gentle. I need this. I need you. I want it all… with you. I've been patient long enough. *We've been patient long enough. Just rock my world, okay?"

He nodded and shifted to the side, grabbing a condom from the nightstand.

With deliberate precision, he guided me onto my back. His tip teased my entrance and I purred, the sensation only about to push me to the point of no return.

With his eyes glued to mine, he slid inside me, inch by inch. Frozen, we both looked at each other as my body adjusted to his for the very first time.

Neither of us breathed, too enthralled in the moment.

I smiled. Nick smiled back.

He reached for my face with one hand, and I sucked

on his thumb, desperate to keep my mouth busy to muffle the cries I knew would soon tumble out.

Nick thrust slowly, gauging my reactions.

I locked my ankles around his back, changing the angle, pulling him deeper inside me, relishing how his body grazed my clit with each roll of his hips.

His eyes darkened under heavy lids as if he was trying to prolong the pleasure, to stitch himself to me, to live in this moment forever.

Snapping out of my daze, I threaded my fingers through the hair at the nape of his neck and pulled him down to me, desperate for his mouth on mine—and every part of him against me. I kissed him with fieriness.

With a moan, I detached our mouths and pushed my chest forward and his head down, silently begging Nick to cherish my breasts. He tugged at the sensitive tips with his teeth, drawing a loud gasp from me, his hands busy kneading my achy flesh.

Blazing fire set up there while he toyed with the hard tips with his tongue, as if to tame the flames.

Once satisfied, I propped myself up on my elbows and devoured his mouth, unable to go slow. I slid further up, and with open palms, I pushed Nick onto his back and impaled myself on his erection. A series of curses left his luscious lips as a whimper left mine once I rolled my hips over his in an erotic tango.

"Dahlia, fuck—"

Nick fused one hand around my waist, the other tracing every curve of my face, his gaze traveling from my lips to my eyes.

This, this moment with this man, was one I would cherish forever.

I felt more alive than I had in years—and more womanly than I'd known in just as long. I felt beautiful in the way he looked at me, in the heat burning behind his gaze. I lost myself in the amber of his eyes, in every sensation his body stirred within me.

With my hands splayed across his toned chest, I started moving up and down. Short gasps left my mouth while I rode him like I'd pictured doing so many times since we kissed for the first time.

Spasmodic groans escaped him as he clenched his teeth.

Increasing the friction, he lifted his pelvis, and with quick jerks of his hips, I welcomed him further inside me.

I closed my eyes as pleasure built in every fiber of my being, and my spine buzzed.

We both lost ourselves in the bliss we brought to each other.

"Dahlia, I won't... I-I can't..." He breathed fast. "You're beautiful. Look at me."

I opened my eyes, and without breaking contact, I lay back, pulling him down with me in the tumble. Positioned between my legs with my knees spread on each side, Nick pounded faster. His lips firmed in a thin line, his features taut, and his eyes focused on my face the entire time.

"Like this... Don't stop. I...I... *Yesss.*" The orgasm tore through me as I surrendered myself to him completely.

He slowed his movements, clamping my hips, keeping me still as he emptied his load in jolts.

He grunted as we both convulsed in each other's embrace, our hearts beating to the same rhythm, our breaths fighting for the same air.

His hands anchored me at the waist, keeping me flush against him, while his lips rained gentle kisses over my eyelids. "You're beautiful. All of you. It was...you are..." —he sucked in a puff of air, trying to even his breathing— "amazing."

My emotions fought to spill out all at once. What we'd just shared was out of this world, making everything between us feel more real than ever. "Don't go, okay? Don't leave. Don't die. Stay with me." The words, mixed with tears, left my mouth before I could hold them back. Or think them over. "I've been alone for so long…and… and now that you're here, I never wanna be alone again. What we share is special. It's ours…us. It's everything. What we just did only cemented that feeling."

A sob wheezed out. Nick had a way of making me feel vulnerable, a sensation that had felt foreign ever since I'd had to steel myself to keep going three years ago.

He dried my tears with his thumbs. "Hey, I'm here. With you. I'm not going anywhere. As long as you'll have me in your life. This. What we just did…you're right. It welded something between us. A force neither of us can deny."

His words felt as if he could read my deepest thoughts and the language of my soul.

It stole the last particle of air from my lungs.

Words I hadn't spoken in years resurfaced in my head —and my heart. I pushed them down, not ready to assess what we were to each other or what we could be, but knowing it wasn't a dream. A mirage. Or a figment of my imagination.

No, these words had now planted seeds in my heart.

And they wouldn't go away.

Chapter 10

Nick handed me a sausage he'd just grilled over the campfire. Jack and Buddy rested on a blanket behind us, the dog being used as a play mat and a car track once more.

"Naughtiest thing you did as a kid?" I asked.

Nick's eyes flicked up toward me, and he hiccupped a laugh. "Easy. One night, I found my Christmas presents and unwrapped them all," he whispered.

"Oh no," I exclaimed, slapping a hand over my mouth. "Did you get caught?"

"I was very careful to wrap them back up afterward. But somehow, I mixed the name tags. My parents had a long talk with my sister and me about Santa. And nosiness."

"Is your sister in Chicago?"

"No. She was in Europe for a while. Came back, somewhere on the East Coast. Met a guy… A surfer. One who escaped the expectations his family had put on him and moved to Australia. Last I knew, they lived in a van on the beach and were happy."

"Oh, this sounds fun. I wish I could live like that." I paused. "Santa, huh? I can't imagine you being naughty."

Nick shrugged. "I had my moments growing up. Tucker got himself into lots of fights—mostly about girls— and I had to jump in to save his ass more often than I can remember. This scar on my eyebrow, I got it after Tuck was assaulted by the entire football team in junior year because he made out with the quarterback's girlfriend under the bleachers and everyone saw it. I couldn't let him get his ass kicked—again. Not that he couldn't defend himself, but he's my friend, so we always had each other's back. We still do." He snickered. "He loved that. No, I take my words back. He still loves that. Trouble. And girls."

"Oh, this is terrible. I can't wait to meet him. He sounds like an…huh…interesting guy."

"Believe me, he is. But he's also the most loyal person I know. And there's nothing he wouldn't do for the people he loves. He's the best, and you're right. You can't be bored with a friend like that."

"Addison is the same. She was the popular girl in high school. Always having a boyfriend. Attending parties. Experimenting with everything before anyone else our age even dared. She got me my first beer at fifteen. Whenever we're together, it's like no time has passed since high school. She pushes me to try new things…to be more adventurous. To follow my instincts." I shook my head as some of Addison's and my best memories flashed in my mind. "What are your parents like? Are you close?"

"No, they live in Italy. I don't see them very often. They rarely come to visit me. Maybe once a year at the most. I try to fly there when I have some free time. Tuck feels more like family to me. But you should see my parents together. They're the real deal. Love at first sight. They were made for each other. Even after all this time, they're still madly in love. They're the definition of couple goals. Sometimes I think they love each other more than the idea of having a family. It's okay, though. As long as they are happy. Are your folks around?"

"Still living in White Crest. In my childhood home. My dad's a lawyer. He used to manage Carter's and my career when we first started. Got us our big break contract when we signed up with Riley. They come here from time to time, but usually, I'm the one driving there to see them. After Jeff died, I pulled away from everybody I loved because it hurt too much. All those memories… Carter refused to gimme my space. In a way, I'm happy he didn't. He prevented me from drowning."

I averted my eyes, memories of my past hitting me at full force.

Nick scooted his chair closer to mine and held my hand in his. "It's okay to be sad. I already told you. How was he?"

I met his eyes. "Who? Jeff?"

"Yeah."

A warm laugh came out. "Where do I even begin? I'd known him all my life. He was almost three years older than Carter and me. The three of us grew up together, but never did it occur to me that we could be more someday. Jeff always volunteered to help Carter and me whenever we needed anything… Always gravitating around us. He used to brag he was our biggest fan. And honestly, he was. From day one. Thumbs-ups, smiles, driving us around. He never missed a show unless he had to. He's the one who got us on Riley's radar. He would have done pretty much anything to see us succeed."

"Did he sing too?"

I shook my head, grinning at the memory. "Nah. And he couldn't figure out a guitar either. If he had, we would have been unstoppable the three of us. Our chemistry was through the roof. He only sang while doing hands-on work around the house, and believed me, it was bad. Really bad." I paused. "From the outside, he looked fearless and always in control. He knew what he wanted, and no one could change his mind if it were set on something. But with me—and Cart—he showed that softer side of him… his vulnerability. And huge heart. He was smart, caring, hardworking. He struggled to find his place in this world. Somehow, even when we tried to include him as much as we could in the band, he felt like a third wheel. So, he decided to follow a path he thought to be his calling. War changed him, though. Jeff wasn't cut for the army, and deep down I'm sure he knew it too, but he hoped to make a difference and leave his mark on the world. To make it a better place…in his own way."

I breathed out with a tight smile.

"That's pretty noble of him. How did you two happen?"

"One day, I was at his home, and he paraded in front of me, half-naked, still wet from his shower, only a towel wrapped low around his hips. He told me years later he had had a crush on me for years but had no idea how to tell me, so he came up with this idea to catch my attention. I was fifteen."

"Did it work?"

"Oh yes. After that, I couldn't stop thinking about him. He woke up my dormant hormones, and I became obsessed with him. He asked me to prom, and things evolved between us after that. Our relationship changed the dynamic of our trio, and we never went back to what we used to be. For a long time, Carter resented us. He acted as if it was all fine, but deep down, he was hurting. A lot."

"But he stayed by your side, no matter what, no?"

I nodded. "Yeah." I lost myself in my thoughts. "Jeff was my first everything. We grew up together. We'd been through so much. Just when we finally figured out how to be with each other for the long run, his heart stopped. I never got a chance to tell him goodbye. Never got the opportunity to tell him all that he meant to me. How sorry I was for the years we missed being happy, too busy fighting." A lump filled the back of my throat. "We had it all—*I* had it all—and it crashed and burned without any notice."

I used the shoulder of Nick's hoodie I'd borrowed to wipe the tears welling up in my eyes and sniffled. My heart shattered in my chest. It turned to dust.

Nick squeezed my hand a little harder, letting me know he was there, then smiled at me. He didn't have to say anything. Everything I needed to mend the remaining fractures of my broken heart swept through his eyes. It warmed me up. With him, I felt more alive than I had in years. The particles of my heart flying around in my chest found their way back together. They built my heart back up, piece by piece, until it felt whole again. I flipped my hand into his and returned his squeeze.

"Any ex-girlfriend who broke your heart? A lost love? Anyone who got away?"

Nick's shoulders dropped as he sighed. "There was this girl. Zoey. Like you and Jeff, we started dating in high school. Back in the day, I thought what we had was true love…that she was the one for me. Until one day, after college, she packed her stuff and moved to California to be with a guy she'd met online. I wanted us to move in together. We had dreams…or so I thought. Turned out she had dreams of her own, and they didn't include me. I took it hard. Met all kinds of girls afterward, thanks to Tucker being on the prowl almost every night, but it always felt wrong. Then I started seeing Pamela on a regular basis. We weren't dating, just being exclusive. After a year she hinted for more. I couldn't see myself going the distance with her. Just to piss me off, she hooked up with one of my two best friends—who apparently had a huge crush on her I knew nothing about—and they eloped months later. She's kinda controlling and crazy at times, but Jace loves her. If he's happy, what else could I want for them?"

I pivoted to face him. "Your ex-girlfriend—or whatever you were—married one of your best friends and you're okay with that?"

"I aim for what my parents have, and I won't settle for any less. If they're happy together, that's fine by me. I would've never married her, anyway."

"Okay, I knew you were amazing, but that, right now, blows my mind. Can I send Pamela a *thank-you* card?" My smile washed off, and I brought my attention back to Nick. "Does this mean you can see yourself going the distance with me?"

His eyes found mine, gleaming with so much heat and power, I had a hard time swallowing. "Yes. I do."

We stared at each other, and flutters danced around in my belly. My pulse kicked up.

Nick's lips parted, but Jack joined us before he could add anything else, and broke the moment.

He tugged at Nick's sleeve. "Play with me? Buddy sleepy. Go swing."

Nick squatted to align his face with my son's. "Oh, you want me to push you on the swing?"

My baby's eyes filled with delight, and he bobbed his head fast.

"You sure you're brave enough to go high?"

He nodded again.

"Okay. Come on then, little guy. Let's see if your toes can touch the sky."

With both hands over my heart to prevent it from running away or combusting, I watched my men sauntering away, hand in hand, toward the swing set Nick had built for Jack last weekend.

My men.

When did I start referring to Nick as mine?

I had no clue, but the thought didn't scare me. No. Instead, it soothed another chunk of my bruised heart.

The realization struck me hard, knocking the air out of my lungs.

Chapter 11

"**S**coot closer," I said to Dahlia as we positioned ourselves on our stargazing deck, Jack sleeping beside her, tucked in a red sleeping bag, Buddy snoring on his right. With my phone, I snapped a picture of the four of us. "I'll get it framed."

Dahlia pressed a kiss to my chin as I took another shot of us. "Thanks for letting Jack and I be a part of Derek's list. I had fun today. I'm glad Joan could take over the shop all afternoon. She's been amazing so far and knows everyone in town. I found someone I could count on, and she's exactly the right person."

"It's all you. You make people want to be the best versions of themselves. It's a gift you possess, Dahlia Ellis. I know because it's rubbing off on me too."

"Thanks, but look who's talking. You're pretty *extra* extraordinary yourself, Nicholas Peterson. We make a great pair, you and I."

I kissed the nape of her neck, pushing the copper tresses over her shoulder and relishing the floral scent of her. With her back to my front, I hooked an arm around the curve of her waist and pulled her against me, my body hardening at the mere thought of spending the night together.

"You're lucky we have company, or I would've made you scream my name right here. All night long."

Dahlia writhed her ass against my erection, testing the limits of my willpower.

"Thanks for the double sleeping bag you got us, by the way. This makes camping so much more worth it." I rolled onto my other side and flicked off the fairy lights with the switch I'd installed beside my head on the platform. Darkness settled around us.

Nestled in my arms, the woman I never knew could steal my heart turned to face me. Entangled, we stared at the dark sky, the stars shining like someone had sprinkled diamonds from space.

"This is perfect," she said.

I ventured a hand under her shirt, sliding my fingertips along the length of her ribcage, then back up to trace the line of her spine, repeating the motion like a slow, deliberate dance.

A low quivering gasp left her mouth and her body tense.

I kept going, savoring the shivers that blossomed beneath the pads of my fingers. Dahlia squirmed against me, pressing herself deeper into my arms.

"Now this is perfect," I said, my palm molded to her backside, holding her close.

In the pitch-black darkness, we couldn't see each other clearly, but by instinct, my mouth found hers, and I swallowed the soft whimpers that escaped her lips.

We pulled apart before things escalated, and she anchored herself to me, clutching my shirt. In the safety of each other's arms, we sank into the quiet.

My eyelids fluttered as I tried to stay awake, but I lost the battle, lulled to sleep by the gentle rhythm of her breaths.

"Nick?"

I blinked, unsure if it was part of a dream or not. "Hmm."

"I really like us together. Thanks for everything you do for us. It means a lot, and I'm thankful for all of it. I'll never take anything for granted ever again. This is me telling you I'm grateful to have you in my life…in our lives."

"It all comes naturally with you and Jack…as if you've always been a part of my life. I'm the lucky one. Now sleep. I'm watching over you," I said, as she sank her body into mine, fastening my grip around her. "I'm glad I found you too. I'll never wish to be anywhere else. And I'll always make sure you're happy and safe."

———

"You expecting someone?" Dahlia asked as I got up to answer the door the next afternoon.

I shrugged.

The pounding intensified on the other side.

"No. None of the guys from work said anything about coming over, and the neighbors are gone for the day. Everyone else I know is here."

My eyes traveled to Jack drawing in the living room, Buddy napping next to him, and Dahlia sitting at the kitchen table, looking over the paint samples I'd picked up for the bedroom.

Another knock on the door.

My grin stretched from ear to ear as I yanked it open. My best friend stood on the front porch, a duffle bag slung over his shoulder, looking like his preppy self, dressed in dark trousers and a purple button-up shirt with the sleeves rolled up to the elbows.

"Hey, man. What are you doing here?" I asked, pulling Tucker into a hug. I failed at holding back the smile curling my lips. "Are you lost? Those clothes have no place around here."

He took a step back and tsk-tsked. "You're just jealous that I'm better looking than you, man. I thought coming to town for a surprise visit would be a good idea. You know, just to throw away any plan you might have."

I stepped aside to let him in.

As if his eyes were magnets only attracted to the opposite sex, Tucker's gaze landed on Dahlia. "Oh, you have company." He elbowed me in the arm, probably thinking he was being subtle.

Jack, curious, came to me, and I picked him up and kissed his cheek.

"Man, how long have you been here? Did time fly by and I didn't get the memo? Whoa, you've got yourself a family." Tucker bunched his dark eyebrows, giving me a what-the-hell stare. "Did I miss an entire episode of Nick Peterson's life?"

Tucker slapped his chest, his dramatic side on full display, and I rolled my eyes as Dahlia rose to her feet to meet him.

"This little guy here is Jack. Jack, this is my friend, Tuck. Don't listen to anything he says. He's a troublemaker."

They both studied each other with frowns, but Jack held out his fist for Tucker to bump, just like we practiced all the time. My friend and I burst out laughing. And like a dad, pride overflowed in me.

"Nice to meet you, Jack. I see you already know the secret code to our friendship." He ruffled the boy's hair. "You can call me Uncle Tuck."

I flipped a palm over, glancing at my friend. "Uncle Tuck?"

He shrugged. "Yeah, thought it sounds good."

I shook my head but ended up laughing along with him.

My woman neared us, interrupting our chuckles.

Tucker gave her a slow once-over, panty-melting smirk in place, his playboy ways untamed. "Hey there. I'm Tuck, Nick's best friend. And the most handsome between the two of us."

Dahlia furrowed her brows, looking at him, unimpressed.

I silenced my snicker with a closed fist.

With round eyes, Jack watched the interaction as closely as I did.

"Dahlia," my girl finally said, shaking his hand. With a loud sigh, she shook her head. "You see, I thought I was Nick's best friend. This isn't working. We've already agreed that in this town, I get to hold the best friend title. Sorry, man. You're now second best."

"Did you just *man* me?" Tucker asked with a stunned expression.

Dahlia failed to reel in the grin spreading across her lips. "Yep. I think I did. *Man.*"

Tucker pivoted to face me, his eyes wide. "Nick, I like her. She's a keeper. Are you single?" he asked in his most flirty tone—the one he used every time he tried to hook up with someone.

I clapped his shoulders. "Off-limits, man. Sorry. She's too good for you."

Dahlia's gaze traveled between us, her smirk getting bigger by the second. "And I'm already taken," she said, locking lips with me.

Those words pinned me to the floor. The way she said she was taken—as if it were the most natural thing to announce—sent my heart into overdrive. Dahlia had staked her claim on me in front of my best friend. This meant a lot. At least, to me, it did. Her words replayed in my head, and my body sizzled. The thought of sending Tucker away and kissing her until her lips caught fire popped into my head, but I pushed it away. For now. *Later*, I promised myself. Instead, I pulled Dahlia against my chest and pressed a kiss to the top of her head.

"Welcome to Green Mountain, Nick's friend," she said to Tucker.

"Thanks. Staying for the weekend. Hope you guys have room. I thought I should make sure Nick here was thriving far from the city. He kept ignoring my calls, and it didn't sit well with me."

"Drink?" I asked.

"Beer, please." He brought his attention back to Dahlia. "Tell me all about you," he said, a hand on her lower back, leading her to the table and taking a seat next to her.

Thirty minutes later, we were alone on the deck, enjoying a drink under the warm, late spring sunshine.

"Man, no wonder you didn't tell me anything about your relationship," my friend said. "Fuck, you've got yourself a rock star. Is this a prank? Am I hallucinating?"

I huffed a laugh through my nose. "She's the best thing that has happened to me in a long time. We clicked. From the moment we met. Hard to explain. It's more than just…

simple attraction." I let the words simmer between us. "It's everything."

"You're aware she has a kid, right?"

"Thanks for the heads-up." I shook my head. "Didn't notice."

"Are you ready for this? Being a dad and everything. Because that boy will look up to you. Like Derek did."

I took a sip, searching for the right thing to say. "It doesn't have anything to do with my being ready or not, man. All this," I said, waving my free hand around me, "fits. It's where I'm supposed to be. Where I belong. It came naturally with Derek. And it is with Jack too."

"Whoa. You, the city boy, turned into a country man. Damn, you have it hard for that girl. I never saw this one coming. I thought you'd be ready to leave town before the six-month mark. Tell me. Are you pussy-whipped like Jace?"

"You met her, man. Dahlia is nothing like Pam. She's her own woman. If you haven't noticed, she does pretty good for herself—and I do too. But together, we're great. We're thriving. This thing between us, I can't describe it. It's rare. Addictive. Something I lack the words to explain. Something bigger than us."

"Okay, why do I feel like I'll hear the L-O-V-E word soon coming out of your mouth?"

I took a sip. "You're just jealous."

Tucker tilted his head back, laughter spilling out. "Keep trying to convince yourself, man. Hey, speaking of her, where did your woman go?"

"On a walk to get Jack to sleep. Should be back soon. Do you wanna go out for dinner or stay in? We could order in too."

"In. I want to get to know the woman who's about to

own your heart—and your balls—and that little boy you can't stop gushing about."

"Fine by me. Let's hit the grocery store then." I jumped to my feet. "Come on, follow me."

Tucker halted before we made it down the deck. "Did you tell her about Derek?"

I scratched the side of my face. "I did. Even showed her the list." I inhaled through my mouth to calm the jitters waking up inside me at the mention of my deceased friend. "I didn't give her all the details, though. I will… When the time is right. It's still hard to talk about him. Baby steps, okay? Right now, I'm happy—we're happy— and it's all that matters. I've decided to focus on that."

Tucker downed the rest of his beer and got in step with me as we sauntered down the driveway toward my truck.

———

I attacked the dishes while Dahlia put the leftovers away, and Tucker hung out in the living room with Jack. My friend had never been a baby person, but Jack had won him over pretty quickly.

Perhaps it helped that Tucker was about five in his head most of the time.

"Got an idea. I should be awarded the *best friend of the year* title. Hope you'll vote for me when the time comes," he called out from where he sat, his tone serious. "You two should go out for a few hours. Enjoy each other."

I stopped breathing. At least, I'm pretty sure I did. I should get my ears checked. Perhaps I heard him wrong.

"Me and my friend, Jack, we'll play with his car toys or watch some TV shows meant for us guys. Aka cartoons meant for kids under five because they're my favorites too," he added with a wink.

"Good one, man. Even I believed you for a second. Don't repeat it or I'll take your words for granted."

Tucker sighed in the most dramatic way. Yeah, he should get a degree in theater, he was that good. "You want to spend some time with Uncle Tuck?" he asked the boy.

Jack, now perched on his lap, nodded.

"See? Even he can't resist me. Go out, make out, do whatever you want. We'll be fine. There are no bottles or diapers involved, so I'm capable of babysitting this little guy." As if to prove his point, Jack leaned back against my friend's chest, completely at ease. "Say bye Mama, bye Nick," Tucker said.

Jack echoed his words, waving his tiny hand at us, watching my best friend as if he'd painted the moon—and the stars.

"Are you sick? You're not trying to bribe me to go out with you like you usually do? Something is wrong."

"Bah, me and Jack-Man are bonding. I'll go out some other time. I'll still be here tomorrow night. Anyway, the nightlife in this town looks a bit boring. No offense. I also don't feel like hanging out with Uncle Mike in his semi-retired community." He brought his beer bottle to his lips and offered me the smuggest smirk.

I leaned in and brought my mouth close to Dahlia's ear. "Babe, if we wanna go out, now is the time. I understand you don't know Tuck, but I vouch for him. And Jack will be asleep by the time we leave. It's your call."

"Won't he feel left out?" Her heart, big and selfless, made another appearance. My chest brimmed with pride.

"Nah, I'm sure he already has a woman on speed dial, whom he can't wait to call later."

Dahlia rolled her lips and chewed on them, looking hesitant for a second. "Okay, let's do this, but tomorrow you'll spend time with him. He's your best friend. He came all the way here to check up on you."

"You've got yourself a deal. Now let's go before he changes his mind."

"Where are we going?" Dahlia asked once we tucked a sleepy Jack in and kissed him goodnight.

With our fingers knitted together, I brought our joined hands to my lips and kissed her knuckles. "I was thinking we could head to your place and have dirty sex because my mind has been entertaining the idea all day."

Her face flushed with excitement as if powered by a thousand volts. "Oh, I like how you think, Nick Peterson. Drive us home then."

Home. I liked the sound of it.

Derek's Bucket List – ~~23. Nick. Feeling like the cracks in my world are healing~~

Chapter 12
Dahlia

Warm lips teased my nipple through the fabric of my shirt. A yelp came out, and I arched my back, pleasure traveling through me in addictive waves.

"I'll never get tired of this," Nick said.

His deep voice stirred something wild inside me. His grin set every nerve in me alight. The heat between us blazed hotter than ever, and my skin tingled wherever his eyes lingered.

I squirmed on the bed, my resolve hanging by a thread.

Clutching the hem, I tugged my shirt over my head.

Nick traced a path with his lips from my breasts to my belly. He hooked his thumbs into the waistband of my jeans, and in the most painfully slow movement I'd ever witnessed, he lowered them to my ankles. I shimmied out of them and kicked them off, unable to wait any longer.

We only had a few hours to ourselves, and I intended to make the most of them.

Nick eye-fucked me as he stood by the bed, undressing as if he had all the time in the world, his irises gleaming.

"God, you're so hot when you stare at me like you wanna eat me up." The moan escaping me sounded foreign. "Don't leave me like this, all worked up. It's cruel."

Now naked as the day he was born, he hovered over me and used the back of his hand to skim the skin between my breasts, moving down to my stomach and grazing the junction between my thighs.

Shivers ran through me. My hips bucked off the mattress.

His hand ventured south, tracing the length of one leg, then the other.

My nipples were so stiff they tingled. My clit pulsed from all the prickling sensations shooting inside me and all the dirty promises I could read on his face.

I gasped. "Fuck me or kill me, choice is yours, but stop messing with me, Peterson. Give it to me already."

Nick snickered and bit one nipple. I grunted...or purred. I wasn't sure. Pain and pleasure blurred together.

"Did you just *Peterson* me?"

I nodded.

"Oh, I see you mean business."

I extended my arm to caress the wooden piece of him begging for my attention, but he jerked away from my reach. "Hey. Not fair." My breathing turned shallow, and scorching hot desire flew through my bloodstream.

"Listen, I have a plan, and you'll love it. So much that you'll ask for more. Want to hear all about it?" Nick's smirk widened. "You know that friend of yours?" He tipped one eyebrow, looking devilishly handsome in the moonlight spilling through the window.

"Which one?" I blew the words out, tremors of unfulfilled need rippling through my body.

"The one you told me all about. You know, the one who has been warming up my place for the last three years. That vibrating thing you like…"

"*Yesss,*" I murmured, clenching my thighs together, barely able to stay put. "What about it?"

"Tonight, he'll join the party. Funny fact, I've never had a threesome before. Have you?"

Did I dissolve on my bed? Yeah, I probably did.

Nick's gaze fixated on me, waiting for me to say something.

"I've never had one before either." I breathed in slowly, focusing on his lips that I couldn't wait to feel all over me. "Being naughty with you, you think I'd like that?" I asked, my voice out of tune.

He cupped my cheeks and pulled my bottom lip between his teeth."Oh, believe me. I know you will, baby. Until you're so satisfied, you'll beg me to end you."

My breath hitched on its way in. Nick hadn't even started feasting on me, and I was already insatiable, every inch of me combusting with need. "Peterson, stop wasting my time and touch me already."

Relishing the idea of messing with him too, I dipped one finger between my thighs, and Nick's face turned a dark shade of purple. I flicked a nipple between my moist digits and thought he'd explode before my eyes.

"God, you're the hottest thing I've ever seen right now. Dahlia, no cheating, though. Don't start your fun without me."

With his body positioned over mine, he kissed me senseless, leaving me light-headed. At some point, we had to break apart to catch some fresh air, my lips sensitive and numb.

"Where's that friend? I can't wait to meet him."

With his hands locked around my waist, as if he feared I'd vanish, I slid to my side and opened the drawer of my nightstand. With one hand, I rummaged inside until I presented a very-expectant Nick with a neon-pink silicone dildo.

His eyes flared, and his tongue darted out.

He studied the toy, and with his hands still clinging to my body, he glided me further back on the mattress. "Ready to play?" he asked, every word and glance dripping with naughty promises.

I blinked, drunk on the hunger pulsing in his eyes. That was the moment all hell broke loose—the moment I lost touch with reality, and gravity abandoned me.

Without waiting for an answer, my man dived forward and spread my legs with his muscular hands. He lapped my soaked center with his greedy tongue, and I shivered underneath him.

He increased the pace, fucking me with his tongue.

A train of unintelligible words, mixed with cries, left my mouth, turning him into a starving man. Without letting me catch a single breath or savor the heat building inside and along my skin, Nick grabbed the pink toy from my hand and pushed a button. It played a vibrating rhythm in his fist, and he stared at it with awe. When he recovered from his daze, he coated the toy with my damp heat, sliding it inside me with ease, my vagina convulsing around the shaft.

Holding the vibrating toy in one hand, gliding it in and out of me at a dizzying pace, he plunged back between my legs and sucked my clit harder, my bundle of nerves feeling raw between his lips.

The few brain cells I still owned left my body.

My breathless whimpers echoed in the room as my

entire body stiffened for a moment, then melted, satiated and spent. I fisted the sheet at my sides, trying to anchor myself to this world and stay grounded in the moment.

Nick moved over me, thirsty for my mouth. "You like this dirty, don't you?"

While he kissed me, he kept maneuvering the toy in and out of my tight channel at a steady pace.

Throaty moans spilled out of me, wild and unrestrained, creating a chaotic symphony. My cheeks flared, a rush of heat radiating through me.

Our eyes met.

The affection pouring from him healed every remaining scar on my heart—even the deepest ones.

"Dahlia, you've seen nothing yet." His voice cracked on the last word.

How had I been lucky enough to find a man like him? What could I have done to deserve him? Why was life granting me this second chance at happiness?

I looped a hand around his neck and pulled him down to me. My mouth ravened his, pouring into him all the particles of love dancing inside me. Yeah, love. What we shared looked a lot like it—and felt a lot like it too. In every possible way.

"Gimme a sec," he said, lifting himself off me and reaching for his discarded pants on the floor.

"Listen…I-I was thinking," I said as he froze, a condom in hand, waiting for me to continue. "You're clean. I'm clean. Except with you, I haven't had sex in years, and I'm on the pill. What do you think about ditching this?" My gaze zeroed in on the foil package. "Only if you feel comfortable."

I heard his sharp intake of breath as he studied me, furrowing his brows.

"Or we can use it. I just thought… I don't know…"

Without a word, Nick tossed the condom over his shoulder, looking hotter than ever, determination tightening his features, a lopsided smirk tugging at his lips.

I swallowed, my head spinning from all the unspoken promises etched across his face.

The sexual energy radiating off him was so intense, I swore I could've gone up in flames

He crawled over me, and I held my breath.

Discarding the vibrator, he dived inside me, where he belonged, in a long slick thrust. Where our bodies and souls merged, and we became one. Goose bumps bloomed all over my skin at the feel of him, bare and swollen, making me his.

I shivered as he pounded into me and circled my puckered nipples with his tongue, alternating between them both, until I shuddered underneath him. His name, a whispered breath, trickled from my lips, pleading for him to stop, my flesh too tender, and imploring him to never stop, my yearning for him untamable. Insatiable.

Longing for ecstasy, I ground my hips against his.

Nick cursed when I dug my fingernails into his biceps.

I locked my legs around his waist, keeping him close to me.

His body rubbed against my clit and wiped out every bit of fight I had left, making me feel alive—and about to explode in euphoria.

Unable to process anything anymore, I begged him. "Never stop… Deeper… Faster… Fuck me harder. Yes… like that. More… Oh, *yesss*…"

"Keep talking dirty. That's sexy."

I shook my head. "No talking. More kissing."

His irises turned almost black as he plunged forward, allowing me no time to catch my breath, his tongue showing me just how turned on he was. Our hips moved together, a perfectly rehearsed choreography, drawing me toward my climax with each thrust.

Nick grabbed a fistful of my hair as I braced myself on my forearms, keeping our mouths fused together.

He moved to sit on his ankles, bringing me up with him. I straddled him and circled his waist with my legs as he rammed inside me from beneath me, never missing a beat. I kept him close, my arms locked around his neck while he gripped my ass, anchoring me to him.

We surrendered to the pleasure coursing through us, until the world beyond the bedroom vanished.

Nick's fingers traveled all over my back as if he couldn't get enough and had to touch me everywhere.

Breathless, he kept the pace steady, my body bouncing over his, all the sensations he brought to me clashing together until I cried his name and came undone against him. He fastened his arms around me, holding me upright as I tried to come back from the rush.

When our eyes met, the air between us crackled, every flicker reflected in his gaze. My heart sizzled at the realization.

Before I drowned in the golden depths of his eyes, I reluctantly drew my body back, fighting the pull of him. The hollow ache between my thighs throbbed, a raw reminder of the void.

Nick's lips pursed, but I silenced him with a finger. Under the weight of his watchful and confused gaze, I bent forward, taking him all in my mouth. His dick twitched at the contact of my tongue.

"Fuck… Dahlia… Wow… Jesus…"

Pride filled me as I stole his ability to form a complete sentence.

A taut expression painted his face, and it almost looked painful. He fucked my mouth for a few minutes, then halted the rocking of his hips. With a string of curses, he ran a hand over his face and tilted his neck back, granting me all the power.

With one hand curled around the base, I pumped him, enjoying the tremor of his erection every time my tongue laved the tip. I took him all in, sucking him with vigor until his cock lengthened to reach the back of my throat.

Nick breathed in—and out. His control stretched thin, until it shattered. With one swift movement, he flipped me around, and I had to release him. He positioned himself underneath me until my soaked center rested against his mouth.

He lapped at me with his tongue, and shivers skated the length of my back. My mouth returned to his dick, sucking it so hard, he stiffened under me. His mouth continued his teasing of my flesh, and I purred in bliss. Nick patted the bed, grabbing his newfound friend. With the hammering vibration on, he brought it back between my thighs until I shook, unable to stay still as surges of pleasure washed through me. And then he let go, a loud animalistic grunt escaping his mouth, as we came undone together. I gulped every drop of milk flowing from him in jolts, my tongue licking and teasing the now oversensitive tip. Until he couldn't take it anymore and had to writhe from underneath me.

Two could play this little game he was indulging in, and it turned out the bedroom sins were my ultimate weakness.

Moving back, I wiped my mouth with the back of my hand. We locked eyes, both panting. My chest rose and fell in a quick tempo as I tried to get a full breath in.

On his knees, Nick inched closer and kissed me with

everything he possessed, no doubt tasting himself on my lips. "Dahlia, you have something that belongs to me right here," he said, licking the corner of my lips clean of any trace of him.

And I died right about there.

Chapter 13

"Okay, here's the thing," I said when I stopped by Dahlia's shop before the opening hours. "I've learned from a very reliable source that today is Buddy's birthday. How about we throw him a party tonight? I'm sure Jack would love that."

Dahlia moved to my right, removing wrinkles from yet another gown with a portable vapor machine.

"It looks good," I said, taking a step back and admiring the wooden shelf I'd just fixed on the wall next to the shoe display, making sure it was level.

"I love it," she said, a smile in her voice. "What do you have in mind?"

I gave her a grin laced with mischief. "Lots of things."

She poked my arm with a finger. "Buddy's birthday, Nick. Focus." My gaze traveled down her body. "My eyes are up here," she said, pointing to her face with two fingers. "You seem to love planning stuff, so I'm all ears."

"How about we bake him some dog cookies? I found a recipe online, and it's super easy. We could get party hats and balloons and all the silly things kids love. My neighbors are away for the weekend, so Buddy is staying over with me."

"Would it be just us three?"

My hands found her hips, and I drew her to me. "Only Jack, you, and me. And Buddy, of course. I'm sure Jack would love the party setup."

Dahlia skimmed her lips over mine. "He will. And thank you for always thinking about him and making him feel special."

"You two deserve the best. I'm the lucky one. Would tonight work? If you guys can make it."

When did I get excited at the idea of throwing an old dog a birthday party?

"Yep," Dahlia said. "Very important question, though. Will we be able to kiss after the party?" She quirked a brow, offering me a cock-awakening smile, her eyes glistening.

I removed the vapor thingy from her hand and placed it back on the rack, looping my arms around her. "You're right. I love plans. Always have. Right now, I can tell you I did a lot of strategizing this week, and most of them involved a very naked me and a very naked you and a lot of kissing. Last weekend seems like ages ago."

I leaned in to claim her mouth, her pink lips tasting like cherry. My balls tightened as she rubbed my junk over the fabric of my shorts.

"Birthday party for the kids, then naked after-party for us. That's the plan."

She purred into my ear, the sound almost bringing me to my knees."Keep planning, Nicholas Peterson. I can already tell you're mastering the art quite perfectly. Do you need me to bring anything?"

I motioned *no* with my head. "Everything's covered. Recipe printed. Shopping list is on my phone. And the girl has agreed to be my date."

Dahlia laughed in my arms, and I got harder for her.

"Anything else you want me to take care of before I get going?"

"Oh yes. I almost forgot. There's a light bulb to change at the back, and I got some black and white framed pictures I'd like you to hang on the wall between the dressing rooms."

"I'm on it. Show me the way."

"And if you have a little more time to spare, there are some heavy boxes to move around. They're piled up in front of the emergency exit. If the fire department stops by, I'll get fined."

I flexed my biceps, and we kissed some more before Dahlia led me to the back of the store after calling me a show-off.

"What time do you open today?"

"In about forty minutes. We still have time."

Once in the backroom, before I could catch up with what was happening, Dahlia jumped into my arms and wrapped her legs around my waist.

I clutched her ass, and she kissed me until I had to lean back to breathe on my own. "I love it when you're not wasting any time. Want to do this here?" I asked, lost in her starving eyes.

She nodded and pushed the straps of her dress down, exposing her bare chest. Her nipples, puckered and pink, pointed at me, begging me to feast on them. "One week is far too long," she whispered against my mouth.

I freed my cock with one hand, and I sat Dahlia on a

pile of boxes. I lifted her maxi dress until the fabric bunched around her waist, kissed her with purpose until my lips hurt, and rammed into her, my pants low around my ankles. I kneaded her breasts with my hands the entire time while she tipped her head back and cried my name over and over. We moved together in flawless rhythm until we both came in a tangle of pleasure and contentment.

"Wow," I said between kisses as we both free-fell back to Earth.

I zipped myself up after I lowered Dahlia down onto her feet. She swayed, and I offered a hand to steady her.

"I'm drunk," she said with a smirk, a dark blush coloring her cheeks, and her eyes glossy. "Drunk on you."

"Don't say stuff like that because I'll never get out of here."

"I'm glad we got it out of our systems. Now I'll be able to focus. It wasn't fair having you around, looking all sexy with your tool belt, and doing nothing about it."

I turned my head to kiss her again. This woman.

Together, we moved the boxes with a shared awareness, our gazes speaking the unspoken language of our hearts.

———

Hours later, Dahlia, Jack, and I stood around the kitchen island, Jack perched on a stool, molding dog cookie dough into bone shapes.

The boy's arm fell to his side, and Buddy got to his feet to lick the sticky dough from his fingers. He giggled, the sound pure and heartwarming, and we joined in. "Buddy likes cake. His tongue wet."

After we put our creations in the oven, I sat the toddler on my shoulders, and together we hung red balloons and a

Happy birthday banner over the door leading to the back deck.

"If this house were mine, I'd move the kitchen to the north side and the living room here, where we can look over the mountains through those giant windows. I'd paint the walls white to light up the space like you did at your place but keep the old hardwood floors and planked ceilings, though. They give this place its charm. I'd also build a barn where the garage stands. It's old and must be replaced soon, anyway. All white, like the house, with black shutters and teal doors. Maybe get a horse…or two. Or use it as a wood workshop or a place to have people over," I said. "I haven't really thought about that part. It's just an idea… The way I see it in my head. The land is big and flat. It has so much potential."

"Ohmygod, I can see it all too. It would look amazing. Your vision is very similar to mine. Except for the barn, which, to be honest, I hadn't thought about, but it would be the perfect addition. One day, when you start your own construction business, you'll be able to build houses the way you see them in your head. You could even use a barn as an office."

I gave Dahlia a pointed look. "How are you so sure I'll own a business one day?"

She shrugged. "Call it instinct, but I just know it."

"Let's make a pact. If I do, I'll name you president of the interior design department. Mike wants to retire in about a year. He talked to me about taking over. We'll see."

Dahlia wound her arms around me. "It's sexy when you're making plans to stay in Green Mountain. By the way, I would love to join your business. You're kinda hard to resist when you're in construction mode. That tool belt… Think you could wear it more often?"

I snickered, tucking her hair behind her ear.

The air tensed.

I looked between her lips and her eyes, torn between holding her gaze and kissing her. "Dahlia, you're making it hard for a man to walk away. The mountain air is great, but you're greater. My home is here now. I can't imagine living anywhere else."

That was the truth. I didn't miss Chicago. I loved the new life I was building for myself here, and as long as Dahlia and Jack were in it, I'd never be able to be anywhere else. No matter how I missed my friends back in Illinois.

Dahlia batted her lashes, her big moss-green eyes locked on mine. "I'm very glad you feel this way. Now that I've found you, I'm not ready to let go of you. I kinda like having you around." She buried her face into my chest and took a big whiff before lifting her gaze back in my direction.

"You do?"

"Yeah. You're kind of nice. And good-looking. And skilled with your hands. And you smell great too."

I mirrored her lopsided smile before claiming her lips, our mouths fusing in a slow, intoxicating tango.

Time stood still as we lost ourselves in each other's embrace.

"About that tool belt, I'm pretty sure we can put it to good use," I said.

Dahlia's eyes became stars.

We kissed until Jack bounced our way, Buddy in tow. "Buddy wants cake now. Cake, cake, cake," he singsonged.

"Let's see," I said, lifting Jack into my arms and turning to check the timer on the oven. "Five more minutes." I opened my palm, holding up all five fingers. "But it'll be too hot. Tell Buddy he has to wait twenty minutes, okay?"

I lowered Jack back onto his feet, and he raised one finger. "Buddy, wait twenty minutes. *Nicksaid.*"

The dog hung his head and let out a huff.

I squatted before the bloodhound, rubbing him behind the ears, just the way he liked it. "Come on, Buddy. Don't be sad. It's still your birthday. Just get some fresh air, and I'll come get you in a few minutes."

He sat, his gaze set on me.

"Okay, time to get real, my friend. To have a discussion man to man. Or rather, man to dog. Or whatever. We're throwing you a surprise party here. If you could spend the next twenty minutes outside, it would help us put the finishing touches on things."

Jack perched himself on my bent knee, looping one arm around my neck. He bobbed his head. "Surprise, Buddy. No peeking."

I pinched my lips together to hold back the snicker threatening to escape. My eyes drifted to Dahlia, who shrugged. I found it adorable whenever Jack repeated her words.

With his head hanging low, the dog tottered outside when Jack moved to his feet to hold the door open. "Surprise Buddy. And cake. No peeking, okay? Go play."

About ten minutes later, the rains started, and Jack called Buddy in. Greta said he was half-deaf, but I wasn't so sure. Every time Jack called his name, he came running. Well, not running, but he came. In his old and slow dog version of a jog.

"Buddy, Buddy. Buddy," the boy yelled through the ajar door. "Birthday cake ready. Come eat, Buddy. Peek now. Buddy. *Budddddddy. Nicksayitsokay.*"

The downpour intensified, and I grabbed a rain jacket. "I'll go get him. I'm sure he can't hear us through the rain.

He must be hiding somewhere. Old fellows like him don't like getting wet and stinky."

Jack giggled.

"Buddy doesn't deserve to catch a cold on his birthday, does he?"

The boy shook his head. I ruffled his hair before making it to the front porch.

Outside, I rounded the house, looking for the birthday boy. No trace of him anywhere. I searched under the back deck. No sign of him there either.

Rain streamed down my face.

The property was big, but most of the grown trees outlined the perimeter so I could see far ahead. Anyway, Buddy never ventured away from the house. No doubt he hated the walk back whenever he ventured too far, his body quickly wearing out.

After I looked behind the garage and the firewood shed, I went to his house next door. Greta and Brett were still away, and there was no trace of Buddy there either.

"Where are you, old pal?" I asked, mostly to myself. "C'mon, Bud, time for your party. Stop hiding."

I circled the perimeter. Still nothing.

Jack's voice resonated through the rain as he kept calling Buddy's name from the back door. "Buddy. *Buddddy.* Cake ready."

My heart drowned in my chest.

Sweat lined up my spine.

A nagging feeling twisted my stomach.

This wasn't good. This was fucking not good.

It couldn't be happening. Not tonight. Not on his birthday. I wasn't ready to say goodbye to another friend.

I would never be able to face Jack again if I came back inside without Buddy.

I rounded the house to the left and locked eyes with

Dahlia from the kitchen window. She pursed her lips. I shook my head, and her face fell. Even through the pouring rain, I caught the panic taking hold in her eyes.

"Buddy, where are you? Come back home now. It's cake time. I'm sorry I asked you to wait." My voice cracked on the last word. Why wouldn't this sick feeling go away? Why was my stomach tied so tight it hurt?

I turned around just in time to witness Jack running in the rain to meet me, Dahlia after him.

"Guys, go back inside. You'll get soaked."

"Buddy, your cake ready," Jack yelled.

I caught him and picked him up, using my body to shield him from the downpour.

Dahlia neared us and lifted him into her arms.

"Mama, want Buddy," he said, a tremolo in his voice. "Buddy my friend. Where's Buddy? *Buddddy.*"

"I don't know, baby," she said, pulling him close, unable to protect him from the rain.

"We'll find him." I removed my jacket and placed it over their heads. Better. With the sleeve of my T-shirt, I wiped my drenched face. The rain picked up, each drop feeling like a tiny needle as it prickled my skin.

With one arm around Dahlia's shoulders, I urged her to go back inside. "Don't worry, I'll keep looking." A clap of thunder startled us, and she didn't argue, hurrying into the house, her footsteps splashing around as she retreated. I was about to give up too when I heard a muffled yap. "Come on, Buddy, talk to me."

That sound again.

My heart hit the ground. I swallowed the giant lump down my throat. Tears burned the back of my eyes. On my knees, I looked under my truck, and there he was, huddled down, his eyelids half-shut, his breathing fastidious.

"Oh God, Buddy. What happened? Come here, big guy, let's get you inside." On my front, I stretched my body until I could pull him into my arms.

In the entryway, Dahlia waited for me with a pile of towels in her hands. We glanced at each other, no words required to understand how bad the situation was.

Jack put a blanket over Buddy as I laid him on the living room floor next to him, now dressed in his PJs, in the same exact spot they always had their playdates.

"I sing you a song, Buddy. *Cattter* sings to me when I sick."

Buddy butted Jack's tiny hand as if to say, "Okay."

My eyes brimmed with more tears. Right about now, I would've done anything to ease all their pain.

Dahlia's arms rounded my waist from behind. I cocked my head to watch her, tears flowing down her face at the sight of her son and his dog friend together. Both of them saying goodbye to each other, even if Jack couldn't truly understand the magnitude of the situation.

Holding on to each other, Dahlia and I stood there, watching them, neither of us able to speak. The emotions soared in my throat, choking me. Dahlia's shoulders heaved.

Jack finished his song and kissed Buddy on the head. "I love you, Buddy. You my most *bestest* best friend."

I dried my tears with the hem of my still drenched shirt.

"You should go home," I said, spinning around to face Dahlia, rubbing her upper arms with my hands. The sight of her broke me. "Don't cry. It'll be okay." I pulled her into my arms, hugged her like my life depended on it, and kissed her forehead. I was a liar. It wouldn't be okay. None of this was. And honestly, I wanted her by my side. But I didn't tell her that. "I'll take him to the vet. I don't want him to suffer. You don't have to go through this. It's unfair to you. Buddy is my responsibility. I'm the one who offered to babysit him for a few days."

"Nick, I'll stay. We're doing this together. I'm not going anywhere. When you get back, I'll be here. I'll wait for you." Dahlia choked on her words. "I know how much he means to you. We'll…we'll wait for you."

I bowed my head. "Let's get Jack to bed first, then I'll take Buddy to my truck."

Dahlia nodded and lifted her son, now fast asleep beside the dying dog. "Say goodbye to Buddy, Jack," she said, waking him up. Sobs shook her body, but she kept them in, for her baby's sake.

Through my broken heart, all I hoped for was to soothe her pain. To add permanent sunlight to her life… and to her heart. Jack and Dahlia had already been through so much together. My instincts kicked in every time they were around, asking to protect them to make sure they'd be safe and sound.

When did I get so attached to this family?

How did it happen?

Jack's eyelids fluttered open, and he petted Buddy's head for what would be the last time. "Good night, Buddy. Sweet dreams. Be a good boy," he said, echoing the words his Mama told him every night.

A piece of my heart unglued itself and bled onto the floor, leaving a trace of me behind.

I bit my inner cheek to avoid crying.

With deep breaths in and out, I kept some sort of control over my own broken heart.

In the playroom that had become Jack's bedroom whenever he stayed over, Dahlia laid him on the sofa-bed and tucked a blanket around him. With her fingers laced through mine, we made it to my bedroom. I put a pile of clean clothes on the bed. "Take a shower and change. You can sleep in here. Or downstairs. I have no idea how long it'll take."

"Nick, I wish I could go with you…"

"I know. But I gotta do this on my own. As long as I know you and Jack are safe here, things will be fine."

She nestled her body in my embrace, and we stood there, our heartbeats fusing through our chests.

In a foggy state of mind, I changed and kissed Dahlia one last time before lifting the dog into my arms and settling him in the backseat of my truck. I found a veterinary clinic still open at this hour, a forty-minute drive from here, and followed the instructions once I entered the address into the GPS on my phone.

Time stopped. Had I been sitting here at the clinic for two hours—or six? I had no idea, no sense of how the moments had passed.

"I'm sorry. Buddy won't make it through the night. His body is too old and tired," the vet explained. "There's nothing we can do except make him comfortable."

In the privacy of an exam room, I fished my phone out to make a call, and the idea of being the one breaking the heart-crushing news shook every cell of my body. I inhaled. Air barely made it to my lungs before it wheezed out.

Greta picked up on the fourth ring. "Hey, Nick. Is everything all right?"

I swallowed, trying to speak the words tying my organs in knots.

I exhaled, pinching the bridge of my nose, my head bowed forward. "Sorry to…huh…bother you at this late hour. It's just…"

I heard the hitch in her breath. "It's Buddy, isn't it? It's okay, Nick. We knew this day was coming. You can tell me."

Keeping my eyelids sealed to force my racing heart to calm down, I muttered a breathy, "Yes." I could do this. I had to. My neighbors deserved the right to say goodbye to a dear member of their family, and my friend deserved the right to hear their voice one last time.

"Is he gone?" Greta asked.

I swallowed. "Not yet. We're at the vet. Nothing… nothing they can do. I'm so sorry."

"Can we see him?"

I nodded as if they were standing right beside me. "Sure."

"Gimme a sec. I'll get the guys in the other room."

I rubbed the heels of my hands over my burning eyes before switching to a video call, angling my phone so all they could see was their dog. In an attempt to offer them some privacy, I pushed the chair I'd been sitting on into a corner by the door, leaned forward, elbows on my knees, and buried my face in my palms.

"Hey, Buddy," Greta's voice resonated from the other end. It sounded more emotional than before. "I hope you can hear us."

The dog's head twitched a little, his eyelids fluttering as to reply he could.

"I'm sorry we're away. You're…" Her voice drowned away, the pounding in my skull blocking most sounds out.

With both hands, I scratched the back of my head, my fingers unable to erase the tingling sensation spreading to my scalp.

The buzzing in my ears lessened, and Chaz's voice made it through. "Life will never be the same without you, Bud. I'll always remember you. I-I love you so much."

The sound of his sobs hijacked my heart.

Greta's voice, now strained and wobbly, spoke next. "Nick?" I cleared my throat and took my place next to

Buddy and picked up the phone. "Thank you. Thank you for giving us the opportunity to say goodbye." Sobs strangled her words. "Buddy was lucky to have you too. I know you two had a strong connection, and you'll miss him. Also, I'm sad for that little boy. I could tell Buddy loved him very much."

The lump in my throat had turned into a rock.

I said nothing. Because I lacked soothing words.

"Thank you, Nick," Chaz echoed. "At least he's not alone."

We exchanged a few more words and hung up.

For a moment, I watched Buddy, trying to comprehend everything that was happening. To make sense of the idea of losing another friend.

With his soft paw resting in my palm, I stayed by his side as the minutes quietly slipped away. I'd never leave him when he needed me the most. His eyes gleamed in the golden light as we held each other's gaze. Then they closed, and his breathing slowed, turning shallow. I rested my hand over his ribcage, making sure he was still alive.

I bit the inside of my cheek and finally let the words out—the words coming from my heart. "Hey, Bud. I don't know if you can still hear me, but I wanted to say thank you. For being my friend… And…and for watching over Jack. You welcomed me the moment I came to town and never left my side, even though I wasn't family… You accepted me, and you accepted Jack and Dahlia as if they were family too. Every morning after the sun rose, you joined me…as if—God, this is hard—as if you knew I needed someone to lean on after talking to Derek and telling him about my life here. You said nothing, but you were there, listening to me. And that…that was priceless. True friendship."

I closed my eyes and evened my breathing.

"I'm sorry... I'm sorry you have to go. Our time together has been too short, but it has been great. You'll finally meet Derek, okay? He's a nice kid. I'm sure he's already waiting for you up there. Yeah, I'm sure. Please watch over him. He needs a friend too...a best friend. The kind he's been wishing for, for a very long time. Please say *hi* to him for me, would you?"

I wiped my eyes with the heels of my hands.

"I can't believe I'm doing this again... Losing a friend is hard. Losing a second one in a matter of months is fucking impossible. I know I'm not alone. I-I have Dahlia. And Jack. If I'm allowed to ask you one last thing, can you watch over them too? I know Jeff is doing just that. How... how could he not? He had the most amazing family a guy could dream of. But maybe, just maybe, you could help him too... Or be his friend. Everyone needs a friend, and I'm sure he'd like the company. He must feel alone up there all by himself."

I cleared my throat.

"I don't know him, and never did, but he must have been quite a man. Tell him I'll take care of those he loved the most. Because I love them too. With all my heart. I-I'm sorry for rambling. I have no idea how all of this works."

With my forehead pressed against the fur of his neck, I squeezed his paw harder.

Buddy took his last breath, blinking as if to thank me—as if telling me he would be all right, not to worry, that he heard me.

My throat clenched.

I pressed a final kiss to the top of his head.

"You can go now, old pal. You've earned your rest. Thanks for being my friend. I'll forever miss you..." I tried to swallow, but couldn't. My throat was raw, tight, almost sealed shut. Breathing felt like work.

Tears burned behind my eyes before spilling freely down my face.

My very first friend here in Green Mountain had left me.

Somehow, it felt like he took a piece of me with him. The first piece of my heart that made all this move-across-the-country journey thing worth it. Somehow, in the short time we'd spent together, Buddy gave me my hope back. He made me believe I could do this. Start afresh. Start over. Be happy.

A little over an hour later, with Buddy's collar hanging from my fingers, I made it home. Rain was still pouring outside, and I was drenched and cold by the time I made it inside.

Dahlia was waiting for me in the kitchen, a cup of tea cradled in her hands.

Her lips looked thinner than usual, and sadness lingered in her green eyes.

She lifted her head as I entered, and I gave a small shake of my head.

Without a word, she padded toward me and wrapped me in her arms. I pressed my forehead to hers, savoring the warmth and closeness of her body against mine.

After a moment, she leaned back. "You're all wet. Let's get those clothes off you. Follow me." Holding my hand, Dahlia led me to the upstairs bathroom. I had gotten rid of the tiled floor, but the shower was still usable.

In the middle of the room, I stood frozen, as if I couldn't remember what I was meant to do.

Dahlia turned on the water, then peeled my shirt off, her fingers scorching against my cold skin.

She unbuttoned my jeans next and helped me shimmy out of them.

After she pushed me under the hot stream, she

removed her own clothes and snaked her arms around me from behind, the hot steam of the shower cascading over us.

"It's okay to be sad…just don't be sad alone."

"How's Jack?" I asked after a long moment.

"Asleep. He'll be fine."

"I'm so sorry. That's not how I planned the night—"

"Plans don't always work out, Nick. And it's okay. It's life. You gotta learn to let go and ride the tide once in a while."

I shuffled on my feet, and with my woman in my arms, we stayed like this, bringing each other comfort.

The water turned cold, and after we stepped out of the glass box, we dried ourselves in comforting silence.

"Do you have to go home?"

Dahlia shook her head.

"Good. I want you here. With me." I pressed a gentle kiss to the tip of her nose, my knuckles skimming the soft skin of her bare arms. "I think we have to mourn Buddy together. The three of us."

I put on cotton shorts and a clean shirt and watched Dahlia tug at the T-shirt I had loaned her, along with the panties she had washed earlier, heat rising in me imagining her bare legs wrapped around me.

"I can't believe I didn't notice earlier how sexy you look dressed in these. You should raid my closet more often. I might actually like my clothes better on you."

We exchanged a smile, and I led the way downstairs. In the kitchen, I cut a large piece of the birthday cake I'd bought, and side by side, we attacked the chocolate dessert with our forks, sitting at the island.

"Why do you think he chose to die here? With me? With us?"

Dahlia shrugged. "Buddy felt safe with you. We all do.

It kinda makes sense." Tears glistened in her eyes. "You made him feel special."

I put my fork down, too many knots strangling my stomach to eat another bite. "I'll miss him… This place will never be the same without that dog around."

Dahlia scooted closer and rested her head on my upper arm. "You're a good man, Nicholas Peterson. You're strong. Fearless. And wise." She pressed a kiss to my shoulder. "And you're incredibly sexy."

"You think I'm sexy?" I pushed back, studying her expression.

She bobbed her head the same way Jack always did. "Yeah. And it's distracting. Let me show you the effect your sexiness has on me." Her eyes undressed me as they roamed over me in tantalizing slow motion. She bit her bottom lip, looking utterly irresistible.

I blinked, still amazed by the connection and chemistry we shared—and by the intensity spiraling between us.

In the most enticing way, and without breaking eye contact, she lifted the T-shirt over her head and dropped it on the floor.

My gaze lowered to her plump rose-tipped breasts and her center barely covered by her panties.

My throat worked.

"God, you're beautiful."

"Touch me, Nick. I can't stand not being in your arms any longer. We both need this. To feel better."

Fuck. This woman. She had a way of burning down the last thread of my willpower. Every single time.

I tipped her chin up with my finger.

Dahlia smiled. The kind of smile that could make me do nasty things to her.

Sadness lingered in her gaze, but now desire was taking over. Pure and raw.

My heart was bruised, but my body came to life. Scorching heat coursed through my blood, igniting each one of my cells.

My lips found Dahlia's, and a gasp left her mouth when our tongues touched. Desire shot through me, shaking my foundation and playing with my restraints.

My girl tasted as good as she looked. Exceptional. Sweet. Brave. One of a kind.

We explored each other's mouths with our tongues, taking our time to memorize every corner as if it was the first time.

All the pain that had been clinging to me since I ran away from Chicago died.

I wasn't scared anymore.

Everything in my life clicked into place.

I was where I was supposed to be.

Dahlia Ellis *was* where I was supposed to be.

All the puzzle pieces now made sense together. They had a purpose. I could finally see the big picture. Nothing that had happened was in vain.

I lowered my head and licked the swell of her breasts as I pushed them up toward my greedy lips with my hands. She shivered underneath my touch. My lips couldn't get enough of her as I feasted on her body.

With the pad of my thumb, I rubbed one pebbled nipple, and the moan that escaped her mouth got me even harder for her.

We moved to our feet, and with a step forward, I pushed Dahlia against the wall and lifted one of her legs, wrapping it around my waist. I ground my hips against hers, and nested my erection between her thighs. I cursed under my breath as she anchored herself to me.

"You're all I want, Nick. All the time. It's like you're

born from my fantasies. My wildest dreams. And I can't get enough of you," she whispered. "Ever."

I kissed my way down her throat, sucking and nibbling her skin, leaving my mark."You'll be the end of me."

Her fingers moved down.

I let out a loud growl as she freed my erection and curled her hand around it.

Every inch of me trembled.

She moved her hand up and down—in the most torturing, yet excruciatingly good way.

In that moment, it hit me. Every curve, every inch of me had been made to fit hers.

My thoughts bounced around in my head. All the things I'd wished we could be together now seemed possible.

"Bed?" I asked as we devoured each other with our mouths, voracious and burning with lust.

It was as if all the emotions we had been bottling up had erupted into a storm of passion neither of us could contain. Yearning. Desire. Need. And something bigger—more potent, almost hellish, yet beautiful. Something we had to face together.

Dahlia raised her eyes to mine. They had turned into molten emeralds. "No. Right here. Right now. I can't wait." The words trembled as they slipped from her reddened lips.

Her touch, soft and delicate, as she stroked my throbbing hard-on, sent ripples down to my toes. With her fingers, she shifted her panties to the side, exposing herself, and I groaned at the sight.

I replaced her hand with mine and pushed one finger inside her wet heat, testing how ready she was for me. Her warm arousal coating my digit was all the encouragement I needed. With one hand still holding her leg locked around my waist, I used the other to guide my way in, and entered her in one hard thrust.

Dahlia gasped.

I growled.

I dug my fingers into her ass cheek as we adjusted to each other.

Longing and lust overflowed from her eyes as I searched them to make sure she was all right.

She nodded, killing me and bringing me back to life all at the same time.

Without breaking eye contact, Dahlia pinched one of her stiff nipples.

The vision shattered me, and I could have shot my load right there without even having to move inside her.

She flicked the hard pebble between her thumb and forefinger, the sight propelling my hormones into overdrive.

Every nerve in my body sparked, my muscles tensing to the point of no return.

Shivering, electrified and taut, my body teetered on the edge of explosion.

My hand found her other breast, and I played with the tip the same way she did.

She let out a string of unintelligible words as she arched against me, clenching around my shaft, making me her prisoner.

Lifting both her legs around my waist, I slid in and out of her, unable to go slow any longer. "You're mine," I said, breathless, all the oxygen now busy fueling my dick.

"I'm all yours. God, I won't last long. Nick, don't stop." She breathed hard, her tone brooking no arguments, shattering the last of my restraints.

Without another word and with my mouth glued to hers, swallowing all her whimpers, I rammed into her.

Her back hit the wall behind. Again and again.

My balls were rock tight, ready to explode, stealing every shred of my common sense. Yeah, my brain had left the building, and only my body was in charge.

I lowered my head and ravaged her mouth. My entire being vibrated as her body swallowed me deeper. Until I could almost touch the deep end of her. Until I was about to be fused to her forever.

"There. Don't stop," Dahlia cried, her pupils dilated, and her lips swollen.

I ventured one hand down, and when my fingers connected with her clit, she detonated against me.

The walls of her vagina strangled my dick as they tightened around it.

She froze for a moment, her eyes closed, bliss painting her face.

When she opened her eyes, something had taken over her gaze. Something wild. An urgency.

"Fuck me harder, Nick. I'm not made of glass." Her voice, husky and low, unleashed something wild within me. I ripped her panties off, not wanting them in the way anymore. With my hands attached to her ass, I pounded into her harder.

The wall behind her quaked every time I speared into her.

Another orgasm hit her. Stronger. Her skin glowed in the low-lit kitchen. I lost myself in her eyes.

It took Dahlia almost a minute this time to come back from the rush as I licked a trail from her breasts to her jaw, relishing the tremors shaking her body.

She whimpered as I pushed into her with everything I had. Until my legs weakened when I came, and she collapsed into my arms, on the verge of fainting.

We both caught our breath before talking again.

"Evidence submitted. Case closed. Proved you are sexy." She claimed my mouth, stealing my breath away, and I forgot even my own name. "The sexiest. I hope you recharge fast because we're not done. I still need you," she said, with a twinkle in her eyes. "And you need me too."

"Don't worry about me. I have plenty to give. We'll see who calls it quits first." We untangled from each other's arms, and I guided her upstairs, toward the shower. "This time, I won't be gentle with you. I'll imprint myself on every square inch of your flesh, and you'll feel me in all your cells."

"I can't wait," she said, running away, her hearty laughter enveloping me.

"Don't hide. There are a million things I still wanna do to you."

Dahlia circled back toward me, splaying her hands across my chest, her naked body all shiny from sweat. "Then you better start now 'cause I won't be the one stopping you."

In the most natural way, Dahlia healed more pieces of my broken heart as if she were born to. As if she could soothe me just by being here.

With me.

And she had a magical way of keeping the darkness of the night at bay.

Derek's Bucket List — ~~24. Nick. Being brave even when it scares me~~

Chapter 14

Dahlia

I lay in bed, my mind replaying the last few hours on a loop. My body ached in the most delicious way. The man curled around me slept, his soft snores brushing my skin.

When Nick had returned home earlier, I had no idea how to comfort a man so completely shattered, standing in the doorway with his wet clothes clinging to him like a second skin. Shoulders slumped, chin lowered, he looked soul-weary. Saying goodbye to his dog-friend hadn't been easy for him. Buddy's collar was dangling from his fingers, and something inside me had twisted at the sight. Buddy was gone. Forever. The realization had hit me hard, a crushing weight squeezing the air from my lungs.

One glance at him was enough. I saw the hurt, deep and unspoken, churning within him and knew how helpless he must have felt.

My words were useless. Nothing I could have said at the time could have erased or eased the turmoil inside him. On my feet, I'd hugged him instead. In all the years I'd fought with my late husband, after he came back a changed man from the war, I'd learned that our bodies were much better at communicating pain and sadness than our words.

In that instant, I hadn't planned to shower with Nick, but with the anguish that had flashed in his eyes when I'd undressed him, his body rigid and unresponsive, I'd figured he might need this. Affection. And warmth.

Both naked, our bodies had been pressed together in the most intimate way, and yet there had been nothing sexual about it. I'd let my hand rest over his heart as mine had beaten steadily against his back.

I had the certainty in that moment that this man had infiltrated every corner of my mind, my heart, and my soul.

His sorrow had become mine.

Nothing could have broken us apart, not when grief had held us prisoner.

I watched Nick's sleeping form beside me, my stomach twisting at the thought of telling Jack about Buddy's passing the next morning. I didn't know how to explain death to a toddler. He still didn't understand the part where his own daddy had died. My heart shrank in my chest at the thought of breaking his, my pulse faltering.

In the kitchen earlier, I'd studied Nick as he ate a slice of the cake meant to celebrate Buddy's birthday. Only one thing could fix us. Love. No matter the form or how it was expressed.

Under his watch, I'd removed the shirt he'd given me and let it fall to the floor. Nick's smoldering gaze had drunk me in, his irises darkening, his lips pulling into a thin line.

He had scanned me from head to toe, and an ache had built low in my belly. Heat—hot, rousing—had rolled off him, the sexual tension between us rising to a peak.

"God, you're beautiful." The tone of Nick's raucous whiskey voice had warmed each inch of me.

"Touch me, Nick. I can't stand not being in your arms any longer. We both need this. To feel better."

At my words, something in his expression had turned feral, and I'd wondered if I could dissolve with only one sweep of his tongue?

Or from the intensity with which he was eye-fucking me?

He had stood still, my body quaking from the lack of attention.

Days when my vibrator was my best friend had become insignificant. Not when I'd experienced the real thing—warm flesh, whispered promises, lingering kisses. I would never go back.

I had brought one finger between my legs, and fire had burned in Nick's gaze. The animalistic side of him had taken over, and his own finger, thicker and longer than mine, had replaced my digit. Waves of unleashed ecstasy had surged through me. Why was Nick's touch always better? As if his fingers had a sixth sense when they fucked me. As if he could get me high just by embedding them inside my body.

A loud gasp had escaped my lips, mixing with his groan.

I had come, chasing the last waves of nirvana, my back hitting the wall as I drifted in the aftershock of bliss.

I'd yelped when he'd ripped my panties off, and that was the sexiest thing I'd seen in a long time. This man. One request, and Nick had turned into an unapologetic, dominating alpha. Gone was the sensitive, careful man I usually encountered. He'd gripped a handful of my ass and rammed into me until my vision blurred, and I believed I would never get down from this high.

Afterward, we had showered together for the second time in less than an hour, but this time around, the sexual tension between us had reached a new height. Nick's mouth was all over my skin, biting, teasing, licking, and kissing. My head had spun, desire and pleasure rushing through me in delicious waves. I'd spread my arms to either side, bracing myself against the shower walls to stay upright. My legs had felt like jelly, my pulse racing, my heart banging against my ribs.

"Stay with me, Dahlia. I'm not done yet. You woke up the beast in me. Now you'll have to tame it, or I'll eat you up all night. I'm ravenous and can go on for hours. Nothing will make me stop. Except you begging me to. You taste too fucking good, and only you can sate this thirst I have for you that's urging me to continue."

I'd swallowed hard as Nick had whispered dirty promises in my ear, making me even hotter for him.

All my wishes were being granted, here and now.

I'd swayed at the touch of his lips over the seam between my thighs, and Nick had caught my hips to steady me, his warm breath teasing my bare flesh.

"Hold on to me. You've seen nothing yet."

Another surge of heat washed through me as the memory faded, and I watched him for a few seconds, looking peaceful in his sleep.

When I finally followed him into his dreams, the grin curling my lips hadn't left, and the feeling rooted deep inside my heart had only increased.

It had only amplified my will to come clean. To be honest. And to take a leap of faith.

The next morning, I woke up early, and Nick was still asleep. The man who normally got up at the crack of dawn had been undone by the events of the previous night. I watched him for a long minute, making sure the worried lines that had marred the skin around his eyes last night had truly disappeared. Once satisfied, I snuck out of bed. Careful not to disturb him, I tiptoed outside the room and went to check on Jack. Through the ajar door, I peeked into the small bedroom that had become his. He was still deep in sleep, his fist clutching his fluffy blanket. The sight of him made my heart quiver and my eyes well up with tears. When I'd learned I was pregnant at twenty, it had been such a shock, but now I couldn't imagine a life without my baby in it. He was my whole world.

Strong arms locked around my waist, and warm lips trailed kisses down my neck. I shivered. If only I could wake up like this every day. With the man I loved next to me. I swallowed the words, spun around, and wrapped my arms around Nick's neck.

"Good morning," I said, kissing him back. My pulse sprinted. Yeah, I loved him. More than I ever could have imagined. My stupid heart was messing with me. In many ways, it didn't make any sense. Our relationship was still brand new. Yet, it felt right in every way. The other day, I wondered if my heart had mistaken the bond we shared for affection—because it had been starved of love for so long and couldn't process the rush of flutters invading me every time my mind drifted to Nick...or whenever we spent time together. No. I knew all about love. I had it. I had lost it. And now I could feel it again, burgeoning inside me, its branches spreading, their sap coursing through my veins.

"Good morning. Sleep well?"

I smiled against his lips. "I did. What about you?"

"As if in a dream. I can't believe we slept for less than four hours, and you look this good in the morning. It's unfair," he said.

"You should get in front of a mirror. You'll see you look way much better than I do," I said, combing his hair back with my fingers. "Are we ready to do this?"

"What?"

I straightened my back, trying to infuse myself with the courage I feared I lacked. "Tell Jack about Buddy…"

Nick bowed his head. His body stiffened. I kissed him, trying to show him he wasn't alone. That I was right there, by his side. And we could do this together. That we were stronger together. His arms held me closer, and I relaxed in his embrace.

"Yeah. I think I am. Are you?"

"I will be. I'm not sure he'll really get it, though. Death. It's kind of an intangible concept for a child…"

"How about we do something special? To commemorate Buddy's life. When my friend Jace's dog died years ago, we had a little ceremony in the backyard. We made cards and buried them in a hole, saying nice things about him. Perhaps we could do something like this. It's just an idea…"

I fastened my grip around him. "I like it. I'm sure Jack will, and Buddy would too."

We hugged without a word for a beat, losing ourselves in the comfort we brought each other.

The heaviness of the moment evaporated, and I became conscious of every inch of my man's hard body pressed against mine. I swooned in his arms as his lips locked on mine, taking their sweet time cherishing my mouth.

As if he sensed we wouldn't break apart if this dance between us didn't end soon, his hand met with my ass cheek. "Go, shower. I'll make breakfast. There's a special pancake recipe I want you to taste. I'd join you, but I don't want Jack to wake up and be afraid and alone," he said.

"You're too good to us, you know that, right?"

"Nah, Dahlia. I'm the lucky one."

Thirty minutes later, we sat around a plate of pancakes —Kelly's recipe as Nick called it—and fresh fruits, Jack sitting on my lap, not yet reaching the table by himself. I should get him a booster seat like the one he had at home. Yeah, that would make sense, since we spent so much time here these days. I forced my mind into the present and twisted strands of his hair around my finger as I spoke the words I dreaded most.

"Baby, we gotta talk about Buddy." I firmed my back and inhaled through my mouth. "He was really, really old, and last night he left… To become a star." I gestured to the ceiling to emphasize what I was saying.

"Like Daddy," my baby said. Not a question but an affirmation.

"Yeah, like Daddy. I'm sure they're already best friends."

"Me go on star? With Daddy and Buddy?"

I shook my head, a steel clamp strangling my heart. "No, baby. You can't."

Jack's lower lip shuddered. "Buddy my *bestest* friend. I want Buddy. *Buddddy*." Tears shone in his gray eyes, the same color as Carter's.

Unable to speak, I hugged him to my heart as tears made their way down my cheeks. "I know, baby. I know," I whispered, my voice cracking.

My eyes found Nick, and his expression mirrored mine. Holding out my hand, I grabbed his, unable to let go, all of us needing one another to get through this. He offered a small nod. We were in this together. No matter what.

After breakfast, we made cards and wrote nice messages to Buddy. Nick found an old metal coffee bin in the garage, and we placed our treasures inside.

"I'll begin," Nick said as the three of us stood around the little hole he had dug under the bloodhound's favorite tree. "Buddy was my friend. He came to me the moment I arrived in Green Mountain, welcoming me to my new life. He followed me everywhere and made sure I always had a friend around. Just in case. As if he sensed I was alone, heartbroken, and lost. As if he could tell I had no idea why I'd come here and required his guidance. Buddy, you showed me love had no limits and that it was possible to love someone you've just met, even if it made no sense in your mind. When I left Chicago, I did not know what to expect. I embarked on this journey because I had something to gain. Something to accomplish. Something to prove to myself. Now that I'm here," he stretched his hand to intertwine his fingers through mine, "I've never been so sure of where I belong. Thanks for being my friend, Buddy. I'll always remember you."

Nick sniffled and rubbed at his teary eyes with the heel of his hand.

"Jack, do you want to say something?" I asked my son as I squatted to look at him, barely containing my own tears.

He nodded.

"Go ahead, baby."

"I love you, Buddy. You my best, best, *bestest* friend." He kneeled in the dirt and dropped a handful of pebbles, leaves, flowers, and bits he'd gathered minutes ago into the hole. He moved to his feet but bent over to pick up a stone he'd dropped. "Bye," he said, a satisfied expression on his face as he waved at the coffee bin.

The sweet gesture brought a fresh batch of tears to my eyes and permeated my heart with pride and love.

"You did great, little guy," Nick said, fist-bumping him as emotion clogged my throat.

No matter how big or small, grief was something I really struggled to deal with.

With a finger, Jack beckoned my man to lean forward. Nick opened his palm, and my son placed a pebble in it. They stared at each other for a long second. Nick's throat bobbed. Without a word, Jack slipped into his arms. They embraced for a long minute, neither of them speaking.

When they finally pulled apart, Nick's face was a map of tears and tenderness. He lifted my son into his arms, kissed the crown of his head, then threaded his fingers through mine, bringing me comfort.

We exchanged a glance. I'd met only a few people in my life who could read my heart—and my mind—easily. And over the weeks we'd known each other, Nick had become one of them. A look my way and my soul let him in. No questions asked.

With my eyes closed, I inhaled a cleansing breath. "Okay, let's do this," I said, lowering my shoulders as I breathed out. I cleared my throat before speaking. "Buddy, you and I didn't know each other very well, but you brought so much joy to the men I love that I'll be forever grateful to you. I wish I could have known you better, but even if your journey amongst us was brief, you made a great impact on all our lives. Rest in peace, Buddy. And thank you for loving us. Go find Jeff now. And tell him we're doing great. And I'm sure Derek is waiting for you too."

I dried my tears with my fingertips, my shoulders heaving.

Nick released his grip on my hand, and my fingers trembled.

The softness in his eyes when he pressed a kiss to my cheek sealed the tiny fractures of my heart.

"Gimme a minute," he whispered, tucking tendrils of my hair behind my ear.

I nodded, watching as he lowered Jack to his feet, and they both used toy shovels to bury the coffee bin.

When Nick rose back to his feet, he pulled me to his heart and kissed my temple. "I'm here, Dahlia. It's okay. We'll be fine."

I buried my head in his chest, taking comfort in the beating of his heart and the sound of his breathing. He was alive. We were alive.

Jack roamed around, picking more treasures to place on the fresh mound of soil.

Our eyes followed him, matching grins stretching our lips.

My heart was all over the place.

Whirling around, Nick placed himself in front of me and cradled my face with both hands. An anxious laugh bubbled out. "Dahlia, can I ask you something?"

I frowned, trying to decipher the look he gave me. "Sure."

"Did you just tell Buddy you love me?"

I leaned back and covered my face with my hands for a split second, feeling his heavy gaze on me. Oh, he didn't miss that. Through a timid chuckle, I drew in a bit of courage and met his eyes.

"Okay, hear me out. I kinda did. Because I do. I know it's too soon, and I'm sorry if it scared you because that's the last thing I wanted to do. Gosh, I wasn't supposed to say anything yet. It…it just slipped out…in the heat of the moment." I closed my eyes, Nick's stare about to drill holes into my skull. When I opened them again, his irises **sparked**, the glow so bright I had to avert my eyes. "I hope what I said won't change anything between us. Please don't run away. If you wanna panic, it's okay. I'll understand. To be honest, I probably would if I were in your shoes." I winced. "But let's talk first if I freaked you out. I can't take my words back, but we can…I don't know. If you prefer for us to go home so you can deal with everything, just say the word. I won't be upset. Oh gosh, I'm talking nonsense…"

Nick grabbed my upper arms, forcing me to look at him.

His eyes had darkened. The bent in his lips had receded.

I swallowed my uneasiness down as the man I knew I loved bored his heady gaze into mine.

"Dahlia, stop." The tilt of his lips returned. The ones I was dying to kiss to make him forget the last five minutes. "I asked you because I had to make sure I didn't dream it. At the vet last night, I told Buddy how much I love you. And that I hoped it was reciprocated. I don't know how it happened—or when—but my heart is all yours. Every fragment of it. I love you, Dahlia Ellis. Never had I imagined I'd find love here. Certainly not this fast. Yet I can't stop thinking about you… You've become the center of my universe. Knowing I was coming home to you yesterday after Buddy left eased the pain. You were the only one I wanted by my side through it all. Somehow, somewhere along the way, you stole my heart, Dahlia, and I'm thankful. And for what it's worth, I don't want it back. I want you to have it. To keep it. And for you to trust me enough with yours so I can care for it the way it should be."

My voice trembled. "You love me?"

"I do." Nick kissed me, and a kaleidoscope of butterflies took flight deep inside me, turning everything that was gray and dull into a spectrum of bright colors.

Jack came running between us and pushed us apart, snaking an arm around each of our thighs. My fingers met Nick's as we both caressed his hair. As we both stepped back, my son reached for our hands, his little fists curling around our fingers, and the three of us headed back inside.

"Mama kissing Nick." He giggled. "Mama loves Nick."

We all burst into a fit of laughter.

"And Nick loves your Mama," my very hot and perfect boyfriend said. *I love you*, he mouthed my way, and I'm pretty sure I flustered because a wave of heat crawled up my cheeks. "And Nick loves Jack too," he added, picking up my son and nuzzling his neck.

"Nick loves Mama." My little boy hiccupped between giggles.

Nick loves Mama.

I would never get tired of hearing those words.

———

"How about the three of us do something fun today?" I asked as we played with Jack's toy cars in the den, the warm late-morning sun spilling in through the panoramic window. "I need to get home first for a change of clothes, then we can go hiking. See the waterfall. Afterward, we could float down the lazy river in those big inner tubes."

"Is it safe for kids?" Nick asked.

"You know you're cute when you worry about us, right? But yes, it's safe. I walk faster backward in heels than those tubes. He'll wear a lifejacket, and we'll sit him on either one of us. You'll see, it's really fun. Not much adrenaline involved, but it's romantic."

"Do you have one of those hiking backpacks to carry children for the hike?" he asked.

"Cart has one. We'll stop by his place to pick it up."

"Great. Gimme ten minutes to put a picnic together and then we'll get going."

I tugged at Nick's T-shirt and pulled him to me. "I love you." I sighed. "I'm happy it's finally off my chest. Now I can tell you every morning. And every night. And every minute in between."

Nick brushed his lips against mine."I love you. Go relax and let me get to work."

"But I wanna help," I pouted.

He shook his head. "Not this time. If you stay next to me, I won't get any work done. Dahlia, you're way too distracting for my sanity." His hand connected with my ass cheek, and I yelped. Stretching my neck, I kissed him, my lips molding to his. Yeah, I loved him. Way more than I ever thought I could love anybody else.

Nick carried Jack up to the waterfall in the backpack, my son whooping as we spotted a fawn and its mother. My man held my hand the entire time, as if afraid I'd get lost in the woods—or maybe just to make sure we stayed connected. The trail was marked and five feet wide—there was no way I could drift away—but I didn't mind, loving the way he watched over me. Loving how special and important he made me feel.

As if Jack sensed Nick and I were in it for real, he sat on his lap during our picnic, then fell asleep in his arms once we were done.

The sight of them filled my chest to the brim.

"You two look adorable together," I said, snapping a picture of my men. "How did you happen to walk into my life that day? How could you have mistaken my shop for Hilton and Sons?"

Shifting Jack to his right arm, Nick pulled me to his chest and kissed my forehead. "It was you, Dahlia. You blinded me with your smile and your beauty that day. And I just followed you in. Without thinking straight. Because even back then, I could tell you were special. That you held some power over me."

A seed that had been planted in my head—and my heart—weeks ago finally made sense.

I rested my head against his torso, Nick's strong hand pressing against my back. The rhythm of his heart, blending with Jack's soft breathing, soothed the jitters stirring inside me. Fiddling with the lint on the picnic blanket, I tried to muster the courage to speak. My heart thundered in my chest at the idea of giving voice to the thoughts running around in my head.

"Nick, I gotta tell you something," I said.

Leaning back, he searched my eyes until they locked with his, questions swimming in his gaze.

"It's big. I haven't told a lot of people… Huh…in fact, only Addison and Carter know. And…well…Jeff did too." I drew a deep breath through my mouth, attempting to settle the nerves twisting in my stomach. "See? I can't start this relationship without being honest with you first. You said you hate half-truths so… Ohmygod, it's harder than I thought it would be."

A weight pressed against my chest.

With my eyes closed, I inhaled and exhaled.

Nick grazed my cheek with his knuckles, and he forced my glistening eyes toward his. "Dahlia, it's okay. Nothing you say will make me walk away from you…from us. I'm here to stay. For the long run. If that's what you wish too."

I nodded, drying my teary eyes with my fingertips. "It's big. And kinda scary to admit out loud."

He scooted closer until I could sink my body into his. "It's me, Dahlia. You can tell me anything. I promise I won't react if that's what you're scared of."

"You might see me differently. Or think…gosh, please let me explain before jumping to conclusions, okay? It's complicated."

He raised a hand. "Trust me."

I nodded and scooted back, desperate for some fresh air, before telling him the secret that had been haunting my nights for years now. "Here we go. Promise me you won't get mad."

"I promise," he said. I saw the truth flashing in his eyes. The commitment. The love. The trust.

"There's a chance Carter is Jack's biological father." My throat worked as I swallowed the lump clogging it. I slid my now-moist hands under my thighs and hung my head low, avoiding looking at Nick for a few seconds. Until the storm in me dissipated—a little at least.

A strong hand curled around my nape. "Dahlia, look at me," Nick said. I tried to fight it but lost the battle, so I did. My eyes, as if he controlled them, lifted in his direction. "I knew."

"You did?"

He nodded.

"How?"

"To be honest, I didn't know but suspected it. The way Carter acts around you two is much more than just love. When you guys say you are family, it's way more than that. You are *a* family."

We both said nothing for a long moment. Until Nick broke the heavy silence.

"Everything makes so much more sense right now. I'm

glad to know I wasn't being paranoid. Carter behaves like he *is* Jack's father, not just his uncle. And as if you're his girl, not just his childhood best friend."

The words lingered between us, floating in the air as fragile drops that could either make us stronger or break us altogether.

"You said you two never dated…"

I drew in a jagged breath. "We didn't. It was one night. But somehow, that night changed a lot of things between us." I averted my eyes, staring in the distance. "Are you mad? I'd understand if you were." I sealed my eyelids as more tears streamed down my face.

"Jeff knew?"

I bowed my head. "I told him. Before we got married. But, since the day I learned I was pregnant, I've always been sure Jeff was the father. Even now… I don't know how to explain it. It's a gut feeling. After the shock subsided, Jeff and I had a long talk. We cried, we hugged, we cried again. And he finally decided to stay with me. And trust life."

I broke into sobs.

How could this day have turned sour? First Buddy, now this. There were just too many emotions swirling around. With just a spark, I was sure I could set the air on fire.

With my legs folded under me, I buried my face in my hands and let go of all the guilt I'd been keeping in for so long.

"How did Carter react? I don't know him much, but I'm sure the news didn't sit well with him."

I snorted. "We lost him for a moment. Darkness took over his life. He drowned his sorrows, pushed us away, acted recklessly. It was bad… I-I didn't recognize him. Us, as I said, was a one-night thing. A mistake… Something I think had to be settled between us because we would've always wondered if we were meant to be…" I paused. "But then Jeff died. And Carter came back to me." A long silence stretched between us. "There's this paternity test. He has it… I gave it to him after Jack's birth. I would never prevent him from knowing the truth. He deserves the right to. I'm just… I'm just not sure that *I* want to. Or that I can handle the truth if it's different from the story in my heart. The three of us had a complicated but beautiful relationship. Jack is the product of it…of unconditional love. It's precious." I swallowed. "Carter has never looked at the results. Not that I'm aware of…"

I blinked back some of my tears before continuing.

"After Jeff passed away, Carter and I decided we'd raise Jack together. We'd be like co-parenting him. I know Carter has been hoping for more, but I can't give it to him. Even if Jeff is stated as Jack's official father on his birth certificate, Carter is also his. In all the ways that count." With a cock of my head, I stared at Nick. "And now there's you… If we do this, you and I, Jack will consider you his daddy too. You must be willing to play that role. Eventually. He'll become yours too… In all the ways that matter. It's the only way this thing," I said, gesturing to the three of us with my hand, "can work. If we all commit to this child. He might have lost his daddy. He might have never known him—and never will—but Carter, you, and I, together, we can offer him something great. I know it's a lot to ask, but it's my reality."

"I—"

"Don't say anything if it means you'll change your mind afterward. You don't have to decide today. I'm just putting it out there. That's something you'll have to accept if you're with me. And as much as I love you, I'll never force you to a life you're not ready for. We'd both be miserable."

Nick laid Jack on the blanket beside him, extra careful not to wake him up, and on his knees, stalked toward me.

His eyes, amber in the sunlight and full of sparks, bore into mine—into my soul—and I braced myself for whatever words would leave his lips.

———

"Are you staying with us tonight?" I asked Nick as we drove back to my place. "Unless you desire some time on your own. I know the last twenty-four hours have been emotional. And then I dumped that piece of info on you. It wasn't considerate. I should have waited."

He brought our connected hands to his lips and kissed the back of mine. "Don't ever apologize for speaking what's in your heart. I already told you I'm not going anywhere. And no way am I letting you walk away either. We'll make it work, okay? You two are stuck with me."

We exchanged a heartwarming smile before I turned to stare out the window, emotions still filling my eyes. "I love you," I whispered.

"I love you too," he said, leaning in my direction to tug me against his side.

Feeling safe in his embrace, I rested my head on his shoulder and breathed him in. His masculine scent tingled my senses, and I lost myself in the newfound familiarity of him—of us.

"So, are you staying?" I asked again after a beat.

"Wouldn't it be weird...me sleeping over? Waking up together, the three of us?"

"We do it all the time at your place..."

Nick breathed out a soft laugh. "I know. But this is your home, your family nest. I won't feel good barging in."

"But I want you here. With us."

He parked the truck in the driveway and framed my face with both hands. "I know you do, and I love you even more because of it. Because you wanna share all those things with me…as if I'm already part of your family. And I told you, I'm all in. For the long ride…for the entire journey…but there's more than just you and I involved here. Let's not rush things. I'll stay for dinner but go after, okay?"

With my eyes closed, I nodded at his words. A lone tear traced down my cheek.

"It's been an emotional day. Let's order in," Nick offered.

My shoulders felt heavy and tense. With a breath out, I nodded again.

"Go inside, take a bath or anything you do when you wanna relax, and take a nap. Jack and I will take care of everything. We'll take care of *you*. You're always the one thinking about everyone else. Let me be there for you this time."

I hugged him tight against my heart over the center console of the truck before moving to get out. "Thanks, Nick."

With more tears sliding down my cheeks, I walked toward the house.

My heart jammed in my chest, its beats irregular, when I heard Jack and Nick's conversation.

"Mama sad?" Jack asked.

"Mama's tired, little guy. Let's have some fun together while she rests, okay?"

I made my way inside, and from the window, I watched them, laughing together, knowing in my core everything would be all right.

They raced toward the front door, Jack screaming his happiness the entire time. Nick ran after him, lifted him over his head, turning him into an airplane.

Their contagious giggles multiplied and reached my heart as I climbed the stairs to my bedroom.

Later, after we put Jack to bed, Nick and I snuggled on the couch. The day had been an emotional roller coaster and right now, we required each other to calm the storm.

After he made sure Jack was safe and he tucked me into bed, he left. I missed him the moment the front door clicked behind him and the engine of his truck filled the silence of the night.

Chapter 15

Nicholas

Standing in the doorway a month later, I rubbed my hands together, admiring the newly renovated bathroom. Yeah, it looked sharp. Gone were the old tiles and leaking faucets. Mrs. Rutherford had allowed me a decent budget to remodel the room, and thanks to Dahlia's interior design skills, it surpassed anything I'd envisioned.

I hadn't seen my girl in almost a week, and somehow, it felt like forever. With the store thriving and drawing clients from everywhere, she'd been busier than she'd ever hoped for. It didn't make things any easier that her employee Joan was home caring for her sick grandchild. At night, after work, Dahlia spent some time with Jack and went to bed early, exhausted. I didn't mind, though my body was aching in withdrawal, making the most of the time apart to work on the house. At least now I had one less room to worry about. Every day, we talked on the phone in the morning and at night. The last time we saw each other, I brought over pizza, and Dahlia had fallen asleep just minutes into the movie. Even when we hung out at her house, I still didn't spend the night. After I put her to bed and made sure Jack slept tight, I always drove back here— alone in this house too big for one person.

Hungry, I went downstairs and surveyed the place, still struggling with Buddy's absence. Whenever I was home alone, I missed my old pal. Even if he were as active as a piece of furniture, he still brightened up my days.

I dropped my ass on a stool in the kitchen when a knock on the door startled me. I wasn't expecting anyone at this early hour on a Saturday morning. Rising to my feet, I straightened my stained work clothes and ran a hand through my hair, hoping to look somewhat respectable.

My frown transformed into a grin—one I was sure made me look stupid—at the sight of Dahlia cradling a sleeping Jack in her arms, standing on my front porch, her hair falling loosely around her face. My smile vanished the moment I noticed the worry lines around her eyes.

"What's wrong?" I lifted Jack from her arms, inviting her in. "Are you okay?"

Her chest caved, and her voice wavered, devoid of the usual confidence. "Paula is home with a bad case of flu, and I got called at the store because one employee didn't show up because her car broke down. The girl who's there right now can't hold the fort by herself. I hired her a week ago. She's not trained to do everything yet."

I leaned forward and brushed my lips against hers. "Tell me what you need. I'm all yours for the day."

"In fact, I was wondering if you could watch Jack for a few hours." She gave me a once-over. "Oh, you were work- ing. This is so embarrassing. I should've called. Don't worry about it. I'll take him with me and find another solution. I'm sorry I bothered you. Please go back to what you were doing. I'll go now."

I clutched her elbow. "Dahlia, stop. I'm here. Don't ever feel bad asking for my help. I love you and will always be here for you two. You're what matters most to me. Both of you. And no, I wasn't actually working… I was just appreciating the work I'd done last night."

She drew in a nervous breath, fingers fidgeting with the necklace around her neck. "Nick Peterson, you're my hero in more ways than you can imagine." She sagged into a chair at the table. "Gosh, I'm drained. You're a lifesaver. I should only be gone for a few hours. Jack's stuff is in his bag. You can put him down for a nap after lunch. I'll be here as soon as I can."

She rubbed her temples, and the sight of her, overwhelmed and visibly exhausted, with dark circles under her eyes, pained me.

I laid the boy on the couch and took a seat beside her, grabbing her hand in mine. "Don't worry. I've got everything under control. We'll be fine. Do your thing and come back later. I'll cook dinner, and you'll spend the night here. You have to rest. I'll watch over Jack. You can trust me."

Dahlia tilted her head back and met my eyes. "I trust you, Nick. I always do. Thanks for being here. I'm usually better organized than this."

I pressed my forehead to hers, breathing her in as I basked in her energy. Our souls fused for a second, and mine comforted hers.

"You're a great mom. These things happen. As you said, sometimes you've just got to ride the tide. And just so you know, the upstairs bathroom is now fully functional, and the new shower is much bigger." I wiggled my eyebrows, and Dahlia burst out laughing.

There. The wrinkle across her forehead vanished.

Her lips, soft and warm, claimed mine, and I melted into her embrace. Torn between what I had to do and what I craved, I gently pushed her away.

"Go. We'll be here when you get back."

I kissed her one last time, committing every second of her lips on mine to memory before she slipped away.

"You're amazing," she yelled over her shoulder, waving at me. "I love you."

In the living room, Jack was still deep asleep. I observed him for a moment, peaceful, his fist closed around his favorite fluffy blanket.

Minutes later, I placed him in his portable bed, fearing he might fall from the couch like he did the first time he came over.

On the kitchen table, I spread the blueprints for a new development project starting next winter.

Mike said he'd put me in charge of it, and according to him, a project of this size, here in Green Mountain, wasn't a common occurrence. I intended to be ready to impress him, more than ever, with my planning skills, leadership, and dedication. Excitement ran through me. I'd missed those—the big projects with hefty budgets and tight deadlines.

A few weeks back, over the drinks we'd agreed to have when I first moved to town, Mike confided that Tucker had told him about the condo mishap in Chicago—and that he was more interested than ever in selling me parts of the business. Or even the whole thing, whenever I'd be ready. His proposition sounded good, and I promised I'd look into it seriously.

Bent over the table, I studied the plans for over half an hour before Jack woke up. He came to me as soon as his eyes sprang open, his tiny feet padding on the hardwood floor.

"Hey, little guy. How was sleep?"

Jack yawned as he lifted his arms, asking me to pick him up.

I sat him on my lap. "Those are construction blueprints for retirement homes I'll be building. Right now, I'm building cabins. We could ask your mama to bring you to the site one day to see the big trucks," I said, stretching my arms as if to prove my point, "and the excavators. Would you like that?"

He nodded, his face still flushed and innocent from his slumber. "Mama?"

"Your Mama had to go to her store for a few hours. She thought you and I could spend some time together. Do you think it's a good idea?"

He nodded again.

"Great. I might ask for your help later. I'm removing the old disgusting wallpaper in the bedroom upstairs and I could use those big muscles of yours." I scrunched up my nose, and a smile glowed on his face. "Gimme a fist-bump," I said as we connected our balled hands. "Hungry? I could make you something. I'm not sure you had break-fast earlier."

"Hungry," he echoed.

"Let's see what we've got." I sat Jack on the kitchen countertop, a hand around his waist to prevent him from falling, as I rummaged through the refrigerator.

Jack poked my arm, and when I turned around, he held a banana in his hand.

"You want that." He nodded. "With toast?" He smiled. "I'll bring your toys down here, and you can play while I make you a five-star restaurant worth breakfast."

Ten minutes later, with Jack perched on my lap, we ate breakfast together. I studied the blueprints still spread before me, making calculations so Mike could produce an estimate.

The sippy cup tumbled onto the floor, and when I leaned forward to grab it, my eyes took Jack in, and my breath hitched.

My heart plummeted to my stomach, and my body froze. Everything came to a standstill. Time stopped yet moved at supersonic speed.

Jack's face was turning blueish. His body stiffened as he tried to take a breath. He brought one hand to his mouth, and his body slumped.

"Breathe, little guy. Breathe."

All my movements seemed too sluggish.

Jack's eyelids fluttered.

No air came in and out of his lungs—nor mine.

As if he'd forfeited the fight, his tiny body turned limp in my arms.

"Stay with me, Jack. Oh God, stay with me. Please, hold on. Come on, little guy."

Life had a twisted sense of humor. Derek, Buddy. And now Jack. No way. Not under my watch. I'd give my life for this boy. Any day. Any time.

My last CPR class had been back when I'd started working for Cody years ago, and it only covered what to do on a construction site—not in a kitchen with a child.

Even though I knew the basics, I had no idea what technique to use on a toddler.

My body woke up. Adrenaline stirred in my blood.

The numbing of my mind washed away, and I jumped to my feet and laid Jack on the floor.

Taking the phone in my hand, I called nine-one-one.

"…must be choking. Have you checked his mouth? How old is he? Do you know CPR?"

I put the device on speaker. My bent finger swept Jack's

mouth cavity, searching for a piece of food lodged there. Images flashed before my eyes. Yes, I had cut the banana into small bites. And the toast too. That I was certain. Still, was it enough for him to choke on it? Or could he have swallowed something else?

"Sir, please confirm your address. We'll send an ambulance." I did, and the lady kept talking to me, assisting me as I hunted for a piece of food clogging Jack's airways.

Nothing.

I flipped him over my forearm as instructed, his head low, and hit his back at an angle with the side of my other hand.

"Breathe, little guy. Breathe. Come on. Do it. One breath. That's all I'm asking for."

My eyes were trained on his lifeless body. I could do this. We could do this.

My chest hurt, my aching heart about to rip it open, twisting on itself. Now wasn't the time. I kept my focus on the child.

I hit his back again. And again.

"Breathe, Jack."

I hit his back once more.

"Don't even think about not breathing. That's not an option. Not while I'm here. Spit whatever is in there. And breathe. Do it. Now." I refocused on my technique. "Derek, help me here. Please. I can't go through this again," I muttered through clenched teeth. Because right now, I needed to believe in every saint.

Holding my breath, I hit his back one last time.

A tiny half-chewed piece of banana flew out of his mouth. Jack squirmed in my arms, color returning to his cheeks.

My heart untangled itself. I coughed, whizzing air.

Oh God, he's breathing. He's alive.

"I'm sorry. I'm so sorry, little guy," I said, pulling him close to my chest, tears scorching the back of my eyes, raw from not blinking, my adrenaline running high in my bloodstream, as a mix of relief, fear, and helplessness stirred inside me. "I'm so, so sorry. I don't know what happened."

All my thoughts went chaotic inside my head.

How could Jack choke on such a tiny piece of food?

I exhaled my relief, my heart thrumming in my chest.

With my fingers, I combed his hair back.

"Sir, the ambulance is on its way. Wait for it. How's the boy? Please check for any signs of breathing distress."

I bobbed my head as if the dispatcher could see me. "Thank you. I'm fine… We're…we're fine."

She kept talking, reassuring me, making sure we really were okay.

I hung up as the sound of sirens got closer.

"Thanks, bro," I said, looking at the ceiling. I kissed two fingers and saluted over my head. "Thanks for watching over us."

A tightness grew in my chest, and a sensation of dread filled the cavity.

I could have lost Jack. *You didn't,* a voice in my head said. *Jack is okay. He's alive. Stop worrying. He's here. With you. Breathing.* But still, I had trouble believing it. The reassurance did nothing to calm my jittery nerves.

While Jack and I waited, I gasped to control my shallow breaths, my emotions swirling so fast inside me I couldn't get a grip on them.

With my eyes squeezed shut, I took a deep whiff of his hair, the baby-shampooed chamomile scent laying a balm over my thundering heart.

With both hands, Jack pushed back. Was I hugging him too tight?

We stared at each other for a moment.

Without looking away, he framed my face with his tiny hands as if I were the one who had to be comforted. The one who'd stopped breathing. "No cry, Nick. No cry. It's okay. No tears, okay?"

How could he be so calm? He was the one who had almost choked to death.

The ambulance arrived a few seconds later, and the paramedics checked Jack's vitals before laying him on a stretcher.

Rushing to the living room, I grabbed his blanket before joining them.

When we settled at the back of the emergency vehicle, I relaxed my stance. Soon enough, I dreaded the phone call I knew could change everything.

"Sir, you did good. The boy is fine. We're taking him in just for observation. He should be released quickly," the paramedic, a man in his late fifties, said, clapping my shoulder. "He's lucky to have you." His smile resuscitated me, and the giant clamp that was crushing my insides released its grasp a little.

Jack wrapped his fingers around mine.

My eyes drifted to our joined hands, and I blew out a long breath.

The boy was alive. Nothing else mattered.

"It will be okay. I'm here." I ruffled his hair, kissed the side of his head, and grabbed my phone, knowing I'd potentially just lied to him.

With a roll of my shoulders, I cleared my throat. "Hey, Dahlia, it's me. Listen…" I paused my breathing until I drew in enough courage to deliver the news.

She screamed. She cried.

And I died a little more inside.

Chapter 16
Dahlia

In the middle of my shop, I crumpled to my knees, my legs too weak to support my weight. Nick's words played on a loop in my head.

"Jack choked."

"Couldn't breathe."

"Turned blue."

"Called the paramedics."

"Ambulance."

"Hospital."

No one was around. The only employee was busy hanging gowns we'd just received in the back of the store.

My eyes burned from all the tears I shed.

My throat itched from all the cries I let out.

My heart was bruised from all the times it banged against my ribcage, beating too loud and too fast.

My stomach hurt, tied too tight with bands of thorns coiled around it.

The little angel living in my head, the one I could trust, told me Jack was okay.

Jack was breathing.

Breathing.

Breathing.

Breathing.

My brain reset, and some of the fog around me dissipated. That was when I remembered Nick, still on the line.

On all fours, I reached for the phone I'd dropped seconds—or was it minutes?—ago and brought it to my ear.

"Nick?" My voice sounded so far away and weak. So not-me. "Are you still there?"

His voice—masculine and unmistakably his, yet missing its usual self-assurance—grounded me. "Yes. I'm here. Not going anywhere."

"Thank you."

"No. You can't thank me. I almost cost your baby his life."

"Nick. Stop. He's fine. He's alive. It wasn't your fault."

Sobs strangled his next few words. "If you decide I should go when you get here, just say it. I'll understand. I messed up. Big time."

"No," I said, my voice catching and distorted as it left me. "You're one of us. I need you. We both need you. Please don't go. Don't leave. I love you."

How could he blame himself?

How could he not see he'd saved Jack's precious life?

I wanted to be by his side, by both my men's sides, to hug them. Kiss them. Love them.

Nick exchanged a couple of words with a man—probably the paramedic—then I heard him tell my son, "The ambulance ride is pretty nice, huh, little guy? We'll have to go inside the hospital when we get there with the nice man here. You'll ride on this magic rolling bed, then a doctor will check on you with this thing he uses to listen to your heart. And your Mama will meet us there. How cool is that?"

Jack's voice, the reminder that his life was safe, reached my ears next. "Do the *wee-oww wee-oww*?"

Every crushed part of my heart healed at the sound of his request. Yeah, my baby was fine.

"You want the sirens?" Nick asked.

I pictured my son bobbing his head with too much energy, like he always did. The curl of my lips turned upside.

"I'm sure Johnny here can get you some *wee-oww*."

Seconds later, a high-pitched sound filled the phone for a short moment, followed by Jack's clear laughter.

This man. I had no idea why life had sent him to me, but I'd be grateful for the rest of my life. Someone I treasured. The way he looked at me. And loved me. And how he always made Jack his priority. As if he was his own. How could I not fall in love with him a little more each day?

From the moment Nick and I met, something strong had seared between us. As if we were destined to meet. To love each other and to be together.

"Sorry, Dahlia," Nick said, bringing my attention back to him. "Are you okay to drive?"

I nodded, then remembered he couldn't see me. "Yes. Mary is on her way. I'll be there as soon as she gets here. We have a fitting in thirty minutes." I sighed, feeling so far away from the ones I loved right now. "Thanks for being with Jack. Please kiss him for me a million times."

"Wanna talk to him?"

An invisible vice squeezed my heart. I did, very much, but I knew I shouldn't. "No. It will just make him miserable and cranky. Hold him. Kiss him. And tell him I'm on my way, okay? Don't leave his side." I shut my eyes and swallowed the mountain-big lump down my throat. "I love you guys so much." Tears spilled from my eyes and streamed in silence down my cheeks. "Thanks for being there for my baby." The sound of voices and doors opening resonated on the other end of the line. "Oh, you're already there. I'll be with you as soon as I can. Keep me updated, okay?"

"Of course. Drive safe, please."

"I will." We hung up, and after I found some of my composure back, I called Carter. I needed him and his strength, and he needed to know. Because no way I'd ever be able to hide anything from him. I knew from where he was he couldn't do anything, but I wanted to hear his voice to find my balance. And it was better he learned it from me than from anyone else—even Jack.

"Hey, Dah. I was about to call you."

The sound of his voice tamed the jitters jumping around inside me.

"Hey, Cart. I miss you." My voice broke. Carter knew me like no one else. No way I'd ever be able to fake being okay around him.

"Fuck, Dah. What's wrong? Is it that guy? He broke your heart, right? I knew he would. Damn it." The sound of his palm hitting a hard surface startled me.

"No. Carter. Don't say that about Nick ever again. He's been nothing but good and selfless around Jack and me."

"What is it then? You sound upset. And I can tell you've been crying."

"It's Jack—" The words died on the tip of my tongue. Even if Jack was okay, I knew Carter wouldn't be. And it broke my heart just thinking about worrying him.

His tone turned serious. "Dah? What about Jack? What happened?" Panic was lightly veining his words.

I had to tread carefully here. Carter had been having panic attacks since Jeff passed away, and everything and anything could trigger them.

I breathed in a big gulp of air and some courage. "Listen to me. Carter, you gotta listen to everything I say. Jack is fine…but something happened… This morning. He choked while eating breakfast. He's okay now. The paramedics said Nick did all the right things—" I bit my tongue as I spoke the words. I cringed. Why did I include Nick in the conversation?

I swallowed the acid rising at the back of my throat.

"Nick?" Anger filled my best friend's voice. "What about Nick? Where were you? Why was Nick with him? Are you fucking with me, Dah?"

"Stop. It's not fair. You aren't here." Wrath sliced my words. "You know nothing."

Rolling my shoulders back, I explained everything. Because no way would I let things get strained between Carter and me. They had been, years ago, and it had almost killed me. Never again.

I could feel every layer of his tension, even from hundreds of miles apart.

"Carter, Nick and I are together. He's a part of Jack's and my life. You better get used to it. You're not allowed to insult him and his intelligence. Imagine how he felt at that moment. How he still feels… Nick loves us, Cart. And we do too. I called you because I thought you deserved to know. Because Jack is yours too. But if you gimme shit, I won't tell you a thing next time."

I blew out a long breath, filled with hurt and anger.

After a moment, Carter spoke again. "Fine. I'm sorry, Dah. You know how I hate not being there for you two.

Most of the time, it kills me. You're the only family I have left. You can't be mad at me for caring about you and Jack." Emotions laced my best friend's voice. "All I'm asking is for you two to thrive and be happy. And safe."

I softened my tone. "I know you do. And that's one of the many reasons why I love you." I paused. "Where are you now? In Canada already?"

Carter told someone to wait and brought his attention back to me. "Landed in Toronto fifteen minutes ago. On my way to Montreal. But change of plans. I'm boarding a flight to Tennessee. Should be there in two hours, okay?"

"Okay," I repeated. The thought of Carter flying to be with us calmed the throbbing of my heart. "Oh, Cart, I must go. Mary just walked in. I'll be able to leave the shop. I'll call you with the updates. Be safe. And don't worry, Jack is all right. They're just keeping him under observation because that's the protocol. Can't wait to see you later."

"Dah, I'll be right there…with you guys."

We hung up, and I gave my employee all the instructions before hurrying to be with the men I loved.

The ones my heart belonged to.

The ones waiting for me right now.

Chapter 17
Nicholas

I padded down the hallway, my fingers interlaced at the nape of my neck, and a frown probably digging trenches across my forehead. Dahlia was inside the room, lying next to Jack on the hospital bed, brushing his hair with her fingers. The image brought painful memories back to the surface. Hospital room. Derek lying on the bed. Murielle by his side. Caressing his bald head.

Air couldn't get through. I was hyperventilating.

With my face turned toward the ceiling and my eyes closed, I drew in a calming breath, trying to steady myself —and my emotions. My stomach twisted. I'd spent too many hours in the hospital in the last few years. My throat tightened with unshed tears at the thought.

I knew I should go in there, but I required some alone time to calm the fuck down. The adrenaline rush I'd experienced earlier had dissipated. Hospital rooms, emergency, doctors. It was just too much for me to take. My insides quivered, spinning at lightning speed, building a tornado and shattering every particle of control and calmness I had left.

I huffed, dragging a hand over my face, rubbing my jaw. The back of my neck prickled, my hair standing on end. My eyes locked on Dahlia, and she smiled at me. A warm, tight-lipped smile that shouldered a lot of meaning. A smile that said *I need you. We need you.* Her gaze bore into me, injecting me with doses of unconditional love. *I'm here for you. Stop worrying, we're all fine. Be with us. Right here. Right now. We're all in this together.*

The sight of the two people I loved more than anything eased some particles of tension inside me, and I mustered a smile back.

The way they looked at me filled my heart and burned it to ashes all at the same time. I had no idea how I should feel. Relieved? Guilty? No, I should not, but yeah, guilty sounded about right because I had messed up, and I lacked the proper word to describe the emotional cyclone killing me inside.

Dahlia walked up to me and grabbed my elbow, stopping me in my tracks as I still debated about my culpability. "Babe, don't. This has to stop. You're making me dizzy."

I tugged at my hair. "Dahlia, Jack is in here because of me," I said, pointing to the room.

Jack waved at me, a curve on his lips, and life shining through his eyes. I returned his wave, and his grin stretched wider.

Peace washed over me, soothing some of my angst.

That boy had a way to connect with my heart in the most raw and powerful way.

"Yeah, because you saved him. You saved my baby's life. He's here, alive, because of you." Dahlia held my hands between hers. Her warmth crept along my arms, reaching my heart and wrapping around it. Like a soft blanket. Like a promise that we'd get through this and a much-needed hug. She lowered her voice, searching my eyes. "Jack is asking for you. They're keeping him for a few more hours, but he's fine. It's just some technicalities. I have to go by the store to drop off the keys, then get his stuff. Can I go to your place afterward? The things he loves the most are all there."

"You should stay here. I'll go."

Dahlia shook her head. "No. He's asking for *you*. I won't be long, and I think you two should spend some time together." She stared at me with trust burning in her eyes.

The thought of staying in that room made nausea reel through me. With a long exhale, I calmed myself down. Yeah, I was stronger than this. No way would I let the last memories of Derek in the hospital haunt me forever. I steeled my back with a new resolve. If required, I could freak out later.

I pulled Dahlia into my arms, filling my nose with her floral scent that made everything better. "Go. And come back. I love you. We'll wait for you, okay? Drive safe."

She nodded, and on her tiptoes, she brushed her lips against mine.

We entered the room hand in hand, and after I fist-bumped with Jack, I lay beside him, stretching my legs before me, crossing them at the ankles. He sank against me, his shoulder pressing into my upper arm.

"Watch dragon with me?" he asked, pointing to the TV mounted on the wall.

"Sure, little guy." I ruffled his hair with my fingers as he settled in closer by my side.

Jack linked our hands, his head resting against my chest as my arm curled around his innocent body, his quiet breathing the only sound reaching my ears.

He's breathing. He's breathing. He. Is. Breathing. Jack will be fine.

The tornado inside me dropped in intensity. Yeah, we'd get through this.

———

DAHLIA

Are you ok? I'm needed at the store. Bridal party just walked in. The girls are overwhelmed.

ME

Jack's napping now. Take your time. Did you know Ross the dragon had magical fire coming out of his mouth? Pretty amazing, if you ask me.

I could hear her snicker in my head.

DAHLIA

You didn't know? It's a shame. Okay, we'll do a dragon marathon. Pizza, ice cream, and us three. That's a date.

ME

Sounds good. Can't wait.

DAHLIA

Forgot to tell you earlier. Carter's on his way. I called him after you contacted me. Took the first flight out. Was north of the border. Should arrive soon. I'll try to come back before he gets there.

ME

Take your time. Don't worry.

DAHLIA

Love you. Hope you know.

I surfed the channels, Jack wheezing softly in his sleep beside me, now nestled against my chest, his fingers still wrapped around mine.

A knock on the door, and a nurse dressed in colorful scrubs walked in. "Oh, he's sleeping."

I nodded.

"We should be able to discharge him soon. Has Ms. Ellis returned yet?"

"She had an emergency at work. She'll be here as soon as possible. Do you want me to call her?"

The nurse, about my mother's age, smiled and shook her head. "Let the boy sleep. Let us know when she gets here."

She left and seconds later, another knock. Carter Hills walked in, his tall self taking the room hostage with his presence and stealing all the viable oxygen with one breath.

His dark gaze landed on me, and the panic swirling in his melted-steel irises switched to wrath. He didn't even have to say a word. It emanated from every inch of him. Careful not to wake up the child, I swept my legs over the edge of the bed and untangled my body from his, positioning him on the pillow and tucking a blanket around him.

"Hey, Carter," I said, holding out my hand to shake his.

His eyes lowered to where my hand floated between us, but he didn't meet it.

Great. This was going to be fun.

"Let's talk outside," I suggested.

The door hadn't even closed behind me when Carter's

harsh tone broke the silence. "Man, you should go home. I'm here now," he said, his hushed icy tone wakening chills along my spine. "Where is Dah? After what happened, I can't believe she left you here to watch over Jack." He blinked as if to make sure it wasn't a dream. Then shook his head in disbelief.

Without budging, I raised my hands between us. "Whoa, stop right here. I'm not a threat. You're serious now? You can't judge me for what happened this morning. You weren't there. And there's no way I'll let you insult me, my character, or my actions."

Carter looked away. I hoped my voice held more conviction than I did. Not that Carter Hills's presence or anger affected me, but more like I still felt responsible for Jack choking earlier. Even so, Carter wouldn't get the last word.

"You and I started our relationship on the wrong foot, but you know what? I respect you. A lot," I said. "I know what you and Dahlia went through and how painful it was. I've never lost my brother, but I've lost someone as important to me. Grief is fucking hard. I get that. And I know you love them, and they mean a lot to you, but they mean a lot to me too. And I love them. With all my heart. Maybe that's not what you wanna hear, but that's the truth. They're not just yours to care for anymore."

Carter's eyes nearly popped out of their sockets, but he quickly composed himself, drawing in a noisy breath as his jaw flexed and his gaze drifted into the distance.

We both turned our heads to make sure Jack was still asleep. The boy's chest rose and fell under the blanket. Once we were both satisfied, we returned to our heated conversation.

Carter said nothing. He just twisted his lips into a scowl, so I continued.

"Dahlia and I connected from the second we met. We both can't explain it. I have no idea what it's like for you guys, and I don't care. All I want is to be there for her…for them." Carter stayed silent, so I pressed on. "You three are family, and I respect that. I'll never break you apart, but I can be their family too. Eventually." There. I said my piece.

The country music star's gaze stayed fixed on me for a long moment as I tried to decipher the meaning behind his dark stare.

"Listen, you can try to push me away or come between us, but all it'll do is bring us closer together. I have no intention to fight with you. What Dahlia and I share is bigger and stronger than us. I know you love her… It oozes from every bit of your being, and you do a shit job hiding it. And it's okay. I won't play games. I could be jealous and threaten you, but I won't go there. I'm not here to shove our happiness in your face either. What you two have is amazing. The thing is… I won't go away. Dahlia is my soul mate. The one I'm supposed to be with. I'll fight for us. Until I bleed. Because that's what soul mates do. They share the same heart."

Carter cleared his throat, averting his eyes for an instant.

When he brought his attention back to me, the lines around his eyes had softened. "She loves you, you know? I could tell from the moment she talked about you the very first time, that you'd be more than just friends…" He sighed, and his shoulders dropped. He cast a glance down, kicking the linoleum floor with the sole of his shoe. After a beat, he brought his focus back to me. "When Dahlia loves, she loves with all her heart. It's powerful. And I wish I could be on the other end of that love. I would give every-thing I own for a chance…but she doesn't love *love* me the same way." His voice cracked, a contrast to the heavy stare locked on me. "Don't break her heart. This will be my only warning."

"I won't." My eyes drifted to Jack, still asleep, and I sighed. "If you wanna spend some time with him, one-on-one, I'll go home and wait for Dahlia to stop by my place once she's done at the shop. Then I'll drive her back here so she can sign the discharge papers. I know Jack will be excited to see you. He talks about you all the time."

"He does?"

"Carter, Jack's your biggest fan. He looks up to you. He sings your songs and tells me all about what you guys do when you're together. You're his dad. In every way that is important."

Carter pinched the bridge of his nose, glancing down. "Thanks for saying that." His eyes followed Jack's silhouette. "It means a lot. Most times, I'm upset for not being around as much as I should…" His Adam's apple bobbed, and he rubbed the back of his neck. "Thank you for allowing us time together. I freaking miss him. All the time. He's such a huge part of my life…of me…and of my brother. He reminds me so much of him." The fight left him. "Go. We'll be here when you get back."

I nodded and tiptoed inside the room to pick up my stuff. Hovering over the bed, I whispered, "Bye, little guy. You'll have a surprise when you wake up. Sleep for a bit longer. I'll see you later." I laid a kiss on his forehead. "Love you." And left.

Outside, I welcomed the breeze sweeping across my face. My angst returned as I climbed into my truck. All the emotions I'd bottled in for the last few hours reached the surface before I could even shut the door.

With a flat palm, I hit the steering wheel as I pulled out of the hospital parking lot.

"Derek, tell me this is a joke. A stupid prank or a dream I'll wake up from. Please, bro. This day can't be real —" I inhaled a shaky breath, trying to ebb the frustration tinting my words. My anger bled into helplessness. "I can't take it anymore. I wish you could tell me it was the last test…or whatever it was."

My heart sank low in my chest as I pulled into my driveway. It took me a couple of minutes before finding the courage to go inside. My legs weighed like they were made of concrete.

A chill zinged through me.

I stared at the sky. "I know it's not your fault, bro. I'm sorry, you didn't deserve my wrath. I love you." I kissed my fingers and saluted the sky. "I'll be okay. Maybe not today, but I will. I promise. Talk later."

Once inside my home, my eyes landed on the sippy cup on the floor and the half-eaten breakfast still on the table.

Knots I thought had previously loosened tied up my insides.

A weight—something big and heavy—pressed my chest, making it almost impossible for me to breathe.

My entire body shook. Images of Jack's inert body played before my eyes, and I sucked in a breath, trying not to shatter into pieces.

With languid movements and a sluggish mind, as if I were here but also a thousand miles away, I opened the kitchen cabinet to grab a bottle and a glass.

With a drink in hand, I slouched in a chair, elbows resting on the tabletop.

Without overthinking it, I dug my phone out and dialed a number I knew all too well.

The gentle voice, with traces of sleep laced in it, that answered after three rings, soothed the emotional wildfire raging inside me somehow.

"Hey, Nick. It's been a while. Is everything all right?"

"I'm sorry. Did I wake you up?"

"Nick, you can call me anytime. I told you. Whenever you feel the need, no matter how late it is."

I gulped some air but ended up sobbing. The woman on the other end of the line said nothing. We messaged each other once or twice a week, but we hadn't talked to each other in over a month.

She let me empty the tears seeping from my heart, her steady breaths bringing me much-needed comfort.

Once I cooled off, she spoke again. "Having a bad day?"

"Huh…you could say that. God… This is so messed up. You know the boy I told you about?" I asked, my voice unsteady.

Tremors rattled my body, and I placed my phone on the table, pressing the speaker button. With my face buried in my hands, I swallowed, squeezing my eyes shut as if it could prevent the despair to sink in.

"Jack? What about him?"

"He almost died, Murielle. I was watching him, and he choked on a piece of banana. He almost died because of me."

"But he didn't. What happened? Tell me everything."

I gave her a recap of everything that had gone wrong this morning.

"You saved his life. I hope you know that. You saved that boy's life, Nick. Why are you guilt-tripping yourself?"

I tried to speak, but the words got stuck in my throat. My breathing idled in my lungs as my muscles spasmed.

After a minute, I cleared my throat. "It's not…it's… huh, I don't know." My elbows dug further into the wooden tabletop, and I sank my face further into my hands, tears spilling from my burning eyes. "Derek was a child… Jack is a child… They're both too young to have to deal with death. When it all went down, Derek's face kept flashing through my mind. As if…as if it were him I wasn't able to save. As if… Why is this so hard? As if I couldn't do anything to save him. Jack was safe and sound. Still, I kept picturing myself switching Derek's ventilator off. Stealing the…stealing the life from him. Stealing his last breath. Forever."

Sobs tinted Murielle's voice. She blew her nose before speaking again. "You freed Derek, Nick, okay? Don't you ever tell yourself otherwise. Y-you set him free… You were the only one strong enough to grant him his last wish. If Derek were here, he'd tell you himself. Because of you, he…he doesn't suffer anymore. He's not stuck in a hospital bed when he should have been playing outside like kids his own age."

More sobs clogged my throat.

"Nick, for both these boys, you are a hero… A true hero… No, you couldn't save Derek—his fate wasn't in our hands—but you saved Jack. This time, you were allowed to try."

I snorted.

"You really are a true hero, Nick Peterson. Go hug that kid now. You and he both deserve to put this incident behind you and move forward. You…you can't let what happened this morning define your relationship with him, okay?" She paused. "What about his mother? How are things going?"

"Perfect. More than perfect. I love her…like I've never loved anyone before."

"Then be with her too. She needs you right now. Trust me."

We exchanged a few other words, and I promised to call her back the next day to keep her updated. The lining of my throat, raw and itchy, burned. I chugged half my whiskey down, trying to chase the pain away.

A movement by the door caught my eye. I lifted my gaze, and as if pulled by some magnetic force, I found Dahlia standing there, a rivulet drowning her eyes and cheeks.

She watched me with something I couldn't define.

How long had she been here?

How much did she overhear from my conversation with Murielle?

My pulse raced at the idea that she learned things about Derek I hadn't told her yet.

Without a word, she ate the space between us in a few strides. I yanked my chair back and rose to my feet, my body trembling.

Dahlia looped her arms around me, enveloping my body with hers.

I hugged her back. With everything I had.

We stood there in silence for a long time, neither one of us brave enough to talk about what she'd just heard. Our tears mixed. Our breathing blurred together, and our bodies fused.

Time halted.

Once I regained some of my composure, I stepped back and searched for her hands, craving her love and her warmth.

"Why didn't you tell me you were the one who unplugged Derek?" she asked. "I didn't mean to eavesdrop. Carter texted me to tell me you offered him a chance to take over, and I wanted to make sure you were okay. I was worried about you. Nick, you should've told me. Now I understand things I didn't earlier."

A cocktail of hurt, sadness, empathy, and love bled from her glassy moss-green irises.

My throat worked, but I couldn't swallow.

"Nick, I know grief. And how much it can shatter someone. I want to be there for you. For the good parts but also the bad and the ugly," she said, cradling my face and forcing me to look at her.

"Dahlia, I wasn't ready. I'm still struggling. Sometimes… Those last images of him flash back when I'm alone. In my truck… In the shower… Early in the morning…" I shrugged. "They used to haunt me. Th-they don't anymore, but I'm still learning to live with them. And, huh, accept the reality. Jack choking, lying in a hospital bed, wearing that blue gown… Tore open scars I thought were mostly healed… I'm sorry I didn't share the complete story with you before."

I laced our fingers together and led her to the couch. With her body hugging mine and my arms locked around her waist, I told Dahlia all about Derek. We laughed as I narrated incidents of our friendship. We cried together when it came down to the moment I turned off his respirator and how I couldn't say a proper goodbye, since the last night I'd visited him, he'd slept the entire time.

Dahlia sniffled through her tears. "Ohmygod, I'm sorry it happened to you. I can't imagine how hard today must have been." She fastened her grip on me, protecting and loving me. "Nick, I never perceived Derek and you were that close." She pulled my head to her chest, and the beat of her heart was the anchor I needed, the calm in my storm.

"Dahlia, I can't bear to lose another person I love. Derek… Buddy… I couldn't fathom the idea of losing Jack too this morning."

The woman I loved with every chunk of my heart got to her feet and held out her hand for me to grab. Together we made it upstairs. She pushed my shoulders until I sat on the edge of the bed and uncapped the marker she took from the kitchen table on our way up. The one I used this morning while I worked on the construction blueprints.

She clutched it between her teeth, and with both hands, she rummaged through my dresser.

I quirked a brow, wondering what she was looking for. There was nothing but boxer briefs, socks, and sweatpants in those.

Her face lit up when she found it. *Derek's list.*

With the pen still clutched between her teeth, she sat beside me and unfolded the sheet of paper. She struck through the eighth item, with more vigor than required.

Derek's Bucket List – 8. Do something deemed impossible

Underneath, she wrote:

I saved Jack's life today. It definitely counts as doing something deemed impossible. Only real heroes can do this. I've been giving myself a hard time about it when I should have been celebrating instead. Jack could have choked on anything at any given time, but lucky for him, he did it with me by his side, and I did all the right things. It's worth something. And the woman I love and who loves me back (a lot), says she has no idea how to repay me because what I did today is an act of pure love. And strength. And bravery. She's telling me here and now I'll be her hero for the rest of time.

Dahlia capped the marker, but something caught her eye, and before one of us could say anything, a big tear rolled down her cheek.

She cocked her head until we stared into each other's souls. "You added your last item?"

I nodded.

"You really believe it?"

I rubbed my fists over my eyes, raw and probably swollen by now. "Already told you, Dahlia. I'm in love with you. And I can't see myself feeling any other way. Ever."

She jumped to her knees and crashed her lips on mine. "You're the real deal too, Nick."

I pushed back, my body igniting under her touch. "We have to go. The doctors are waiting for you to sign the discharge papers."

"I know, but I wanna make sure you're okay first."

I breathed in. "I am… I will be."

Dahlia knitted her fingers through mine, and I followed her downstairs. If she'd asked me to, I would've followed her to the end of the world.

Derek's Bucket List — 25. Nick. Find the one

Derek, I'm pretty sure I've found my person. My soul mate. The one I've been put on this Earth to be with. The one making my days and nights better. I had no clue my heart had been missing one half until she walked into my life. Actually, I walked into hers, but it's just semantics, right? Dahlia completes me. In every way. She's the love of my life. I'll keep you updated. I just hope she feels the same way...

Chapter 18
Nicholas

"Hey, baby. Ready to go home?" Dahlia asked Jack when we entered his hospital room, our hands linked together. The boy nodded, and Dahlia brought her gaze to Carter. "Hey, Cart." She let go of me and jumped into her best friend's arms.

He hugged her tight, and his lips lingered on the top of her head.

My heart trembled in my chest. I'd have to get used to this. Their chemistry. Their proximity. Their love.

"Dah, I was so scared." He stepped back and ran his hands over his face. "I hate it when I'm far away and the distance makes me feel powerless."

Dahlia held his face, her eyes fixed on his. I'd never seen them like this. So close. So… I missed the right word.

Carter pressed his forehead against hers, and for a minute, time stood still. With their eyes shut, they just stayed like that, bringing each other the comfort they both required without even saying a word.

I was amazed as much as I was bothered by this display of affection playing before me.

Jack must have sensed it because he jumped from the bed and came to me, holding his arms above his head until I picked him up.

"Hey, little guy. How are you doing?"

He offered me a *too big for his tiny face* warm smile.

As if he spread magic inside me, the wounds of my heart healed. For good this time.

"Go in the *ambuladalance* again?" he asked.

I shook my head, unable to stop chuckling. "I wish. But we can't. It's only for emergencies. And sick people."

"Like Buddy?"

My insides tightened up. "Yeah. Like Buddy." I squeezed him against my heart. "You wanna get out of here?" I lowered my voice. "Let me tell you a secret. I'm super hungry. I could eat a hippopotamus."

He snickered.

"What about pizza? I'm sure your Mama and Carter would love to join us. I think we should celebrate right now."

"Pizza, pizza, pizza," Jack singsonged, his arms circling my neck.

"Let's go then," Carter added, turning to face us. "I'm starving."

"Gimme a sec, boys. I'll go sign all those papers," Dahlia said, exiting the room.

A silence fell between us. Every breath between us was audible.

After a few seconds, Carter extended his arm. "Thanks, Nick. For saving Jack's life. I'm sorry for giving you shit earlier."

I blinked. Was I dreaming? Carter Hills was thanking me? *Note this day, Derek.* My palm slid into his, but he pulled me into some sort of bro hug instead when our hands connected. That lasted about half a second, but still, maybe we could make it work after all.

Carter blinked what looked like tears away and grabbed Jack's stuff.

Dahlia returned, and we all got going.

In the hallway, I lowered Jack to his feet, and he reached for Carter's hand. After a second, he reached for mine too.

My eyes found Dahlia, and emotions filled hers.

I love you, she mouthed.

I grabbed her hand in mine, and the four of us left together.

Back home, because Dahlia and Jack were spending the night at my place—no way I'd sleep away from them after the day we had—I took Jack aside. We sat cross-legged on the living room floor, facing each other.

"Okay, I have a special someone for you to meet. His name is Rex." I fished out the stuffed dinosaur that used to be Derek's from behind my back. "He used to belong to a friend of mine. A little boy, just like you."

Jack grabbed the toy, kissed his head, and brought it to his heart as if he could feel how important it had been to another child before.

"I want you to have it. Derek would have wanted that too."

Jack glanced at me with his round steel-gray eyes.

"Rex is magic. He'll watch over you at night. To make sure you're safe and sound. You want him?"

He bobbed his head, his eyes still on me. "No cry, Nick. No cry," he said, moving to his feet and brushing my hair.

I wiped my eyes with the back of my hand. I hadn't

even noticed the tears pooling there. "You're right, little guy. Let's be happy."

Jack latched onto my neck. "Rex my friend. Rex my best *bestest* friend."

A smile tugged at my lips. "Yes, he is. And this one won't go away. Ever."

I raised my eyes to the ceiling as if Derek could see us in that instant—from his cloud. As if he were here with us. A part of him living through my actions. With my head tilted back, I winked. "Cheers, bro."

I fastened my arms around Jack, and we hugged before joining Dahlia and Carter on the back deck.

Yeah, the country music star had to come over and make sure my house was good enough for his family. *Our* family.

Jack climbed up Carter's long legs to sit on his lap. "Look, *Cattter*," he said, pushing the stuffed animal into his face. "Rex my *bestest* friend. *Nicksaidhemagical*. I love Rex. I love Nick."

An arm snaked around mine. *Dahlia's*.

The way she stared at me...with love and lust. And something more. I got starstruck. Yeah, Dahlia Ellis was the one for me. My person. My soul mate. My everything.

"Derek's?" she asked, her voice soft as a whisper.

I nodded. Because emotions blocked my airways, and I had nothing more to say.

She pressed her head against my shoulder. "I love you, Nicholas Peterson. I'm crazy about you."

I enveloped her in my arms as we watched Carter push Jack on the swing set, both of them laughing their hearts out and goofing around.

Yeah, the four of us were family. For better or for worse.

Kissing my fingers, I saluted the sky.

Chapter 19
Nicholas

Four months later, with a straight back, my hands shoved into my pockets, and my heart having a party inside my chest, I walked toward the lawyer's office. This sounded so official. Hair prickled across my nape at the idea of doing something meaningful. Something big. Something I had never pictured myself doing short-term before moving to Green Mountain.

I breathed out my angst as I pushed the door open. Soft music welcomed me as I entered the office. I glanced around me. Okay, this place looked nothing like the cold and straight-lined law firms did back in Chicago with their over-expensive furniture and interiors. Here the decor was simple and country-chic. A five-chair waiting room, wooden walls, and a latte-beige carpet. It was inviting, almost cozy.

The secretary greeted me with a warm smile. "Mr. Peterson?"

I nodded before finding my voice, my vocal cords sounding rusty as stress took root inside me. I cleared my throat and croaked the words. "Hi, yes, it's me."

She moved to her feet and pointed a finger in the opposite direction of where I stood, showing me the way. "Follow me. They're waiting for you."

I nodded and walked behind her in the corridor toward a closed door at the end. My heart was racing a thousand miles an hour, and I had to press a hand against my chest to calm its hyperactivity.

The woman tapped her knuckles against the wooden door, and I rolled my shoulders back. Yes, I could do this. Everything was coming together, and this last piece would just make it all more real. She exchanged a few words with the people inside the room and motioned me in.

"Thank you," I said, my voice now sounding stronger and steadier.

A man in his early sixties sat behind a desk. "I'm Eduardo Miller, an old friend of Mrs. Jeanine here. It's so nice to meet you, Mr. Peterson. I've heard great things about you."

We exchanged handshakes before I spun and met Mrs. Rutherford.

I offered my hand, but she stepped closer and wrapped her frail body around me in a hug. "Oh, Nicholas, I'm so happy to finally meet you in person. I saw the pictures of the house you sent. It looks absolutely divine. You brought her charm back. I'll never be able to thank you enough."

She patted my forearm before sitting back into the chair she'd vacated seconds ago.

We exchanged small talk, the tension releasing from my back, and my stance becoming less rigid as I learned a few interesting things about the house I'd been living in and the town that had become mine over the last few months.

"Nicholas, I'm so excited you wanna buy the house," Mrs. Rutherford exclaimed, clasping her hands before her, watching me with stars in her eyes. "From the beginning, call me crazy, but I had a feeling you two would be a perfect match."

"It's a beautiful home. I could picture myself living there the moment I stepped inside for the first time. You're right. This house is special. I don't wanna let it go. Well, I'm not ready to let it go."

The storm inside me calmed down when the words exited my mouth. Yeah, putting roots down in Green Mountain felt natural and like the logical next step. And the farmhouse was where I wanted to live.

Last month, Mike had agreed to sell me his business by the end of next spring.

Since that instant, every piece of my life had slotted in its rightful place.

I had a family. Dahlia and Jack were now fully part of my daily life. Soon enough, I'd also be a business owner. The only thing missing, for my life to feel fulfilled—for now—was that house.

In the small amount of time I'd been in town, it had accumulated a lot of memories. Good and bad. Happy and sad. But it was home, and I refused to move and live elsewhere. Everywhere I looked, I could see Jack running into my arms and Dahlia's touches on the walls. Buddy following me around. The night Dahlia and I had realized we could no longer just be friends, and the one when the dog had left us. The bed where we'd made love for the first time, and the yard where we'd exchanged our first *I love yous*. The stargazing nights in the summer, and the swing I'd pushed Jack on countless times. The moments of intimacy when we had confided about our dreams, our heartaches, and our hopes, and the ones that had us holding on to each other or promising each other the world.

This was the house where I aspired to raise my family. Have more kids. Grow old with the woman I loved.

A pinched sensation gripped my heart.

No way would I let this house go. It was my home...*our* home.

"Shall we begin?" I asked, eager to find out if my offer had been accepted so we could proceed with the transaction.

Mr. Miller and Mrs. Rutherford exchanged a glance.

What was that all about? When I spoke to the owner on the phone last week, she had assured me my offer stood and was being taken seriously. The house hadn't been put on the market yet, so I was pretty sure they hadn't received any other offer.

"Something wrong?" I asked, struggling to even my breathing, trying to look—and sound—casual, though I was anything but.

There. They glanced at each other again.

Mr. Miller cleared his throat. "Mr. Peterson..."

"Call me Nick. Please."

"Well, Nick. All the ownership documents were being prepared when Mrs. Rutherford received a call."

I didn't understand. I had spent the past month researching comparable properties currently on the market in Green Mountain, as well as those recently sold. Tucker had helped me with the financial stuff, so I was already pre-qualified for the loan. As my friend had said, my proposition looked sharp and really fucking amazing.

"Someone put up a second offer. I'm sorry, Nicholas," Mrs. Rutherford began. "I just can't ignore it. We'll—"

A soft knock on the door interrupted her.

The secretary peeked in as she opened the door. "Mr. Miller, your next appointment is here."

"Let her in," the lawyer said.

The scene before me unfolded in slow motion.

Mr. Miller moved to his feet to greet the newcomer.

A familiar scent permeated my nostrils, enveloping me. My heart drummed faster. I scratched my nape, unsure what was going on.

My eyes met Mrs. Rutherford's, and she looked at me with an expectant gaze.

The somber look she bore seconds ago had vanished, replaced by a joyful expression.

Mr. Miller exchanged a few words with the visitor, and I pivoted in my chair to see who it was, but well aware of the presence I could distinguish from a million others.

My body recognized her before my eyes saw her.

In the doorway, Dahlia exchanged a handshake with the lawyer, Jack squirming in her arms. She lowered the boy to his feet, and he ran my way, clutching a toy truck in his hand.

"Hey, little guy. What are you doing here?"

Jack said nothing as he held out his arms for me to lift him.

He settled on my lap. "*Nickkk. MissyouNick,*" he finally said as his tiny arms wrapped around my neck, and he dropped a moist kiss on my cheek.

"I've missed you too," I said, hugging him close to my heart. We'd seen each other this morning, but every hour away from the people I loved felt like a lifetime. Since he'd choked almost four months ago, Jack and Dahlia had spent almost every night at my place, and we'd got ourselves into a comfortable routine.

"Surprise. It's surprise. *Shhh,*" he said in a low voice,

bringing his forefinger over his lips, as if I were in on what was going on.

"A surprise? You sure?"

He bobbed his head fast.

Mr. Miller shut the door, and Dahlia took the seat next to mine.

"Hey, babe. What are you doing here?" I asked, with my eyebrows probably touching my hairline, reaching for her hand and intertwining our fingers together. I breathed easier. Her touch always brought me peace. I hadn't hinted about my wish to buy the house to Dahlia, but I knew how much it meant to her too. I wanted to make sure it was a done deal before asking her to move in with me.

Shifting in my seat to give Jack more room to roll his toy car all over my legs and torso, I watched her as she angled her upper body my way and grinned at me.

She closed her eyes and shook her head. When she opened them again, she smiled at me. "Here's the thing," she said before taking a big inhale. "I contacted Mrs. Rutherford last week. Call it a hunch, but I was pretty sure you'd make an offer on the house. By now, I know you pretty well, Nicolas Peterson. Anyway, I didn't want you to buy us a house. I wanted *us* to buy *us* a house. Together. Make it official. Build something. A nest. Our family… eventually. You can refuse if you think it's too soon or if you prefer to be the sole owner. It's up to you. No matter what, I will be okay with your decision. No hard feelings. I just hope this is a dream we can share. A beginning to our future. If you will have me as a co-owner… As a partner. As your other half."

Jack had stopped wriggling in my arms and was watching his mother with as much intensity as I did, his widened stare probably matching mine.

"You're already all of these things—"

"I'm all in, Nick. I want everything with you. And I want to start dreaming with you. Not in six months or two years from now. Never will I take anything for granted ever again, already told you. I want us to be a family. From this day on."

I swallowed the lump lodged in my throat and blinked. "Are you serious? You wanna own the house with me?"

Dahlia nodded. "Told you the other night. This house feels like home to me. And you're there. My soul already lives there. It's been for months. This house has a heart, and the man with the biggest heart I know and with whom I'm kinda in love with also happens to live within its walls. How could I wish to live elsewhere? Just so we're on the same wavelength here, I'm not going anywhere. Let's make this home *ours*. The way you see it in your head. The way we picture it together when we go to sleep at night. Those walls already have a story, but just the beginning of ours. Let's give them the entire novel—every chapter—so that one day, they tell our story too."

A whirlwind of thoughts raced through my mind, mixed with all my emotions and so many things I wished I could tell the woman beside me if we were alone in this office.

"Mama crying," Jack said. "No cry, Mama. Surprise. Be happy."

We all laughed at his words. Using the pad of my thumb, I wiped the tears welling up in her eyes and moved closer to kiss her eyelids.

"God, I love you right now. So much. Let's do this," I said. With my free hand, I pulled her in for a kiss. "I want this. With you too."

"Do you wanna think about it first?" she asked.

"No, this is perfect. It feels right. I can't wish for any

better scenario than owning the farmhouse together—as a family."

Dahlia sniffled, and I placed my hand on her leg above the knee, unable to resist touching her, and cementing the bond we shared. The leap of faith we were about to take together.

"Mama sad," Jack said.

I shook my head, nuzzling his neck until he burst out laughing, relishing the sound. "No, your Mama is happy, little guy. And so am I."

Jack's gaze drifted between his mother and me.

"Mama happy?"

A smile spread on Dahlia's face when she leaned back and bobbed her head, Jack style. "Yes. Mama is happy," she echoed. "Mama is where she's supposed to be. And Mama loves Nick. And Jack."

Jack clapped his hands, giggling. "Mama loves Nick," he chanted. "Mama always kisses Nick."

"Yes. And we're all moving in together."

———

The next morning, I woke up early, showered, and made coffee while I studied the papers making me a homeowner for the first time in my life. Pride flooded every part of me. Like a complete idiot, I couldn't stop smiling.

Dahlia met me and circled my waist from behind, resting her head against my bare back.

"Did you sleep at all?" she asked.

I swiveled in her embrace. "I did. Because when you're in bed beside me, I sleep like a baby." I planted a kiss on the tip of her nose. "You?"

"Oh, I slept perfectly."

With a quick gesture, she stole the caffeinated beverage from my hand and brought it to her lips with a grimace.

"I can't understand why you'd drink that." A chill ran through her. "It tastes awful. Tea tastes much better."

I twirled a loose strand of her hair around my finger, my eyes traveling down her body, admiring her naked thighs, the shirt of mine she wore falling just below her bottom.

I was right that night, a while back, when I'd told her my clothes fit her better.

With my free hand, I fished out the mug of tea I had prepared for her and placed it in her hand. "Here."

Her grin widened.

I ventured a hand under her shirt, stroking the soft flesh of her lower back, moving in circles, molding her ass cheek to my greedy hand.

She gasped. "Careful. This thing is scorching hot," she said, gesturing to the mug in her hand.

"It's even better," I said, smoothing her lips with mine. "Are you able to stay put while I explore these delicious curves of you?"

"Nick—" My name sounded more like a whimper coming through her lips. Her eyes turned darker, gleaming in the morning light. "Please…"

"Please what?" I asked, my voice sounding more like a growl.

She sucked in a breath, her eyelids fluttering close. "Nick, I—"

I removed the cup from her hands and discarded it on the counter beside mine.

"Fuck, you're already wet," I grunted as my hand reached between her trembling thighs, tracing the moist seam over the cotton fabric of her panties.

"Take me here," Dahlia ordered. "Now." She wouldn't

need to ask me twice. Her tone had lost all playfulness. She had become a puddle of lust, and I hadn't even touched her the way I craved yet. "We gotta christen this house."

"We did just that yesterday before going to bed," I said with a crooked smile, images of last night coming back to me. Bedroom. Bathroom. Walk-in closet. The staircase.

"Yeah, but we haven't done it here yet."

"What about before?"

She shook her head, her voice a shuddering whisper. Yes, my girl was passionate and irresistible, just the way I liked it. "It doesn't count. We weren't owners back then."

"Gosh, I'll never get tired of listening to your super smart naked ideas."

I skimmed the column of her throat with the tip of my nose, and Dahlia shivered. *Yes, I'd never get tired of this.*

Weighing next to nothing in my arms, I placed her on a stool, yanked her panties down her legs, and let my sweatpants billow at my ankles. With both hands, I flipped her until her back faced my front, and angled her until I could spear into her, my hardened flesh burning for her.

A moan broke the silence, followed by a guttural sound coming from my core. The feel of my steeled length sliding between her velvet lips almost shattered me on the spot.

"Oh, Nick," she said, turning her head and sealing her lips with mine.

I swallowed every sound leaving our hungry mouths.

We waltzed together, our bodies in sync.

Dahlia dug her nails into my skin when I pushed deeper inside her.

I shucked my pants away and peeled her shirt off when she twirled around in my arms. After I repositioned her, I glided back into her warm channel, my home in our home.

With a fistful of her hair, I tugged her to me, kissing the life out of her.

The seconds froze around us.

With my palm, I caressed her flaming cheek, losing myself in the lushness of her irises. "I love you," I murmured, so entranced by her beauty, her wisdom, and her whole being, unable to look away.

She held my gaze for an entire minute as we admired each other, welding our connection for the rest of time.

I pounded a little faster, a little harder. She arched her back in response, and I devoured her neck, supporting her weight with my arms to keep her upright.

In that instant of bliss, my heart broke free. Free from the past. Free from any suffering it had ever endured. Free from all restraint.

Its hasty beats shook the center of me, the cadence intoxicating, hoping to fuse to hers and live in her chest, where I knew it would be safe—and loved. If Dahlia looked closely enough, I bet she could see its hammering through my skin.

Carrying my other half in my arms, I laid her on the floor, careful to place her shirt underneath her head.

Balancing over her, our stares never breaking apart, I rammed into her.

Every expression of pleasure across her face played with the strings of my heart. The display of love on her lips made it swell a little more behind my ribs. The promises dancing in her eyes increased its addictive rhythm.

Dahlia tilted her head back, and together, we inched closer to the edge, nearing the precipice. Holding on. Until it couldn't be contained anymore. Until neither of us was strong enough to resist the pleasure building in our cores. Her walls clenched around me as we unraveled, wringing every last drop out of me. A muffled purr broke the orgasmic silence as our bodies convulsed together, and it took a few minutes for our breathing to go back to normal.

In this time, we lost ourselves in each other, chests heaving, satisfied smirks pasted on our faces.

Dahlia propped herself up on one arm and pressed a kiss to my chin, a soft laugh tumbling out.

I gave her a quizzical look. "What's so funny?"

"You. You have that look. The plenitude of being. Your eyelids are half-closed, and you're so handsome right now."

I kissed the corner of her lips, her eyebrows, and the freckles sprinkling her nose. "You think I'm handsome?"

She snickered. "Don't play dumb, Nicholas Peterson. You know I'm obsessed with you, and I think you're very good-looking."

I winked.

"Oh God, stop. Your level of smugness just multiplied. If I thought you looked vain after what we just did, now it's another game entirely."

"I had no idea you thought I was hot, Dahlia Ellis," I said with a shake of my head, no conviction in my words.

She blushed, pink being my favorite color on her. "Don't be all conceited now."

"Never," I promised, claiming her mouth in the slowest possible kiss, relishing the sensations it awoke inside me like it did every single time our lips touched.

I dropped beside her, and with my arm locked around her waist, we rested like that for a while. Just enjoying being with each other, and the after-sex rapture that enveloped us.

Dahlia, Jack, and I were about to become a family, for real.

A lightness settled in my chest at the idea.

When I'd left Chicago, I was broken and lost. And now

I felt better than I ever did. And complete. Positive about my life and the future.

Dahlia went to shower while I attacked breakfast. She came back downstairs a little later, carrying a still half-asleep Jack in her arms.

Picture perfect.

My family. Mine. Mine to love and to protect.

With a satisfied sigh, I let my gaze roam over the space around us.

This house was ours. Because this was where we belonged—together.

The moment he saw me, the boy stretched out his arms, silently asking me to scoop him up. "Nick," he said in his sleepy voice. "*Bakefast* with me?"

My lips found the top of his head. "Yes, I'll have breakfast with you. Hungry?"

He nodded.

"Almost ready, little guy. Will you help me out?"

He nodded again.

With him perched on my hip, we poured orange juice into glasses and set the table together.

"To us," Dahlia said, raising her glass once we sat down to eat.

"To love and family. And to us," I repeated, leaning in to kiss her lips. "I'm happy we're doing this together."

Her gaze found mine. "I wouldn't have it any other way."

She grabbed my hand in hers, kissed my fingers, and I saluted the sky, my eyes trained on her. "Thanks, bro. It's all because of you. Cheers."

Chapter 20
Nicholas

"Y**ou're sure he'd want me here? In his house? While he's here too?" I asked Dahlia as she emptied the suitcase and hung our clothes in the wardrobe, a few weeks later.

"Yes. We're together. And I love you both. In different ways, but all the same. You're part of my life, and Carter has to accept it. It's a tradition of ours. If he plays in town, we stay here, all of us. Now just get ready so we can go."

"What about Jack? Are you sure he'll be okay tonight?"

"With Addi? You're kidding, right? She loves him as her own. They will be fine. Stop being a helicopter parent, would you?"

I elbowed her, and she batted her lashes. Now I knew the power of those. The first time I picked her up for our date, she batted them at Carter, and he stopped fighting with her. Now she used them on me too whenever she wished to have the last word—and it worked. I had no idea why. It just did. I just stopped arguing every time Dahlia used her weapon of choice. I was pussy-whipped, as Tucker would say. I kinda liked it, though.

"Whoa, I can't believe you went there," I teased, pulling her against me. "Helicopter parent, really?"

"This new role suits you."

"You think?"

"Ohmygod, stop with the whiskey voice already. You have no idea the effect it has on me."

I blinked. "Whiskey voice? You're still stuck on that one?"

"Yeah. When your voice is half-smooth, half-husky. It's just like you. All calm and in control on the outside, strong and passionate on the inside. Like the liquor. It fits you. And it's the color of your eyes. Whiskey, I mean. It's also a color, so…"

I tipped a brow. "Oh, and my eyes are whiskey too?"

"Yeah. Lucky for me, it's also your drink of choice. I think that should be my name for you from now on."

"Whiskey? You kidding, right? It sounds like a dog's name."

Dahlia shrugged, laughing. She looped her arms around my neck and closed the distance between our bodies. "Okay, you're right. It sounds terrible." She scrunched up her face. "I'll have to find something more fitting, I guess. Anyway, I love both sides of you."

Oh, I owned a weapon of choice too then. "You sure?"

"Babe, I'd get drunk on you every day if I could. You're my new obsession. You look all inoffensive and sweet and hot, but you're addictive, Nicholas Peterson. And I can't live without you."

"Did I ever tell you how much I love you?"

She wrinkled her beautiful face. "Not sure. Tell me once more. Just in case."

"I love you, Dahlia Ellis. I love your heart. Your compassion. Your calm. Your quiet. Your wild." I kissed the bone above her eyebrow. "And I love us together. I love your son. And I'll befriend the man who has been by your side from the moment you were born and took care of you all these years. Because I owe him. A lot. He did it with the selflessness of his heart, never asking for anything in return. He was Derek's idol, and now I can see why."

Dahlia dabbed at her watery eyes with her fingers.

"I have no idea how you ended up in my life, but I promise to love you every day."

She reached for a tissue from the box on the nightstand and and gently dried her eyes. "Shoot, my mascara. Stop being so handsome. It's ruining my makeup." She pushed my chest with a hand in a teasing manner.

My fingers laced through hers over my heart. "For what it's worth, thanks. For all you've just said. It means a lot. I just fell deeper in love with you. Who knew it was even possible?"

We kissed, our mouths rehearsing a languorous dance. I held Dahlia's waist as she dissolved against me. Passion ignited between us. It always escalated quickly every time we were in each other's orbit.

When we broke apart, I chased her away, my hand connecting with her ass as she yelped and flashed me a ten-thousand-buck smile over her shoulder. Trying to tame my aroused self and regain some control over my body, I finished setting up the bedroom that would be ours for the next few days before going to check on Jack who was napping.

He had his own bedroom both at Carter's cabin and his penthouse, here in Nashville. I watched his sleeping form through the ajar door, his tiny fist clutching his favorite blanket to his heart, the sound of his steady breathing bringing me comfort. Since the day he'd choked, I could spend hours just listening to it.

"Hey," Dahlia called from the kitchen, breaking the moment. "I'll prep lunch. Sandwiches?"

I closed the door and went to join her. "Works for me. You need help?"

"Nah, I'm the sandwich queen, remember?" She moved toward the refrigerator, but halted mid-step. "Tell me, I thought Tucker was supposed to fly here for the weekend?"

"He was. Canceled last minute. Said he had a work emergency. I suspect he was afraid we'd force him to come with us tonight."

"It's ridiculous. He could have hung out with Addi and Jack until we got back. Or watched Jack, and Addison could have come with us."

I stopped in my tracks. "Addi and Tuck hanging out together? Nah, it sounds like a recipe for disaster."

Dahlia chuckled. "Oh, you're right. Why didn't I think about it? Luckily for everybody involved, she has a steady boyfriend, so she's off-limits."

I moved behind her and held her hipbones, molding my front to her back. "No woman is off-limits for Tuck, Dahlia."

"Addison can hold her own. Don't worry about her."

I shook my head. "Never underestimate Tucker Philips. You've been warned. But perhaps having them both here would have determined who deserves the craziest friend title. My best friend or yours?"

Dahlia spun between my arms. "Maybe I'm not ready to find out just yet. Let's not force proximity until we're sure we can handle it."

"We have a deal." I held out my hand, and we shook on it.

———

Later that night, we rose from our seats as Carter Hills walked onstage. He had offered us front row tickets, but Tucker had already gotten those seats for me, and they were perfect. Fifth row wasn't bad. As I watched him, I realized something: Carter, the music star, owned the stage. The air in the stadium seemed to hum with his presence. Even my heart raced at the sight of him with a guitar strapped across his chest. Fuck, Tucker had been right, because in that instant, I couldn't help fangirling over him.

"Hi, Nashville. It's good to be home," Carter said as the crowd erupted in cheers and wolf-whistles. "Tonight's show is dedicated to a fan I never got to meet. He fought cancer with all his heart but passed away at just twelve—far too soon to leave this world. Derek, if you can hear me from where you are, this show is all for you. Tonight's net proceeds will go to Chicago Lakeview Children's hospital in your name, supporting research and helping other children in their fight against cancer."

My hands connected in some sort of prayer under my chin. My heart went on break. I tried to breathe, but it came out as a wheeze.

"And because this song was your favorite, here it goes."

Carter waved at the ecstatic crowd before strumming the first chord of "Monkey Business."

That was when my heart dissolved.

"You did this?" I asked Dahlia once some of the shock subsided.

She kissed my lips. "Yes. I thought Derek would like it…and you too. Well, to be honest, I didn't do anything. I just told Carter about Derek. His story touched his heart. He did the rest entirely of his own volition."

Tears filled my eyes. No matter how many times I

blinked, I couldn't chase them away. "You told Carter about me and Derek? About his favorite song?"

She nodded. "He may act like a jerk sometimes, but his heart is usually in the right place. He told me he would have visited Derek at the hospital if he had known about him. He respects you, you know."

My jaw almost hit the floor as I glanced at her, speechless.

"You'll be able to thank him yourself after the show. We have VIP tickets."

"As if you need those," I teased.

"They are for you. To give you the ultimate Carter Hills concert experience."

"Don't try to transform me into a fangirl, babe." I grinned. "Well, to be honest, I may be a little bit starstruck right now," I added, pinching my fingers closed together.

Dahlia chuckled. "Not happening. Reel it in. The only person you're allowed to fangirl over, Nick Peterson, is me," she said with a wink.

"And I wouldn't want it any other way." I kissed her forehead, my heart waltzing inside my chest, filled with joy and gratitude—and so much love I believed it could never be contained. I kissed two fingers and raised them above my head. *All for you, Derek. Thank you.*

"I can't wait to move into our new place," Dahlia said a few months later as we carried more boxes into her house. After living together for quite some time, we had decided to do all the improvements on the farmhouse we'd talked and dreamed about before moving in together officially. In the meantime, we chose to move my stuff to her place.

In addition to relocating the kitchen, installing a new

banister on the staircase, opening walls to let in more sunlight, and building a terrace for the master bedroom, we'd also decided to tear down the old garage and build a barn in its place. A cozy addition with a place for Jack—and hopefully, our other children one day—to play. Some sort of tree house, but not in a tree.

"Dahlia, believe me, I know, but I'm also happy to move in here with you two and be part of the story of this house too. Won't you miss it, though?"

She surveyed the place. "Sure, I will. But I'm ready for something new. With you. To start a new chapter together."

I wrapped my arms around her, brushing my lips against hers. "Will you keep a guitar on the top floor of the barn?"

"Why?"

"Because you'll miss your little secret spot. You won't be able to visit that stable and those horses and play for them as much as you used to do since you'll have to drive there now. So, I figured you could make the top floor yours. We'll bring in haystacks and hang the fairy lights you love so much. We can add anything you want to make the space truly yours"

"Oh, Nick, you serious?"

"Always."

She rose onto her tiptoes to kiss me. "Nick Peterson, you're my person."

We kissed for a little longer.

"Are we still spending Christmas at the farmhouse, as we planned?" I asked after we broke apart.

"Hell, yes."

Later, we picked up takeout and headed home, eager to finish the final Christmas touches before Carter brought Jack back the next morning.

We entered the dark house, and Dahlia flicked the switch, and golden light spilled across the living room. She lowered her hand to grip mine and halted in her tracks. "I was thinking… Can I give you your Christmas present now?"

"Christmas is in two days. I can wait. And you didn't have to get me anything. I have you, and that's all I'll ever need. My biggest wish came true the moment you fell in love with me."

She shook her head, strands of hair brushing her shoulders. "No. I want it to be now. The timing is right. Gimme a sec." She disappeared for a minute and came back with a little, flat, square black box decorated with only a red bow.

"What is it?"

She locked her hands before her, waiting for me to open the lid, chewing on her lower lip.

The sight of her got me nervous. Tingles ran along my spine, and sweat pearled on the nape of my neck. I held my breath as I looked inside.

A small wooden barrel, wrapped in red satin, sat there —just big enough to hang on a keychain.

I lifted it. "What is it?"

"Your own whiskey label."

I blinked. "My what? Huh, are you saying what I think you are?"

Dahlia's grin reached both her ears. "It won't be ready for a while, but I couldn't wait to tell you. I met that expert and we talked about you, your taste, and he came up with a custom recipe. It's been barreled already, so we won't be able to taste it for about three years. See why I couldn't wait to share it with you?"

I rotated the tiny barrel between my fingers and noticed the small inscription engraved on its side.

I watched Dahlia with a raised brow. "Is it?"

She nodded.

"No, you didn't?"

Her smile stretched bigger, and she beamed in the low light of the house. "I did."

"It's you and me?"

"It's us."

Everything in me sizzled with excitement.

Could I be any happier? Could my heart get too big for my chest?

Whiskey and Country.

Whoa, I owned a whiskey label now.

"Thank you. Wow, I'm still speechless. *Whiskey and Country.* It's perfect."

Dahlia inched closer and took my hand in hers. "Nick, there's something else." She paused, inhaled through her mouth, and swiped her tongue across her lips. "Do you want to spend the rest of your life with me?" She kissed my lips before kneeling in front of me.

Time idled.

I was pretty sure air couldn't reach my lungs anymore. The pounding of my heart echoed in my skull.

I blinked, rebooting my confused brain, and dropped to my knees, facing her. "Babe, I was supposed to be the one asking you. I even got you a ring. I was just waiting for the right time. I had it all planned out already."

"Nick, I don't care about the ring. Well, I do, but that's not the point. I don't wanna wait another second to start the rest of our lives together. Here and now, let's promise to love each other until we both shall live. You already own my heart and my present. Let's just make it official, so you'll own my future too."

I dragged a hand over my face, trying to sort out my emotions. "Gosh,I love you so much right now. I can't believe this is happening." I claimed her mouth, wishing I could bask in this state of bliss forever.

Dahlia grinned, and it shook the foundation of me. My heartbeat slowed, matching the rhythm of hers. We were two halves of a soul about to be reunited. About to clash together and shoot stars across the sky.

"I'm lucky I got to ask you first." She wiggled her brows, and I let out a warm chuckle. "If the dark episodes of my life taught me anything, it's to never let love slip through your fingers. Life is too short to have doubts and not aim for what you want when you want it. It can all end too soon. We're already living together. Will you be my husband?"

"I love you, and I'm crazy about you. There's no one else for me in this world. Dahlia Ellis, I know you asked me first, but I'll ask you too. Will you marry me? My life only makes sense when you're in it. When you are beside me. When we plan a life together. When we're in each other's arms. And every time I'm inside you, I'm vibrating to your melody. You're my song. My inspiration. My everything." I paused and cleared my throat. "I'll be your husband. Will you be my wife?"

"Yes."

We kissed on the kitchen floor, unable to unlock our lips as we promised forever to each other.

Chapter 21

My heart overflowed with so much love.

I lifted Nick's shirt over his head and kissed his muscled chest, tracing circles all over his flesh with my tongue.

I bit one of his nipples, and he jumped back.

"Easy, woman."

I chuckled as I entangled my fingers in his hair.

Nick fastened his arms around me, trailing his lips down my throat. His hands moved south, greedy to touch me, kneading my skin. "I should go get your ring first."

"Later. Now just love me."

He undressed me, our mouths never breaking apart. On his feet, he carried me in his arms, honeymoon style, and laid me on the kitchen table, the coldness of the wood top contrasting with the warmth of my skin.

"God, I could devour you all day and all night if you'd let me."

"Please do," I said, my voice weird and high-pitched.

He pushed my knees apart and nested his head between my thighs. I shivered as his tongue licked the length of me. He pushed two fingers inside my warmth, and a wave of heat washed over me. A loud gasp tumbled out as my fiancé dived his fingers into my dampness again, spreading it over my most intimate folds. I rocked my hips, trying to set the pace, but he spread a hand across my stomach to hold me in place.

Ache and need rippled through me, and a loud cry parted my lips.

Nick did the thing I could never get enough of with his tongue around my clit, and fireworks shot behind my closed eyelids.

With both hands, I pulled him to me. "Just get inside me. Gotta feel you. To remember forever the first time I made love to my fiancé. The ring can wait."

He thrust his fingers in and out of me faster, and I tilted my head back, unable to contain all the sensations swirling in me any longer. Pleasure built deep in my core. With my eyes closed and my hot fiancé's tongue inside me, I came as if the Earth had shattered beneath me.

Propped up on his arms, Nick hovered over me, and without breaking eye contact, he pushed his throbbing hardness—softness over steel—inside my sheath. Until it molded to my warmth.

Euphoria filled me.

He watched me with so much heat and lust, my brain went blank, all the dirty thoughts swirling in my head seconds ago gone. *Pouf.* Vanished. Nick stole my ability to think and speak.

He rolled his hips at a slow pace. "God, I love you."

I curled my hand around his nape and tugged him closer to my heart. The one that beat only for him.

"I wouldn't want to be anywhere else. You, this place, it's what I wished for so many times. What I'll always want."

Nick rammed into me faster. My body stiffened.

I wasn't part of this world anymore. I floated somewhere in space, ecstasy shooting through me in blissful jolts.

He pulled me into his arms, and still inside me, carried me to the couch and sat.

We kissed, our tongues desperate for each other.

I rocked my hips over his, yearning for the friction of our naked bodies.

My breasts filled his hands as he massaged them. I leaned back, consumed by the rush of sensations he unleashed.

"Dahlia, I won't last long. I'm almost there. Come with me."

I increased the pace as Nick clutched my hipbones as if to anchor himself to the moment and not miss a beat.

With my thighs tight on each side of him, I ground my hips until he let out a chain of curses and emptied himself inside me, the tremors of his sex sending me over the edge.

We stayed like that, our bodies tangled together, unable to break apart, minutes after we both came down from our rush. As if one of us could vanish or we'd wake up from a dream.

Nick peppered kisses across my bare shoulders, leaving shivers behind. "I love you, Dahlia. I'm so fucking gone for you."

Our lips crashed together, hungry and unrelenting, and I deepened the kiss, hoping he'd understand how bad I was gone for him too.

———

"Can I give you your Christmas present?" Nick asked as we dressed after our shower the next morning.

"You don't have to. I can be patient," I said, echoing the words he'd said to me and twisting my ring—a square whiskey quartz gem surrounded by tiny diamonds mounted on a platinum band—around my finger. It was beautiful. And like the whiskey label name I came up with, it told our story. *Princess and whiskey.* Unable to detach my gaze from it, I relished how it reflected the morning light.

Nick continued, "I can't. But you'll have to wait until Carter gets here. Setting it up is a two-man job."

I furrowed my eyebrows. "You'll ask Cart's help? Are you two getting along better than I anticipated?"

Nick flashed me the most beautiful smile. "We have our moments. Our relationship isn't perfect, but we respect each other. We'll get there…I hope so."

I jumped into his arms, unable to contain all the joy and excitement vibrating through my heart. "Nick, you're the best. Thanks for doing this for me. I know Cart doesn't make it easy for you. Give him time, okay? He'll get around. Not today, but one day."

"He's important to you, so he's important to me too. I don't care about his broodiness or his attitude. Eventually, he'll recognize how charming I can be," he said, batting his eyelashes.

I backhanded his chest. "Don't charm him too much, though. I want to keep you all to myself."

Carter and Jack arrived, and once I went inside with my son, the men of my life worked together, fixing something on the front porch. Curious, I stayed upstairs in the room that would be Jack's to avoid spying on them.

I heard laughter. And a few curses. And more laughter.

Yeah, things would settle between them. I loved them both too much to lose either of them. They were both my family, for now and forever. We were in this together, the four of us.

"Dahlia. Jack. Come take a look," Nick hollered from downstairs.

We hurried down and put our jackets and boots on before meeting him by the front door.

"Where's Cart?" I asked when my best friend was nowhere to be found.

"He decided to give us some alone time together. He went to get lunch. Should be back in thirty minutes."

Carter. Always selfless around me—since the day we'd met—even if it broke his own heart in the process. I breathed, my emotions already swirling fast inside me.

"Ready?" Nick asked.

Jack and I bobbed our heads, Jack style.

A large grin broke free on my fiancé's face, and he sucked in a breath.

We stepped outside, and my eyes rounded.

I released Jack's hand, and he rushed toward our gift. *My* gift.

With both hands, I cupped my chest. "Nick, this is… I lack the words. It…it's everything I've ever wished for."

"You like it?"

"You're kidding, right? It's perfect. You made this for me?"

He mirrored my smile.

With his hand in mine, we neared my Christmas present: a wooden swing, big enough for the three of us to sit, with fairy lights dangling from the porch overhang. On a wooden plate, the words "Nick, Dahlia, Jack, and _____ special place."

Moisture gathered at the corners of my eyes, and my heart danced wildly in its cage.

"What's that about?" I asked, pointing to the blank space between my son's name and *special place.*"

"For our other child."

"What if we have a dozen of them?" I asked.

"We'll just make another plate. A bigger one."

"You're really ready for more children?"

"I'll have it all with you, Dahlia. Until we check every one of our dreams on that bucket list we made together."

I ugly cried at his words. "I desire it too. All of it. This is the most wonderful present you could ever give me."

———

On Christmas Eve, Carter entered the farmhouse, his arms overflowing with presents.

"You know we don't need anything, right? I thought I made a deal with Santa this year, asking him not to be overgenerous?" I wiggled my eyebrows, hoping he'd get the message.

He shrugged. "I know, Dah. These are just kids' stuff that Jack and I will use whenever I'm in town. You're too adult to understand." He offered me his renowned panty-melting grin and kissed my cheek, and I forfeited the idea of arguing.

I signed. "I'm not fighting you over this. You're such a big toddler when you're with him. Anyway, I like the two of you together, so I guess it's fine."

I emptied his arms, placing the gifts under the tree.

I stepped back next to him. "This looks charming."

Carter slung an arm around my shoulder and tugged me to him. I lost myself in the safety of his embrace for a minute.

"Cart, I gotta tell you something. Can we talk?"

He leaned back, and his smile vanished. My heart

hiccupped in my chest as my best friend stuffed his hands into his pockets.

"Sure. Where's Nick?"

"In the garage. I asked for some time alone with you."

"Are you okay? Is Jack sick?"

I squeezed his arm. "We're both fine." With my fingers intertwined with his, I led him to the kitchen and made tea. We sat beside each other, and I enveloped his hand with mine over the table.

"Dah, what is it? I hate when you do this? Talk to me."

My heart flipped in my chest and leaped into my throat. Pearls of sweat popped on my nape.

"Nick and I are getting married." I swallowed hard and tightened my grip on his hand.

Carter blinked, pushing away the truckload of emotions I knew was searing inside him, and breathed out. It wasn't the time for him to have one of his panic attacks.

"Cart, talk to me," I repeated his own words to him. He looked away and brought his gaze back to mine after a few seconds.

"Don't worry, Dah. I'm okay. I knew this day would come. I had time to get used to the idea."

My eyes rounded. "Wait, you knew?"

My best friend nodded.

"How? When?"

"Nick told me. He actually asked for my blessing. About a month ago."

"He did?"

"Yeah. We had *the* talk, he and I."

"Whoa, I'm speechless. What did you tell him?"

Carter sighed and ran a hand over his face. "The truth. That I love you, but you chose him, and he better take good care of you. And that you are in love with him. Not me." His throat worked. "You found a good one, Dah."

No, he found me, but now was not the time to focus on details.

"You're lucky to have him. All I've ever wished is for you to be happy, you know that. If you are, then that's all that matters." Unshed tears shone in his eyes, his stormy irises looking brighter than usual. "But I thought he was supposed to wait."

I offered him a small, lopsided smile. "I asked him first." There, I said it.

"You did?"

I nodded. "Yes. We bought the house…together. We're happy. I'm happy. And I know deep inside me we're meant to be. Why wait? We won't get married next month, but I'm not waiting a year either. We still have stuff to figure out. I have no clue what you guys discussed, but anyway, thank you for what you said to him. I know how you must feel right now, and I'm sorry. Even if it's not what you wanna hear. I love you, and I always will. You and I, we'll be fine, I promise. For the record, nothing will change between you and Jack either."

Carter pushed back. I could read all the hurt swimming in his eyes."Dah, I have to ask." He dragged a hand over his face before meeting my gaze again. "Will you let Nick adopt Jack?" He cringed as if the words burned his tongue. And in a way, I was sure they did.

I shook my head. "We talked about it. If Nick does adopt Jack one day, it will be because the three of us—Nick, you, and I—decide it's the right thing for him. You're the only daddy he's ever known, and I don't want to mess things up. He's still yours, Cart. Always will. When he's old enough, and if we haven't decided by then, I will leave it up to him to choose for himself. If he wants to… For now, let's keep loving him, the three of us, and he'll be the most adored child in the entire world."

Carter sniffled. "Thanks, Dah. Thanks for not taking him away from me. I haven't looked at the paternity results yet… I just can't—" His voice cracked and drowned the last word.

"I know. It's okay. I'll never take him away from you, Cart. The three of us, we're family. Until we're all old and gray. But now there will be four of us."

We rose to our feet and hugged, our foreheads pressing together, our hearts whispering unspoken promises that would carve our new reality. We were changed, but our bond remained unbroken—and would last forever.

Chapter 22

Derek's ~~Bucket List~~ I wish I had experienced in my life list
+ Nick's Bucket List

1. ~~Go to a hockey game with Nick and the guys~~
2. ~~Make 1 new...no, 3 new best friends~~
3. ~~Kiss a girl, until my heart beats fast~~
4. ~~Go camping and sleep under the stars~~
5. ~~Watch the sunrise every morning~~
6. ~~Dip my toes into the ocean, even if jellyfish are gross~~
7. ~~Go to a Carter Hills concert, because duh, he's the best~~
8. ~~Do something deemed impossible~~

9. Build something with my own hands that I'll keep forever or gift someone

10. Nick. Go on an adventure (now you must pick one)

11. Nick. Knowing I can always count on my friends

12. Nick. Be a knight to a damsel in distress, not that the damsel truly needed me.

13. Nick. Work on a ranch (why not?)

14. Nick. Having a meaningful encounter and finding something that makes you truly feel alive

15. Nick. Do something that's right even if it doesn't feel like it at first

16. Nick. Feeling like my life is moving forward and I am floating

17. Nick. Being speechless (in a good way)

18. Nick. Having a soul-connecting experience

19. Nick. Share something with someone I cared about that can't be described with words

20. Nick. Go on a different kind of date

21. Nick. Make someone smile my newfound mission

22. Nick. Share parts of my life with the person who means the most

23. Nick. Feeling like the cracks in my world are healing

24. Nick. Being brave even when it scares me

25. Nick. Find the one

Chapter 23

**Nick and Dahlia's Bucket List
(or the things we want the most from this life)**

1. Have a house full of kids
2. Fill our house with love
3. Adopt a bloodhound
4. Sleep under the star once a month
5. Name Dahlia president of the interior design department of Nick's construction business
6. Go see the ocean as often as possible
7. End each day telling people we care about how much we love them
8. Grow old together

9. Keep dreaming together
10. (This place is reserved for all our other dreams that will come along the way)

Epilogue
Nicholas

Three years later

"Dah, are you sure it's supposed to look like this?" I asked, trying to block the smell by breathing through the fabric of my long-sleeved charcoal sweatshirt. "This is disgusting."

My wife traipsed our way with a warm grin plastered across her face. "Don't worry. It'll be gross for a while." She neared us. "But you're doing great. Look at her smile. She only has eyes for her daddy."

"Yeah, I suppose it's worth every diaper," I said with a wink.

I leaned forward and kissed Violet's chubby cheek. She looked at me with her big golden eyes as if she'd never seen something so amazing, and my heart flip-flopped inside my chest. Our daughter looked like a tiny replica of Dahlia with her fiery copper hair and porcelain skin, but she had my honey-colored eyes—or whiskey-colored as Dahlia called them.

Violet babbled as I picked her up and brushed her soft baby hair with my fingers. "Are you coming to the park with Daddy and Jack?"

She smiled, and I took it as a "Yes, Daddy. Please. I wanna play too."

I grabbed the knitted blanket Barb had gifted me all those years ago and wrapped it around my daughter, exiting her room.

"Hey, son. Get your mitt ready. We're leaving in five," I said as I knocked on Jack's bedroom door.

"Come in, Daddy. I'm almost ready." I opened the door and peeked inside. Royal-blue walls, white trims and ceiling. Carter Hills's album covers, enlarged and framed were next to Derek's signed jersey, above his bed. A large picture of his daddy, Jeff—Carter's older brother, the one Jack never got to know—was set on the opposite wall. Next to it was another one of Dahlia with the Hills brothers when they were teenagers on prom night. Jack's guitar, the one Carter had gifted him on his birthday, stood in a corner, next to a giant stuffed hippopotamus Jeff had gotten for him before he was born, and Jack-the-Bear, the stuffed animal that used to belong to his dad when he was a kid. Rex, the dinosaur, was probably hiding in its usual spot under his pillow.

On his white-painted chest of drawers was a picture of us—him and me—taken the day we hiked to see the waterfall, and another from when he was three, on Dahlia's and my wedding day, when he had become my son in every way that truly mattered. Beside it was a third one of our entire family after Violet was born.

It was a beautiful collage of everyone who cared about him.

Jack had more parent figures at his young age than most people had in their lifetime.

I helped him fix his baseball jersey and held out my hand for him to take.

Baseball was something we bonded over. During the summer months, I was the assistant coach to his Little League team, the Black Bears.

"Is Mama coming?" my son asked.

"Not today. She has to go to the store for a few hours. Violet is coming with us, though."

"Cool."

My heart beat faster.

I had everything I'd ever wished for.

Who knew I would have found it in the middle of Green Mountain, Tennessee, all those years ago?

I watched my kids, my heart full, still thankful to Derek for pushing me to leave my old life behind in Chicago, and go on this journey. To this day, I still kept his bucket list tucked in my drawer, alongside the last letter he had written me and Kelly's card with the pancake recipe. Once in a while, I re-read them, remembering how lucky I was and all the progress I'd made since I chose to turn my life around and start afresh. Reminders of how far I'd come after my world had shattered.

"Can we take Spencer?" Jack asked. Spencer was our bloodhound puppy, the latest addition to our family. "If he stays here by himself, he'll whine all day from his playpen." As if he'd heard his name, the dog rushed to Jack's legs, and the boy squatted to pat his head. "See? He really wants to come with us to the park."

"Sure. Get his stuff and meet me in the car."

My son pumped his fist. "See, Spencer? I told you it would work," I heard him whisper in his new best *bestest* friend's ear as he used to say when he was a toddler.

The memory of him and Buddy, inseparable, flashed through my mind. My lips turned upward. For some reason, it seemed like a lifetime ago. So many things had happened in our lives since.

I stepped outside with a giggling Violet tucked in my arms, her tiny fingers tugging at my ear.

My gaze lingered on the mailbox with the inscription, *The Petersons,* carved on the side. A moving-in-together gift Dahlia had ordered from Stud the day we had visited the lawyer's office and I had found out she had put in an offer on the house so that we could buy it together.

When we had come back to our new home that afternoon, Greta and Brett had hung a *Welcome Home* sign over the front door, where they, along with Mike and a few guys from work, had joined in to celebrate that life-changing event with us.

Dahlia met me after I buckled our daughter in her car seat, cutting my trip down memory lane short. She kissed our baby's rosy cheek and turned her attention to me. "Next time, I'll join you guys," she said as she wound her arms around me. "I'll call you when I'm done. I'm having lunch with April later."

I pulled her into my arms and kissed her with all the love pouring out of my heart.

My wife moaned into my mouth, and my entire body woke up.

I grabbed a handful of her ass, and she gasped. "I promise to love you and take my sweet time tonight."

Dahlia ground her hips against mine. "I can't wait."

She deepened the kiss for a long minute before letting go of me when Jack walked out of the house with the puppy on a leash.

"Have fun with your friend. Tell her I'll give Carter pointers on how to get that baby out of her if she wants.

Lessons free of charge." I winked, and Dahlia kissed me again.

"Is he meeting you there?" she asked.

"Yep. Can you believe it took us years to get there?"

Dahlia's grin widened. "April is good for him. He's happy now. We all are. It was about time we chased that storm away and we all found our place in this world."

"I agree. And you were right. All this time. Carter and I, we're good. Derek would be ecstatic."

"Derek would be proud of you… I'm sure he is from wherever he's watching over you." Yeah, that cloud. A wrinkle crossed Dahlia's forehead. "Have you heard about Tucker lately?"

I paused to think for a moment. "No. Why?"

She shrugged. "I don't know. A feeling. The last time I talked to our friends was almost a month ago. When they're distant for a while, it is usually an unmistakable sign they did something wild. You know, like the last time we were vacationing together without the kids. We should invite them over. To make sure they're okay. And it could be fun. I miss our friends."

"Don't worry. I'm sure they are fine. They have so much on their plate right now. We'd be overwhelmed too if we were in their shoes. Anyway, I'll call him later. I'm sure he won't refuse a weekend in the mountains. Fresh air… and some much-needed help. Anyway, we're scheduled to taste *Whiskey and Country* for the first time two weekends from now. They could come to town early and spend a few days here beforehand. With us. And the kids."

Dahlia clapped her hand. "I like how you think. I can't wait for all our friends to join us. We've been waiting three years for this moment. Riley, June, Stud, and Belle are coming to town in a few days and will be staying all week at one of Cart's cabins."

We exchanged a grin.

"To this day, that private whiskey label is still my favorite Christmas present." I kissed her lips. "About Tuck, don't worry. Let me deal with it, okay? I'm sure everything's fine."

Dahlia nodded, pressing her body against mine. "Is Jace coming too? For the tasting?"

I sighed and shook my head. "Nah. Not that I know of. It's like the wedding all over again."

"I'm sorry," Dahlia said.

"It's fine. He's supposed to be a no-show, but he might surprise us—let's hope so."

"We could visit him next month. We haven't been to Chicago in a long time."

"Dahlia, I love you. So much. And a whole lot more every day," I said. "I'd like that. Thank you."

"I love you more. Now go play with our kids because I want you all to myself tonight."

I kissed her cheek, adjusted the crotch of my pants, and climbed behind the wheel.

My wife waved at us as I drove away.

I eyed the kids through the rearview mirror. Jack was tickling a giggling Violet.

Every piece of my heart belonged here in Green Mountain with my family.

Now.

And forever.

Want more? Grab an invite to Nick and Dahlia's nuptials in ***Wild Encounter***, Tucker and Addison's story.

Read Wild Encounter now

emmanuellesnow.com/products/wild-encounter

———

Thank you for reading Nick and Dahlia's
emotional and beautiful love story.

———

FREE bonus chapter
Want even more? Your bonus chapter awaits here:
emmanuellesnow.com/collections/bonus-chapters

WANT MORE EMOTIONAL LOVE STORIES?

WHICH COUPLE WILL YOU PICK NEXT?

False Promises

★★★★★ "The angst, the utter heartbreak, and protectiveness I felt for Carter during this book is unreal!"

★★★★★ "Emmanuelle Snow really knows how to tug at all of your emotions and does such a great job of bringing her characters to life!"

A gripping story of sizzling passion, lust, and the price of fame.
Start Carter Hills's story now

———

Sweet Agony

★★★★★ "If I could give more than 5 stars, I would."

★★★★★ "This is not a romance, it is a story about first love, first heartbreak and growing up."

A compelling tale of love, friendship, and self-discovery that will tug at your heartstrings.

Start Dahlia's story now

———

Cruel Destiny

★★★★★ "Wow. Just wow. If that could be my review, that is all I would write."

★★★★★ "Emmanuelle has done it yet again. She found a way to slip into my mind and heart with her words and the creation of characters you can't help but fall in love with."

★★★★★ "This book broke my heart in the first twenty five percent and sewed it back together."

A story of healing, second chances, and the risks of opening your heart to someone new. Can they trust each other with their hearts, or will their pasts keep them apart?

Read Nick and Dahlia's love story now

———

Wild Encounter

★★★★★ "This is by far one of the most well-written

book I've read this month. It is dynamic, intriguing, interesting, unafraid to go there and most of all touching."

★★★★★ "I personally wouldn't call this book JUST a romance novel because it's so much more. I 100% recommend it no doubt in mind."

A tale of passion and perseverance that will leave your heart racing and your spirit soaring.

Read Tucker and Addison's love story now

———

Last Hope

★★★★★ "This book was not only about the darkness but it was about pure love, hope, spice, family, and friendships on point with just the right amount without overpowering the storyline at all."

★★★★★ "Devon and Riley's story is a beautiful one with a lot of emotions. The subject matter is intense but it is handled very gently."

A tale of resilience and second chances in a world where love and danger intertwine.

Read Riley and Devon's love story now

———

Midnight Sparks

★★★★★ "The characters, the love, the humor, the steaminess, the emotions… it's everything I hoped and more."

★★★★★ "I think that is one Emmanuelle Snow's sexiest novels yet."

Welcome to the island where Holiday magic meets unexpected romance and a chance at a fresh start.

Read Gavin and Aisha's love story now

––––––

Fallen Legend

★★★★★ ""The love that grows, not only through tough angst but through unconditional moments had my heart. This is a spicy and riveting book"

★★★★★ "Emmanuelle Snow doesn't just tell a story, she creates an entire world."

A poignant and uplifting journey of hope, love, and the power of second chances.

Read Sam and Madison's love story now

––––––

Snowbound

★★★★★ "5 big stars from me for this amazing story. Absolutely loved it!"

★★★★★ "Emmanuelle Snow's stories are always full of angst, and Snowbound is no exception."

The intertwined lives of two strangers bound by fate in the midst of a snowstorm.

Read Anderson and Abigail's love story now

———

All available at emmanuellesnow.com

ACKNOWLEDGMENTS

Oh. My. God. Where do I even begin? Wow, I can't believe *Second Tear* duet (previously titled *Whiskey and Country)* is finally done and published. What a ride. First draft. Rewrites. Tears. Sleepless nights. Edits. Joys. Smiles. Pride. Seriously, this book has been a tough one to write. It's so emotionally charged that I had a hard time capturing the complexity of the journey. Those big emotions were needed to get the importance of where Nick's journey started and where it ended, and how and why he became the guy he is today. But… Wow. I'm lacking a better word. My characters are usually pretty straightforward with me, but for some reason, Nicholas Peterson gave me a hard time. Now I get why. He was stuck in his own grief and was trying to find ways to heal. To soothe the scars of his heart. But we're good now.

Yes, I have that kind of relationship with my characters (haha!) Countless times I wish to invite them over to have a talk or ask them out for a drink.

Nick's journey became mine through each page. Our souls fused for a moment, healing and being brave together.
    In this adventure, I have people to be thankful for.

My husband and kids. Okay, I know I wasn't available sometimes, and you found it hard, but you were always there cheering me up, even when tears were rolling down my cheeks and my vision was so blurry I couldn't type anymore (Yes, this is an emotional book, even for me as an author). We're a team, the six of us, and you mean the world to me.

Shalini. Let's be honest. How many times did I actually have to rewrite scenes to translate in words the poignancy of the story or seek emotions from deep inside me to give Nick the voice he deserved? This was our Everest, as you told me, but we climbed it, never backing down, and now we can look back and high-five. Because, girl, we did it! I'm so proud of the story. But mostly, I'm proud of us. Once again, your book fairy godmother's talent and love are priceless, and I'm lucky to have you in my life, as an editor and a friend. To many more books together!

Virginie. Your words of encouragement and your faith in me are invaluable. Yes, Nick's the story of my life. I was just too close to it to notice it.

Jacynthe. Your optimism is priceless. Thank you for being my friend through it all.

Steph. Thank you for giving me the opportunity to share what I was born to do with your students. Two decades ago, you made me fall in love with the language, the words, and the storytelling. Your passion is contagious. And if all teachers were as enthusiastic as you, school would be a place where dreams are supported and nurtured. When I look back, I realize I've come a long way. And it is partly due to you.

Readers. Without you, I wouldn't be calling myself an author. Your love for my books and my characters means the world to me. Carter Hills Band wouldn't be half the universe it is today without your unconditional support and enjoyment of my stories. And yes, the real-life Carter Hills Band Fan Club is something I have never seen coming! Thank you.

Bloggers. Bookstagrammers. YouTubers. TikTokers. Every one of your reviews and early reviews/publicity gave me goose bumps and brought happy tears to my eyes. Thank you for giving my books a chance and for sharing the love.

Second Tear is a wrap, as my editor and I would say, but I'm super emotional at the idea it's over. Sure, every time I type the word "The End" I'm tearful, but for some reason, this one made me super extra-emotional.

Nick and Dahlia, I love you from the bottom of my heart. And you both deserve your happy ending. And so much love.

To all y'all, cheers!

Emmanuelle

ABOUT THE AUTHOR

Soulfully Beautiful Love Stories

USA Today Bestselling Author Emmanuelle Snow is an author of contemporary YA and women's fiction love stories, who gives life to strong characters who'll fight with all they have to reach their life goals and find their own happiness. She loves her characters to be relatable and realistic.

Emmanuelle is in love with love. Especially complicated, deep, and passionate feelings that make a relationship extraordinary and complex all at the same time.

In her spare time, when she's not writing or reading, she likes to go on road trips—with her four kids and her own soulmate—watch movies, paint, or do some DIY, always with a cup of green tea in her hand and listening to country music.

She splits her time between beautiful Canada and the small US towns she adores.

Find all of Emmanuelle's books here:
emmanuellesnow.com

———

ALSO BY THE AUTHOR

CARTER HILLS BAND UNIVERSE

(suggested reading order)

Carter Hills Band series

False Promises

Heart Song Duet

Blindsided

Forevermore

Whiskey Melody series

Sweet Agony

Second Tear Duet

Cruel Destiny

Beautiful Salvation

Breathless Duet

Wild Encounter

Brittle Scars

Upon A Star Series

Last Hope

Midnight Sparks

Love Song For Two Series

<u>LONESOME HEART DUET</u>

Fallen Legend

Rising Star

<u>TWO OF US DUET</u>

Snowbound

Wicked Love

MEDORA BEACH UNIVERSE

Wrecked series

Cast Away

Ride for a Fall

Touchdown series

Kickoff

Read them all

emmanuellesnow.com

All available on author's bookshop

EMMANUELLE SNOW

USA TODAY BESTSELLING AUTHOR

WILD ENCOUNTER

ADDISON

I slumped down on the couch of the posh hotel we were staying at all weekend and huffed, a wine bottle hanging from my fingers by its neck. Glasses were overrated, anyway. "That's it. I'm over men. I'm done."

My childhood best friend snickered.

"I'm serious, Dah. This time I mean it. You know I do."

I scanned the space around me. Large windows with a direct view of Nashville's busy streets below, high wooden beam ceilings, dark flooring, and handcrafted wood furniture. Chic and tasteful, with an unmistakable country vibe.

"Yeah, right. I'm sure you won't last a week. Two at the most," Dahlia teased.

My friend, and the bride-to-be, inched closer, and I zipped her up. Her cut-out mermaid gown was a gray-lavender hue and looked both sexy and demure, showing just enough skin without being indecent. Perfectly Dahlia Ellis.

Before I could sink back into my lazy position on the couch, she beckoned me to follow her with a finger. Sitting on the edge of the bathtub, I glugged the wine straight from the bottle while I watched her apply mascara.

"Addi, there are good men out there who would appreciate your light. Don't punish all of them because you dated a few who were total dickheads." She grinned at her reflection, but it was meant for me. It warmed my heart as she continued, "I'm confident you won't last in your quest to ignore them all when they turn on the charm."

"Laugh all you want, girlfriend. You'll see. Be prepared to be shocked. This time, I'm not backing down. Anyway, remember Felicia from college? She messaged me last week. It's destiny."

"The one you 'experimented' with?" my friend asked, curving her fingers into elaborate air quotes, her gaze fixed on her eyelashes in the mirror, not sparing me a look.

Another sip. "The same. We could have been in love and lived happily ever after. The timing was just not right back then."

"Huh, you said the same thing about Carter once. Besides, I thought women weren't your thing," Dahlia added with a quirked brow.

"It's not the same. And perhaps I changed my mind. Who knows? I might be into women more than men after all. Think about it, we should have been a couple, you and I. Everything would have been much simpler."

"You think?"

I shrugged. "We get along fine. And we're friends, so our relationship would have had a solid foundation. Look at you and Nick. Friends, then lovers. I believe that's the secret to long-lasting love. Back to business…" I sighed. "Felicia and I experienced some pretty memorable moments together. It's just Shawn happened to cross my path, and I couldn't resist him. Stupid me. Stupid men. I'm telling you their species is old news. You're lucky you found two awesome ones in your lifetime. What are the odds? God knows I've tried. I usually don't back down easily, but hey, maybe it's time I try something else. That I understand once and for all what life has been trying to tell me all these years…"

Dahlia shook her head, focusing her attention on me for the first time since I started the conversation about my disastrous love life. "Addi, you know how much I love it when you're not being overdramatic, right?"

I poked my tongue out, and we both burst out laughing. A sense of peace washed over me. Dahlia Ellis had that effect on me. Her presence was always enough to ease all my doubts and bring a curve to my lips, even when I didn't feel like expressing joy. "That's why you love me. I'm entertaining…despite myself. Anyway, where are the bridal shower festivities taking place? I can't wait to party all weekend. The distraction will do me good."

My best friend reached over and landed a kiss on my cheek, her eyes searching mine. Worry shimmered in them. "You okay?"

I nodded.

"You'd tell me if it wasn't the case, right?" I sensed the apprehension in her question.

"Always. You're the only one I willingly confide in."

With a warm smile that promised everything would turn out just fine, she went back to applying her makeup. "All over town. Tonight, we're having dinner with only the people closest to us. Tomorrow, we'll have a get-together with some friends and the guys on a yacht before splitting up and maybe meeting again later."

"Rewind for a sec. We're having your bridal shower with your future husband and his friends?"

"Yep. His best friend. Guys from work. That's the idea."

"Yeah, I should've been the one organizing the whole thing." Dahlia raised a hand, ready to argue, but I kept going. "For what it's worth, I'm sorry I let you down. I was really looking forward to throwing you the bachelorette party of the century."

A new weight grew heavy on my shoulders. In the fog of my latest relationship blowing up, I had lost focus on what really mattered. This time, my tears had knocked me out more than ever. But I was back now, and no way was I failing the girl I considered a sister again.

Dahlia pulled me into a hug. "It's okay. Don't chastise yourself. It'll still be fun. And you did plan most of the wedding already. You deserve a night off…to enjoy yourself… You, me, booze, music. And the man I love and his friends."

I leaned back, studying her for a moment. Dahlia had no ounce of evilness in her. She really meant everything she'd just said.

"What is it?" she asked, a frown marring her forehead.

"Real sweet, Dah. After I told you I was done with men, you're going to make me spend hours with a bunch of Nick's buddies. And alcohol. If I didn't know your heart, I'd think this was a test. To check my newfound determination." One more sip of wine. *Be strong, Addi,* I repeated in my head. I flicked my hand and pasted a smile on my lips. "Know what? It doesn't matter. I won't back down. I'm done with men, and I'll prove it to you. Tonight. I won't flirt, and I won't kiss. Nope. Nada. D.O.N.E. Just watch and learn, girlfriend."

I held out my hand, and we shook on it.

Read Tucker and Addison's story,
Wild Encounter, now

emmanuellesnow.com/products/wild-encounter

Author's bookstore at emmanuellesnow.com

"Tucker freaking Philips!!! Wow! Emmanuelle Snow has written another beautiful, rollercoaster, sneakily emotional romance."
(Goodreads)

"This is without a doubt Emmanuelle's best work yet!" (Goodreads)

Wild Encounter is book one in the **Breathless** duet.
emmanuellesnow.com/products/wild-encounter

Dahlia's
BRIDA
GREEN MOUNTAIN, TN